AFTER ALL

A Novel

Patricia DeGroot

Published by AM Publishing, NY, NY

Cover designed by Lynnette Bonner

Patricia DeGroot
Visit my website at https://patricia-degroot.com

Printed in the United States of America

First Printing: Aug 2019

ISBN-13 9781070576299

CONTENTS

One generation shall laud Your works to another,
and shall declare Your mighty acts. —PSALM 145:4

PROLOGUE

The wind pressed against him, cold and biting, much like his task. William turned up his coat collar and dismounted. He roped his horse to the post. "This won't take long." He patted the horse's nose, said the words close to his ear lest they were lost to the storm.

Turning, he stared at the white-washed building, the steeple he'd helped erect. No use in delaying, he strode up the walk, opened the church door. The tug of the wind battled his hold. Dirt swirled at his feet. A howling cry echoed in the chamber. He entered, jerked hard with his cold hands and was rewarded when the door shut tight, leaving behind the dust and the noise and the cold.

He was alone inside. The hollowness unnerved him.

Exhaling, he moved forward, his footsteps harsh against the hardwood floor. When he reached the lectern, he stopped. The membership book was open. His name would appear in it over and over again. He and his wives, many of his sixteen children.

After today it would appear no more.

He reached for the writing pen, one his tithe had helped purchase. He hesitated briefly. Would Tilly leave him now? Her fear too much to bear? She knew the truth, he reminded himself. But that didn't always matter.

The ink struck the parchment.

"I William W. Hatcher, on this day of 2 February, 1878, do hereby strike my name from church membership. I can no longer break bread with the likes of liars, cons and thieves."

He scrawled his signature with boldness, dropped the pen and stared at his words. There was no turning back now.

His footsteps took him back to the door.

Outside again he paused and looked skyward.

The bleary winter day was nothing compared to the sorrow in his soul.

CHAPTER 1

Present Day

"Say that again, would you? You *don't* want me to use the word *promise* in your wedding vows?"

There are some conversations that unbalance you. This morning, I'd had one like that.

I write wedding vows for a living. I usually don't meet my clients. Not in this day of internet websites. Brides and grooms usually fill out an online form, the questions I've devised easily giving me enough information to personalize their vows.

But today I'd met with the groom at an over-crowded Denver coffee house.

"I'd prefer a different word, Shelley. Something less restrictive," he'd said from across from me. My laptop and our cups of brew – his expresso, my chai latte – had cluttered our small table as other conversations filtered through the space. The noise and congestion were already making it difficult for me to concentrate and Donovan's demeanor quickly elevated my blood pressure. Had I heard right?

My hands had paused on the computer keyboard. I'd taken a sip of tea and a breath, hoping the heat I felt in my face wasn't radiating across the table. Unfortunately, when I glanced over my computer screen and caught the shrewd gleam in his eyes, I knew he knew I was uncomfortable – and he didn't care. In fact, I could tell he was pretty pleased with himself. He was a good-looking, thirty-something attorney at a prestigious law firm. He wore a black tux, white shirt and unclasped red bow tie. He was getting married in three hours, he'd already informed me. His bride would be in chic red, the wedding a black-tie affair at a prominent Cherry Creek mansion. A five-star reception at Shanahan's Steakhouse would follow. No amount was being spared by the bride's high-powered father.

Donovan had contacted me only an hour ago. I'd let his first five calls go to voice mail. I was on my way out the door, on my way to the airport. My grandmother had unexpectedly died last month. I'd traveled to Texas for her service and promised – there was that word again - my grandfather I'd return to help him sort through her things. Work was the last thing on my mind but on Donovan's sixth call, I'd answered.

"Wedding vows writer." I hadn't tried hard to disguise my annoyed tone. "The office is closed so this better be an emergency."

"It's definitely that," Donovan had replied. But when he'd explained that he'd 'forgotten' to write his vows and needed them ASAP, I'd sighed. "I'm sorry, but that's really not the kind of emergency—"

"How 'bout I double your fee," he'd interrupted. He then made that gets-to-me-every-time "You have no idea how disappointed my bride will be," plea. Since I had a few minutes to spare, I reluctantly gave in. I'd been house-hunting lately, after all, and was still trying to get over the sticker shock. "Do you know where the coffee house is on Main?" At least the area was close to my apartment and wouldn't take me off route to Denver's airport.

By the time we'd met, stood in line for our drinks and sat down, I'd surmised he'd been born into money and law school and the BAR exam had been a breeze. He was already a junior partner. His next step would be to acquire the arm candy and he'd follow that with two-and-a-half gorgeous and brilliant children.

My ability to be dismayed by some of the people who hire me to write their vows had been tinged long ago, but my politeness barely holds when *this* groom vetoes the word 'promise'.

5

I have an immediate instinct to stand up, gather my things and tell him to write his own last-minute-I-forgot-all-about-them wedding vows. Of course, I don't. I maintain my decorum, I swallow my angst. I tell myself he's not the first client I've had who shares his viewpoint. It's not his fault I'm sensitive – overly sensitive – about his I'm-not-in-this-till-death-do-us-part attitude.

I sit up straighter in my chair and tuck my brown, shoulder length hair behind my ear. "How about 'assurance'?" I offer with a smile. I can offer the word 'binder' or 'agreement' as well. It's obvious this attorney is looking for un-sentimental verbiage. 'Contract' or 'deal' would work, too. To me they all mean the same thing – 'promise'; something Donovan is unwilling to pledge.

"'Assurance' fits." He pointed his buffed and polished index finger forward to punctuate his statement.

I'd quickly keyed words into the computer, charged him more than double, and left him as fast as I could, vows in hand. I said a quick prayer for his bride. How long, I wondered, would their 'marriage' last? My impulse to caution her surged, then faltered. Odds were, she wouldn't listen to me.

Now, hours later, having landed in Austin, Texas, I lift my second suitcase into the back of my rental car, slam the trunk shut and still hear Donovan's words echoing in my brain. His behavior should not surprise me. But today it leaves me with a particular unease.

Maybe because my bubble has – at last - burst.

Maybe because now I admit I am not about to find a man who closely resembles a modern-day knight-in-shining-armor. I'd had my doubts for some time, of course. Henry (my first year in college) and Carter (my last year in college), didn't help.

Last-minute grooms didn't either. They are the reason I'm successful – financially and professionally. As the owner of Wedding Vows Writer, LLC., I've grown accustomed to writing wedding vows for the unromantic, un-savvy, illiterate man whose fiancée wants romantic, savvy and original prose for their special day. Grooms-to-be contact me in desperation after realizing they have no clue what to say. They give their vows little thought until it's too late. Lucky for me because it's a lucrative business.

Sadly though, Donovan was in a class all by himself.

I'd wanted to tell him that guys like him should never be allowed to marry – and that their less-than-stellar moral compass has contaminated the well – spread like a virus through the male populace of my generation.

And that, I realize, is why I can't shake our conversation.

I've finally conceded there are more men *like* Donovan than *not*. And my odds of finding one of the few 'good ones' just dropped by major percentage points.

As I get behind the wheel of the car, I rationalize that it's a good thing I'll be focusing on my grandfather for a while. He and my grandmother were committed to each other for more than fifty years. His sorrow is palpable now that she's gone, but I think I might need him as much as he needs me.

I'm calmer by the time I reach his ranch an hour later. I have soothing music blaring through the car radio, the windows rolled down on this warm April afternoon, the balmy Texas breeze while I maneuver the Farm to Market hill country roads blowing my hair and my angst away.

Rock crunches beneath the tires of the car once I turn off the main highway. I continue down the half-mile dirt and gravel road to Granddad's ranch-house. Pulling next to his pick-up truck, I kill the engine and open the car door. I'm greeted by the comfortable sound of silence and a skyline of sunset-orange as I step out of the car.

My grandparents' ranch has always been refreshing. The ranch – Carl and Violet Gatewood's - is twelve-hundred and eighty acres, the reward Captain Isaac Gatewood received in the late 1840's when he fought for Texas in the Mexican War.

Passed down from generation to generation, Granddad is the latest Gatewood to hold title. In the early nineties, he built the newer house that he lives in today. It's set below a ridge of live oak, a sprawling single story with a modern-era red barn filled with horses and a few other outbuildings for supplies. Leafy oak trees shelter it enough to keep it pleasantly cool in the summer, wind-blocked on a gusty day, tranquil always. Remnants of the old house, era 1875, are further west and make for good exploring – something I frequently did every summer - until the year I turned seventeen. Friends, school dances and Friday night football took center stage then. In college it was studies, skiing and one or two guys. Texas visits grew infrequent. Then Gram died suddenly last month and I tasted the guilt of not visiting more, not calling her more.

At her memorial service three weeks ago, I'd realized just how much she was admired and respected. Her garden club friends had plucked and arranged dozens of bouquets with flowers from her own garden and scattered them throughout the house. They're been just as many mourners.

Staring at the ranch-house now, I sense the interior will feel hollow without her. Something Granddad was dealing with every day now.

I hope my arrival will change that.

I see him then, as the front screen squeaks open and he saunters onto the wide wooden porch. He is eighty-five, creaky and slow but he can still ride his horse, plow his field. He still throws hay and makes a mean venison chili.

I exhale, grateful to see him – until he waves with a stiff arm and I notice the white gauze bandage covering his brow. Another man appears behind him; one taller, broader, younger. I swallow as I recognize Ben Anders.

Ben – who was Granddad's neighbor and the sole cause of my childhood vacations' "worst" days.

Until Gram's service I hadn't seen Ben since the summer of my high school graduation ten years ago. But Ben and Granddad, I'd discovered, were now good friends.

When he'd entered Grace Bible Church of Georgetown, I'd been placing another arrangement of flowers in the sanctuary. I'd looked up when I'd heard his voice. Strange that – that I would still know his voice after ten years.

I'd turned before I could stop myself, seeing he was no longer the gangly teen in my mind's eye. He'd filled out. All too nicely. As he shook Pastor Dave's hand my tension went into overdrive. What was he doing there, I wanted to know? I'd put Ben behind me years before and didn't want to relive the past. But I'd find out soon enough that he was a fixture in Granddad's life.

When he turned to catch me staring at him before I could turn away, I quickly focused on the flower arrangement again, furious with myself. I began rearranging peonies even as I felt him approaching me.

"Hey, Shelley."

I cringed and closed my eyes for a brief moment, humiliated, before I faced him with my emotions concealed.

"It's been awhile, huh?"

"Hello, Ben."

"I'm really sorry about Violet," he added. "I'm still in shock."

"Thank you. I think we all are." My tone was calm even though I was shaking inside. Small talk complete, I had to ask, "What are you doing here?" I could not have been more confused by his presence.

His dark brows rose almost imperceptibly, conveying the message that I should have known why he was there. "Carl asked me to give the eulogy," he then answers. "I was just going over the particulars with Pastor Dave."

Eulogy? Ben? He was right; I should have known. Known that Ben was *that* close to my grandparents.

"Of course," I say, unwilling to admit that I was in the dark.

"If there's anything else I can do, any way I can help, just shout."

"Thanks. I think we have everything under control but I'll pass the word."

He reached for my hand then, his touch warm and gentle. Soothing in a way it shouldn't be. For a moment I absorb that touch, lean into it. But the moment he moves his thumb across my palm, I pull away. And he does, too.

I direct my attention to the flowers again as he clears his throat. "I'd better go. See you tomorrow at the service?"

I look up at him again. "Sure." Then he smiled that ridiculous melt-your-heart smile of his. The one that had always been my downfall. I cursed myself for giving him my time, my attention. I fight to recall Ben's flipside instead and touch the indentation on my upper arm. It's the one from the rock he'd whizzed my way with his sling-shot when I was ten. I then remember the sound of my own gasp from the day he'd pushed me into the freezing river two springs later. It had taken me hours to stop shivering and thaw out.

My mind then slides to the sting of rejection I'd felt when, age 15, he'd stood me up for the 4-H Club's summer dance. This after he'd given me a rose and a sweet-smiled invitation that had made it impossible for me to turn him down.

The next day he'd offered a sugar-tongued apology, his grandfather standing over his shoulder, my eyes still red-rimmed.

This is the Ben I know.

He's the grandson of Granddad's oldest friend and grew up living with his grandparents on the adjacent ranch. He'd taunted me every summer, some days pretending to be nice, only to turn on me with some practical joke or prank.

I'd protested loudly when I was told his family would be joining mine on *my* high school graduation trip to Hawaii. By then Ben was in college and I hadn't seen him for two years. That hadn't lessened how he'd permanently scared my psyche so when the adults refused to dis-invite him, I was forced to out-surf him, spot more whales than he did, and find another guy to hang out with.

But I could have saved myself the effort because Ben hadn't noticed one bit.

Now nearly a decade later I find he is well-liked by everyone in the community, G-Q gorgeous, and a part of my past I'd rather not remember.

No one, I tell myself, knows the Ben I know – the Ben who hurt the girl next door more times than could be counted.

Even before grooms like Donovan, Ben Anders had jaded my view on males.

Unfortunately, Ben and Granddad are friends, as well as business partners.

When I'd offered to help Granddad sort through Gram's personal things, I'd inwardly pledged to be a big girl and set aside my prejudices.

I am mature now, after all. Older and wiser. I had the confidence and equilibrium I hadn't had when I was a teenage girl. Ben was *not* going to intimidate me. Everyone else could be fooled, but not me.

I was certain he still had the same mile-wide ego he'd had when he was a teen. And most likely, too many vices to count. He and Donovan probably shared the same viewpoints about 'until-it-doesn't-feel-good-anymore' marriage.

My plan was to be polite when he was around - but keep my distance. At the moment that won't be possible because Ben is with Granddad and Granddad is hurt.

As adrenaline pumps through my veins, I jog across the grass to the flagstone walkway. "Granddad? Are you okay? What happened?"

"Now, now, don't fret." I climb the porch steps. "I'm alright."

Ben's shrug is a non-committal 'I'm not so sure'. "He took a spill while we were in the barn looking at the new colt."

"He's a beaut, Shelley," Granddad says as I give him a careful hug. Hearing him talk helps calm my fear. "I know you wanted to be here when Glory foaled but you're a few hours too late. The boy came early this morning."

I step back, reach for Granddad's arm. "I can't wait to see him. But right now, I'm more concerned about you. Shouldn't you be sitting down? Let's go inside."

He turns without protest – a sign he does need to sit down. I hold his arm as we enter the house and he steers me to the front room where he eases into his old recliner. Ben follows behind, taking a seat on the upholstered couch while I kneel on the floor beside my grandfather. Carl Gatewood is a proud man and I know he won't appreciate me coddling him, so I say, "I guess the floor rose up to meet you?"

"Dang thing," he protests. "Tripped me right up and into the side of the stall I went. Lucky for me Glory didn't panic or I'd have her shoe print on the side of my head for sure."

Glory is one of the newest horses in Granddad's stable. Brown with a splash of white on her chest, she's a gentle mare. I'd found out at Gram's service that Glory was pregnant and I'd hoped to arrive before she foaled. "She trust's you, Granddad."

"Carl never blacked out," Ben offers. "And he hasn't slurred his words. I wanted to take him to the hospital but he said you would be here soon so I gave him some water and checked his eyes. His pupils are normal. So far so good."

"Just a scratch," Granddad says.

I glance at Ben who shrugs again when Granddad isn't looking.

"Okay. What do you say we head over their now just to be sure you didn't rattle something loose?"

"I suppose that'll be fine."

Ben stands and clamps Granddad on the shoulder. "I'll leave you in the very capable hands of your granddaughter then, Carl," he says. To me he adds, "If you have your phone handy, I'll add my number to your contacts. Call if you need anything at all."

I want to refuse him. Tell him I don't need him in my contacts or anywhere else. But, of course I can't; not if doing so puts Granddad at risk. Or clues him in to the fact that I'd prefer Ben wasn't around. "It's in the car. I'll get it for you." To Granddad I add, "Let's get you to the doctor."

As we exit the house, I'm hoping Granddad is okay. I couldn't even imagine losing him so soon after Gram. And I can only hope that Ben's presence isn't a precursor of days to come. I've already come to terms with the fact that Ben and Granddad play chess every afternoon and that they have several business partnerships. I can make myself scarce when they're checkmating each other and discussing heifers. But other times might be more difficult. More noticeable. And I don't want to make myself scarce. I want to be with Granddad.

And want Ben to go away.

CHAPTER 2

I open one eye when I hear Granddad in the hall. The clock on the nightstand is claiming the five-a.m. hour. I'd been alert most of the night, even though the doctor had declared Granddad just fine, so I'm surprised I'd fallen into an early-morning deep-sleep. Foggy, I roll out of bed, telling myself I'll catch up on my sleep tonight.

Granddad is already making coffee when I shuffle into the kitchen.

"Good morning," I greet him. He turns my way before I can ask him how he is feeling.

"Let's go see Glory and her boy."

"Let's do that," I smile, instantly awake. His words calm me, so I hurry back to my room for jeans and boots while the coffee brews, then scramble to keep up with him as he strides from house to barn in the predawn light. He appears to be 'fit as a fiddle' as he would say.

"Mornin', Gail," Granddad says as we enter the barn. Gail Martinez is employed at the ranch. She cleans the barn and cares for the horses. "Mornin' y'all," she returns.

Then a loud neigh commands our attention and we turn to see Glory bobbing her head at the stall door.

"Mornin', girl." Granddad makes haste towards the mare. "How's my girl this morning? How's Glory's Gold?"

"I love his pedigree name, Granddad. Glory's Gold."

"Gram decided on it about a week before she took sick. But we still need a nickname for him." He brushes Glory's brown nose as her colt, all soft fuzzy fur and gangly legs, whinnies and prances behind her.

I blink back tears, say hello to Glory and stare at her colt. "He's beautiful."

The brown colt paws the ground and snorts.

Granddad chuckles. "Why you're a little leadfoot aren't you?"

"That's a catchy nickname. Leadfoot. Hey, little guy," I say to the colt. "You are absolutely precious."

"Leadfoot." Granddad sniffs.

Glory neighs and we all laugh.

"She must agree."

"And is pleased her baby is getting all this attention," Gail adds.

Glory nudges Leadfoot towards the stall door as if giving us permission to pet him. "Thanks, Glory." I reach out my hand and with my first touch I fall in love.

Leadfoot bobs his head and whinnies again, prancing away.

When another horse in a different stall whinnies, it sets off a chorus of whinnies from the rest of the horses in the barn; Gram's mare Malibu (she's been around nearly as long as I have), and Chester (the brown I'd shared my every dream with as we rode the ranch together), and Granddad's paint, Geronimo. He's seventeen hands of solid beast. I turn my attention to each one. When I reach Chester's stall, I enter and give him a fierce hug. Chester had heard every complaint I'd ever had when it came to Ben Anders.

"We'll go for a ride this afternoon," I tell him.

"Time to feed the chickens," Granddad says sooner than I'm ready to leave, but we move back outside – collecting eggs as the sun rises, feeding the chickens before heading back to the house to make breakfast.

Over a bowl of oatmeal and toast I probe my grandfather about today's agenda. "I need to get a few groceries. How about a trip to HEB?"

"We need some bacon and eggs, steak and potatoes," he says.

"I need some yogurt, power bars and salad fixin's," I smile.

"Suit yourself but a bit more flesh on your bones wouldn't hurt none."

"It would hurt a great deal," I tell him. "But thank you. What else?"

"I'm getting my hair trimmed at two. Before Ben arrives."

"Okay. Do you want to make an appointment to see your own doctor while we're out? Dr. Sutter said it might be a good idea."

"But not necessary."

"True."

"I feel fine."

"Okay."

"I'll let you drive the truck into town just the same. Tomorrow we'll take your rental car back and you can start driving Gram's car. I had it washed for you."

"You're the best," I say, meaning it.

By two forty-five we're home, groceries put away and I can retreat to my room to check emails and messages.

I hear Ben arrive just as I close my bedroom door. His muffled voice mingles with my grandfather's. I purposely stay out of sight, managing to slide out to the barn through the kitchen door without notice. I saddle Chester just as if I've been riding him every day. He quivers beneath me and I smile. "You've missed this too, haven't you?" I say as I give him his head and we ride out to explore.

Moving easy in the saddle, the warm breeze caresses my skin. Chester's smooth cadence pounds across the green meadow, relaxing me. I think about the hectic pace I keep at home in Denver, and how I've been struggling with my perpetual single status, the dissatisfied feeling about my life in general.

On Chester's back, it begins to fades away.

◆ ◆ ◆

We fall into a smooth routine of sorts, Granddad and I. For the first few days I watch him closely, looking for any lingering sign of an undiagnosed injury. We feed the chickens together, take the horses to the paddock each day, watch the two-foot high corn stalks begin to leaf, check the watering system and the sky for rain, and run errands. I quickly learn the latter is to re-introduce me to all of his friends – from the owner of the local Feed and Seed, to Lou at Sports Clips or Dale in Walberg. Granddad knows everyone. He's also a baseball fan so there's usually a Rangers or A&M Aggies game on the TV or radio. I retreat to my bedroom when Granddad's either dozing or playing chess with Ben. I find I can work early around the ranch during the cool of the day, then concentrate on wedding vows after supper – supper being four-thirty rather than seven or eight. Granddad enjoys a bag of popcorn or a bowl of ice cream after the watching *Last Man Standing* and off to bed he goes. The routine changes infrequently – such as last week when the crew came to plow and cube the hay field. Granddad greeted one and all atop Geronimo, Chester and I beside them. He seems satisfied every time he can include me in something he enjoys. I've begun to wonder how he'll be when I return to Denver.

And how I'll be.

My house-hunting had begun because the lease is up on my apartment soon. I'd already decided I was not living there another moment longer than necessary before Gram died. But my house search – sticker shock not withstanding - made me realize I didn't quite know what I wanted. The made-over mid-century bungalow that I'd toured in Washington Park had been a bit too urbanite. Likewise, the new build, with its cathedral ceilings and floor-to-ceiling windows, in a community showcased around the amenity center and pool, just didn't feel right either. Steph and Linda, my two life-long friends, wanted me to buy the downtown loft with the twenty-four-seven gym and burger bar. We spent plenty of time in Lower Downtown going to Avalanche games and clubbing. Living in the loft would be a continuum of that.

But it was that lifestyle that I seemed to be growing weary of. Made the song *Looking for Love in All the Wrong Places* hit too close to home.

Saddling-up on Chester every afternoon again gave me a new idea. Maybe I could find a mini-ranch near the Denver city limits. Have a few horses. The best of both worlds.

My housing dilemmas float away when Chester and I ride in the afternoons toward the ruins of the old homestead or down by the river. Just as we'd done in my youth.

Back then my cousin Emory would occasionally join us. Three years younger than me, I'd be charged by my grandmother to look out for her while the adults visited. She'd be riding Malibu and I'd be irritated by their slow pace as we searched for arrowheads or picked daffodils.

On any given hot summer day Ben would appear.

He'd jump out at us from behind a tree, or he'd ride up on his own horse. He usually had a fishing pole with him, sometimes a friend.

Seeing him, or rather him seeing me, always meant trouble. He wasn't exactly a bully but he loved to tease.

And leave a fifteen-year-old girl without a date for the biggest dance of the season.

I purposely refuse to look for Ben when Chester and I ride now. Intellectually, I know he's with Granddad, no longer waiting by the meandering riverbank to jump out and startle me.

Instead, I consider inviting Emory to ride along for the pleasure of her company (strange how three years is no longer a big difference anymore), as I breathe easy while watching red cardinals chase each other and spotted fawns grazing in the meadow.

These afternoons are much more preferable to parking myself in my bleak apartment, scrolling through Facebook or trying to talk Steph and Linda into an outing at the zoo instead of happy hour once again.

Riding every afternoon is also my way of letting Granddad know I'm not pushing him towards going through Gram's possessions.

It's a week and a half before broached the subject by saying, "You haven't gone into Gram's sitting room."

We are eating supper. His eyes are on his plate of pork chops and fried potatoes, the Rangers game coming from the radio on the counter.

I take a sip of my iced tea, knowing I need to tread lightly. Gram's sitting room door has been closed since I arrived. "I wanted you to give me the okay first." I sit across the table from him, avocado salad in front of me.

He clears his throat. "Guess we better get started."

"Okay."

"Not gonna be easy."

"No, it won't. And if we start and you want to stop you just say the word. Alright?"

"Alright then. First thing after chores tomorrow."

"First thing."

Granddad is silent as he opens the door to Gram's sitting room. I enter behind him without breaking the quiet.

Inside, I stop to gaze around at the mid-sixties' décor of ruffled yellow curtains on the window, her pine rocker with floral cushions and a peach and cream afghan draped over the arm. My chest wells up and I blink away fresh tears. Gram's subtly-sweet scent is still lingering in the air as I walk to the pine side-table with the built-in lamp, noting the faded shell-hued shade, Gram's reading glasses still on the wood top, a stack of paper-back novels beside them.

I feel Granddad shift as I lift one book and note it's been ear-marked on page ninety-eight. The title is *Summer Wind*, the cover depicting a young woman hugging the neck of a horse. I decide I might keep the book and read it. I set it back in place and move to the shelves taking up the majority of one paneled wall. There are more books and several porcelain figurines. Granddad is still quiet until he moves beside me and lifts a figurine.

"I bought this piece for her right after I joined the service in 1952," he says, his voice gruff as he stares at a Hummel of a girl in dance; slender, fragile.

I lift another, this one of a girl holding a bouquet of flowers. "They're beautiful figurines."

He shrugs and sniffs, sets the figure down. "She always liked them. Started her collection after the first."

"Gram was a nurse, right?"

"She was. And I was a medic. We were still courting when I enlisted. She joined the Nurses Corp, hoping we might be stationed together. That never happened but she took care of some of the men I shipped stateside. In her letters to me she could tell me how they fared."

"That's pretty incredible."

"It kept us close knit. We could share about our days and know the other one understood. That was important afterwards. Gave us a common bond."

Such intimacy is foreign to me. I'm once again reminded of the condition of my generation. The only common bond I see happening is when the Avalanche or Broncos win a championship. Then, everyone's a sudden fan – until they lose again.

Was there any likelihood I would experience something as special as Gram and Granddad did? When I can count on one hand the men I know who aren't more interested in playing video games than having real conversation? When there are more ways than not to escape from 'real' life into a virtual fantasyland?

I'd once heard that your spouse is like a witness to your life. It applies to my grandparents and most of their generation; people who were committed to one another through thick and thin. Most of it thin.

Unfortunately, that way of life has been replaced with short-lived relationships that end when the going gets rough.

So where does that leave those of us who long for everlasting?

Granddad picks up a framed photo of his and Gram's wedding day and I see him rub his neck. This is going to be so difficult for him.

"I'll go get some boxes," I say with a frog clogging my throat. He merely nods as I leave the room.

◆ ◆ ◆

After he retires that night I quietly return to Gram's room. We have managed to pack a few boxes. They are now stacked under the window and labeled: 'Salvation Army', 'Aunt Nell', 'keep'. Those labeled 'keep' are the items he just couldn't part with yet, like the Hummel's. I'm guessing he never will.

I walk over to the shelf and lift down one of several old photo albums. I'd wanted to go through them earlier but had sensed Granddad just wouldn't be able to be reminded of all that is inside. Now I sit in Gram's rocker. Dust particles catch in the lamp and the bound leather cracks as I open it. Black and white sepia-toned images stare back at me, people I've probably heard about, but I can't put the names and faces together. It's strange to think that these are my roots – my family from the generations before me. I suddenly have a curiosity to know the people inside. Fascinated, I slowly turn the pages.

CHAPTER 3

January 10, 1852

Off the coast of England aboard the steamship Kennebec

We sailed from Liverpool this sunny afternoon, late by two days while we awaited foul weather to clear. I'm still in shock, I believe, as I feel the ship's sway pulling me this way and that. I've yet to gain my balance, emotionally or otherwise.

Much earlier the docks were congested with us travelers, hundreds like Mr. Sarnge, the children and I, eager to be on our way. None of us were assured we would sail and so I'd held our place in line, herding the children close while Mr. Sarnge sought out the captain for his decision. Earlier still, I'd pressed Mr. Sarnge to allow the children and me to remain at the inn where we had stayed these past two nights. It was some distance from the docks and afforded us protection from the chill and dampness that still lay heavy along the shore. But Mr. Sarnge - John – decided we would be best served if we were waiting portside by dawn. A wise decision I would later concur. We did not want to be left behind if the captain ordered the *Kennebec* to sail.

And so, as the children grumbled, I awoke each one, assisting them in insufficient pre-dawn light to prepare for the next leg of our hoped-for journey. Then Mr. Sarnge and I led them out of the two rooms we'd shared; the three girls and me in one, John and the two boys in another. In the still-quiet moist morning, laden with our baggage, we'd made our way through the dark and dank city to the anchored ship. And there we waited.

This came after a disconcerting long week. We'd left London by train three days prior. The gray skies had begun to leak not long thereafter. By the time we'd arrived in Liverpool swollen waves were breaking shore and swaying anchored boats of all shapes and sizes to and fro in the harbor. It wasn't surprising to learn our sea-voyage departure was delayed.

Mr. Sarnge procured for us our lodging and I confined the children to the rooms while he went in search of more news. This even as my charges pressed me sorely to take them about to see the city. Liverpool was known for the pick-pockets and thugs who roamed her streets and I was not going to risk happenstance at this late stage. Instead I turned their attention to the windows and we peered out at the dreary buildings with smoking chimneys and puddled cobblestone streets still crowded with bundled people going about their day. We could only wonder when the sun would shine again.

Then the rain stopped this morning and we all made our way to the dock. We were near the front of the long line of would-be passengers when a sense of cautious excitement began to permeate the air as daybreak neared. This mingled with the scents of dead fish, sea salt, and oddly enough spiced apple cider being sold by a nearby cart vendor. And as the line of would-be passengers lengthened, the sun broke over the black water and a small cheer went up.

My own apprehension quickly followed.

Joseph had until now forced me to keep a sharp eye on him, he, my youngest charge at eight, determined to explore our surroundings at all costs. I'd already pulled him from the edge of the pier, his hands from the rough-hewn anchor ropes, his face from the inside of an open wooden barrel. But once daylight chased the shadows, I stood regarding the massive ship in front of us, Joseph all but forgotten as I considered boarding her.

Then Louisa began to sob, as she, too, eyed the hulk of a vessel. She caused me to give her my full attention. This, thankfully, prevented my own tears.

"Look at the gulls, Louisa," I'd encouraged, drawing her close. "Look how they circle over us, greeting us with a happy welcome."

She, at ten years of age, would have none of my meager attempts to waylay her. She still wishes we were not leaving all behind; her home, grandparents and her mother Ann, long these years in her grave.

Sarah and Ellen, in contrast, scampered about the dock with excitement. They are more reasonable about the future. Sarah, at sixteen, reminds me of her mother; serene and compliant, while twelve-year-old Ellen is exuberant and filled with the possibility of this new venture. Young Joseph is too young to understand we are bound for a new land and a long, laborious journey before our arrival.

When I gazed over Louisa's shoulder to check on him, he was once again trying to climb a pylon.

"Joseph!" my anxious voice rang out.

"Come down from there!" his father added. Joseph's head hung low after he dropped to the ground and his father - my employer - collared him. "You will stay close at hand now," he commanded. "Jonathan, take Joseph's hand and do not let go."

Jonathan, the eldest Sarnge child at seventeen, is just as intrigued by the *Kennebec* as Joseph and I have no doubt the two brothers will probe the captain and crew about her for days to come. He took his brother's hand in his and as we all watched in wonder after the sun emerged, barrels, crates and bags were loaded by ropes and strong sailors and shore men onto the deck and bowels. She is a steamer of great proportions, this ship and, as I found after boarding her, sturdy and clean and modern.

When at last, her nearly three-hundred-and-fifty passengers, this governess Matilda Wyeman and the Sarnge family included, were allowed to embark, the pressing surge of passengers was a bit overwhelming. Urgency lingered in the air.

I was heartened to recognize people I knew from London. Bakers and milliners, dress-makers and laundresses. Their decision to make this journey lessened my anxiety by degrees (could we all be wrong?) and then we were busy acclimating ourselves to the ship. No longer any time for second-guesses.

Now all around me is shifting seawater and fading shoreline. The crew long ago finished loading our worldly possessions, the captain finally giving orders to raise anchor and sail. Liverpool is long behind us, as is England herself.

I am struck by a sudden and intense sense of distress as I consider never seeing my family again. I've left behind my parents and many siblings. The reality is so dire I try instead to concentrate on the care of my five charges, secure, at present, on this, our first night of many, at sea.

All is calm, I remind myself. Mr. Sarnge and his two sons are abed with the other men in a far section of steerage. I reside with the women and girls on the lower deck, all of us clinging to the hope and promises of the missionaries from America who told us about the new world that awaits us. I am writing now, trying to win over my fears, addressing this, my first post to my mama, papa and numerous brothers and sisters who gave me their reserved blessings when I told them of my decision to join John for the journey to America. No candles are allowed below deck for risk of fire, so I write in the dusky light to convey that I am well thus far, safe, my small Bible beside me bringing me comfort. No doubt my family will receive several of my missives at once when I can finally dispatch them. But I write not only to allay their concerns but mine as well.

I write that travel with five children, albeit of a reasonable age, is still a complicated task, made more so by a modest purse. However, Mr. Sarnge is ever thrifty. Our months' long journey will press his pocketbook to the limits but I remind them that he sold his masonry business and house and pre-purchased our way to the Salt Lake Basin and Utah Territory. I also tell them he fore-thought to purchase two wagons and two teams of oxen that will be waiting for us in a place called Council Bluffs, Iowa once our water-crossing to New Orleans, then up the Mississippi and Missouri rivers is complete.

Only weeks ago, John sat me down and explained he would be leaving England for America. I had been a governess in his employ for several years. Until Mrs. Sarnge's death after Joseph's birth I rarely had cause to engage him in matters. Afterward, my role in his household grew. I now consider his children my own, having had a hand in all they are and are becoming. How then, could I let them leave me?

"There was a man on the street teaching about a new way and a new life." John's voice was filled with excitement that day. "I paused to listen and my parched soul was doused with water. I can only hope all he said and all I've since heard and want to believe is true. These people claim they have specific instruction from God Himself and are establishing a new world in a place called the Great Salt Lake Basin. They need all manner of skilled laborers and I want more for the children than what I can provide here. Say you'll come with us Matilda, and embrace the possibility of it all. I can't manage without you."

Explaining to my own family had been more difficult.

"But, truly, Mama, what else am I to do?" I'd argued with her. "Twenty and six, I am, and no better prospects thus far. You and Papa have enough concerns. If there is truly a place where men are good and god-fearing, this Utopia on earth, shant I give it consideration?"

"There is no such place, Tilly." She'd pressed a long thin hand over my own. "But go with my blessing. Just beware of false teachings. And always remember we will be here if you need to return."

I take another deep breath as the ship lists slightly and the ropes groan. Louisa sighs in her sleep, calm now. Ellen rolls to her side in slumber. I arise and smooth the warm coverlet Louisa and Ellen share and check on Sarah who is curled on a pallet beside them.

I tell myself there will be incidences that try me, moments that make me want to flee back home, before I also feel an excitement all the way to the depths of my being. The possibilities once we arrive in this new land will be endless, and it is thrilling to know so.

I remind myself as well that I do have faith in God Almighty and am saved by His mercy and the sacrifice of his Son. I will not be fooled by false promises and false prophecies. But my conviction is that there will be more joy rather than less to confirm the choice I made.

I pray so and rest in it.

That but I could know the future, what trials lay ahead, what burdens, but alas, only God does.

I only know the here and now. We are safe this night.

Was it wrong then for me to leave all behind for the promise of a future? My dear mother and sisters Caroline, Julia and Rachel? My brothers James, Jon, Joseph and Benjamin? My siblings Miles, William, Thomas and Sarah have already gone to heaven (illness, the meager state of my father's purse, stealing them from us), and I miss them all this night. No less my dear papa; I can still see the glimmer of his unshed tears as he and I said our final farewell.

In the quiet of the ship's hull my choice wraps itself around me. I wish to hold on to thoughts of my family back in London yet *this* family – the Sarnge family - is my future. The light of day is only hours away and then I'll be found above deck at the cook stoves the men set up earlier this day. I will attempt in all good faith to make a reasonable porridge for our first breaking of fast on this ship and I will do so with gladness. Five children and their father I have promised to tend and I'm told the port of New Orleans is more than two full moons away. I am determined to be similar to Joseph and Ellen in spirit and embrace our adventure. I will temper my misgivings with good cheer for there is no turning back now. No, none at all.

My course is set.

CHAPTER 4

Present Day

Linda and Stephanie have been my two best friends since grade school. We played teether ball together on the playground. Double-dating was prevalent when we were teens. So was sharing a limo for Senior Prom. I enrolled at the University of Colorado, Boulder first. They both followed but Linda dropped after one year, Steph after two.

We have nursed each other through more painful breakups than I can count.

They both think I'm tinged for staying at Granddad's for so long.

On a three-way phone conversation with them last night Linda tells me so. "You must be bored," she adds. She's never had much tact.

"Yeah," Steph chimes in. "Don't you miss going out for dinner, drinks, dancing?"

A month at the ranch and I have been asking myself these questions. "I'm too busy to miss much of anything," I explain. "I'm still helping Granddad go through Gram's things, and I've renewed a relationship with the love of my life."

"That guy Ben?" Linda asks excitedly.

"No." I frown. "Of course not. Why would you think that? I never had a thing for Ben. With Chester. My horse. He's loyal and snuggly and — "

"Oh, come on, Shelley."

I smile but I'm mostly serious. "And he's a great listener."

"But what happened to you buying a place before your apartment lease is up? Like the loft you toured? I thought you liked the third-floor end unit." Steph laughs. "And *I* sure liked the sales rep."

"I haven't decided one way or the other," I reply. I did like the great views the loft had. The Rockies were visible to the west, Coors Field to the south.

"It's perfectly located in the hub and buzz of the Denver scene," Steph adds.

"And you've both called dibs on the second bedroom on alternating weekends," I add. "I haven't forgotten."

"Remember that incredible gym and smoothie bar?" Linda chimes in. "That was a hotbed of testosterone."

I fight the urge to roll my eyes. "I know you'd love the place."

"You bet we would," Steph states.

But would I, I ask myself.

"Right now, I'm content hanging out with Granddad, writing vows at night and going through these family albums I found."

"Like old pictures and stuff?" Linda says. "Why would you want to go through those? You know, I saw Henry last week. He said to tell you hello. I think you and he—"

"Drop it, Linda. And forget I said anything about family albums." Why had I shared that? I should have known they wouldn't understand. I'm beginning to conclude that my friends are just too shallow, that we don't have much in common any more.

Unlike my cousin, Emory. Tall and slender, Em could be a swimsuit model. She's joined me to ride twice now and – glass of wine in hand and sprawled on the carpeted floor – to look through the old albums. She seems to enjoy this new pastime as much as I do.

"How much longer will you be there?" Linda adds.

"I'm not sure," I deflect. "Some days Granddad is okay going through Gram's things, and others he isn't. I take my cue from him. Ever since the high school baseball season started, he prefers to be at the ball field rather than her sitting room." Granddad had asked me to join him for the season opener. I'd been surprised by how much I enjoyed the game. Even after I'd seen a familiar face in the dugout. He'd been huddled with a player. He'd then clapped the kid on the back and the kid had raced onto the field.

"Is that Ben?" I'd asked Granddad.

"He's an assistant coach."

Of course, he is. "Let me guess," I'd said painfully. "Ben was a star baseball player in college, right?"

"Scholarship to A&M till he wrecked his knee."

Linda's laugh hurts my ears. "High school baseball?"

"More like time with Granddad."

I hang up the phone soon after, annoyed more than I wanted to be. Have my interests shifted so far away from my two friends? Steph and Linda have always been party girls and are proud of it. Regulars at every Lower Downtown pub and nightclub in the Denver area, they know every bouncer, bartender and where every private party will be held. They even have a few Broncos etched on their conquest belts, and are blissfully content with their fly-by-night lives.

I wanted something more.

Something different.

Something better.

I just didn't know what.

The conversation lingers with me throughout the night until I finally stumble into the kitchen for caffeine.

"Morning, Shelley," I hear before I see Ben standing at the coffee pot.

I stop cold, startled and well aware that I'm in baggy sweat pants, and old t-shirt and fluffy pink slippers.

Worse, I have bedhead hair that hasn't been brushed and it's merely – I glance at the stove clock - four fifty-two. Ugh.

I try to smooth my hair down, tuck it behind my ears as I stare at him in his nicely pressed western shirt tucked into starched jeans and Laredo boots. His monthly dry-cleaning bill must be a whopper.

He tips his Stetson, a devious gleam in his green eyes, and I can tell he is enjoying my discomfort.

"Carl and I are riding fence this morning," he offers. "To make repairs on loose posts, broken wire."

I knew this, my brain reminds me – I just hadn't known Granddad and Ben riding fence would mean Ben being in the kitchen so unannounced and so early. Much to my mortification. I make a mental note never to venture around the house again before I've at least brushed my hair. I then mumble something about Granddad getting ready, pour my coffee and quickly retreat, even as I can feel him smiling at my expense.

Damn the man. He always gets the best of me. Even when he isn't trying.

I cower in my room until I hear both men leave the house, wondering if he is still enjoying seeing me humiliated.

Knowing no one would believe me if I tried to "out" him.

Not Ben. He's too cordial. Too polite. He laughs out loud and smiles with his eyes. He is helpful and accommodating, and appears to be genuine.

The Ben I knew as a child told me my braces were blinding him and once loosened Chester's saddle, laughing when it and I fell to the ground.

Yes, these things happened many years ago and yes, he's not that boy any longer – which is the very reason he throws me off-balance. I know how to deal with the other Ben – ignore him, stay away from him.

But *this* Ben –

Granddad relies on him a lot. They have a joint venture raising cattle. Ben handles all the day to day details but he counts on Granddad's experience. They ride together, play chess together, both love baseball and horses and...

I wonder how my grandfather feels about his own son – my dad – living in Denver, a mechanical engineer for Air America Airlines. Had Granddad wanted my dad to stay and work the ranch with him? I question why my dad chose to leave Central Texas, the ranch, his parents. I know so little about my own family. This is why Gram's photo albums have intrigued me. Why the past seems to be pushing its way into the present.

I'd been so wrapped up in my own life for so long I'd given little consideration to anything else. My mom is a hair stylist, has been at the same salon for years. We'd never discussed if she'd ever wanted a different career, more children; she is just, well... Mom. Dad is just Dad; he goes to work, comes home. When I was a kid, they'd watch me play soccer, gave me piano lessons; pretty typical stuff. I had Friday night sleep-overs with Steph and Linda and summer camp. We went to church once or twice a month – the same church not too far from our three-bedroom suburban house. I can't even remember the name of the church. Once I moved onto CU's campus I stopped attending altogether. I hadn't returned to a church until Gram's service. Then, on my first Sunday with Granddad he said, "Church is at ten. We'll go to Sullivan's for brunch afterwards."

I've been joining him ever since. For Grandad, I tell myself, although I find I'm listening to Pastor Dave's messages.

Linda and Steph would roast me if I shared *this* with them. I've given them enough ammo.

Ben, as well; fluffy pink slippers, bedhead hair and all.

If only I had the guts to Google him, find some dirt on him that I could use. But then what? Who would I tell? Granddad really needs him. And I'm not *that* curious.

I'm not.

◆ ◆ ◆

That breezy warm night, after Granddad retires, I carry a bottle of merlot and another photo album out to the porch. The night is simply perfect – seventy-five degrees and a gentle breeze, stars shimmering in the dark sky. The cold Colorado springtime is a distant thought as I curl up on the porch swing and let the warm air caress my skin.

I'd spent the day alone. I'd worked out with my aerobics CD in front of the television, completed all the morning chores, cut fresh azalea's and poppies from Gram's garden and arranged them in one of her vases – all while Granddad and Ben roamed the ranch repairing fence. I hadn't dared saddle up Chester for our afternoon ride for fear I'd stumble onto the two of them. I wasn't ready for another round with Ben yet.

When I heard them return to the yard, I peered through the blinds to see Granddad dismount Geronimo. I stayed inside until they finished talking and Ben rode towards his ranch. Supper had been early and Granddad retired to his room to listen to the radio.

Now Ben and Steph and Linda are far from my mind as I sip from my glass and stare up at the multitude of stars in the sky and listen to a coyote howling in the distance. This place is so special I question why my dad moved away. I think about calling him - asking him some of the questions I now have. Questions about his choices and mom's and if he'd return here one day.

I decide I should ask such things when I return home so instead open the album. I'm beginning to put names to faces. I recognize one of Granddad when he was a boy standing in front of the old house with his parents and siblings. Another sepia-toned shot identifies a man named George as a child of about ten. It appears he is with his own parents, an older couple. Then on an adjacent page is another portrait of the same woman. It is a very old photo, most likely taken around the end of the last century.

I'm intrigued by this woman because of her name. Matilda. My name is Rachel Matilda and I know our family has named the first girl of each generation Matilda for quite some time. My dad's sister is also a Matilda but we call her Nell.

What is bothersome is that I don't know why there is a Matilda in every generation. Is the picture I hold a shot of the first Matilda? Is she our namesake? And if so, why?

CHAPTER 5

January 20, 1852

The creak and groan of the ships' too-tight ropes, the snap of whipping sails and the footfalls of crewmen running to and fro shouting orders, no longer startle me.

We have settled in, I dare say. The children and I now have friendships that, if all goes well, will remain for years to come. We prepare meals together, taking shifts to create dishes of salted pork, potatoes and greens or large pots of oatmeal. Our water supply is plentiful, something I hadn't realized could be an issue until John explained how dire our circumstance would be without it. I am grateful we have a captain who does his job well.

Below decks, we have come to terms with the sparse though dry and warm space that serves as our sleeping areas. It is imperative we keep the area tidy to prevent sickness. There are few complaints about doing so.

Most of our fellow passengers are hard-working and thrifty, traits born by lack and necessity; the reason most of us are on this journey to a new life. Had I not taken the post of governess when I was of age, I would likely still be assisting Papa in his tailor shop as Rachel and Caroline do. Although I can thread a needle well, stitch a hem my father is proud of, I wanted something more. My brother James did, too. James, my eldest brother, opened a London pub my parents are none too pleased with. Now my youngest sister Julia works for him, a shock to us all and further distress for my parents. My other siblings, all on the verge of adulthood struggle to find their way, my father's earnings not going far enough to support us all. Mama, the dearheart, is so vexed by it all. She wants her children and theirs close at hand and yet we have all begun to wander.

I daresay, I am the first to claim a sea voyage and I eagerly share my adventures in my writings to them. They will have my first batch of missives soon. I safeguarded five with the captain of a passing steamer on its return voyage to England. We, the *Kennebec* passengers, were quite astonished when shouts rose yesterday morning and we soon saw the other vessel coming alongside us. Our captains exchanged weather information. Our news was of warm, calm seas behind us, theirs imparted a storm some days out and swells that stir the belly. We exchanged correspondences as well and could only hope the storm they spoke of dissipates before we reach it. The captain promised me he would see my letters delivered, but as the two ships pushed off from one another and the other continued toward my homeland, I wondered if she carried away my last possibility of return.

Still, I am content with my decision, although I long for a strong cup of tea. I did not know that Mormon's forbid tea consumption. I find this preposterous, but will accept it for the time being. In the meanwhile, I cheerfully hum throughout my day, enjoying the camaraderie of our situation, the companionship and exchange of life stories with my new friends - women from all areas of England. The Irish immigrants on board keep to themselves, as if there is an unspoken sad rule in place and we, the Mormons, and they, cannot converse.

However, Louisa is no longer the gloomy girl who boarded ship. And her sisters flourish, as do Jonathan and Joseph. They are busy from dawn till dusk in their explorations and I stimulate their mind with mathematics and a study of the constellations when we can safely remain above deck after dark.

John and I converse every morning and at the evening meal, and throughout each day we find one another, his concern for my welfare and that of his children weighing on him. It is a pleasure to tell him all is well and then witness the anxiety he carries begin to give way.

He is rather a handsome man, still young by some standards yet nearly twice my own years. I've often given thought to why he never remarried after Ann's death; he with five children to raise and a business to manage. I assume he will welcome a wife and likely find one once we arrive in Utah Territory.

I too, long to find a husband. On the shelf at home, John's explanation and my subsequent learning of the new church were my main reasons for agreeing to this voyage. I'm told the men of Utah are all God-seekers; good men of reputation with quality skills and in need of good wives. If they are like John, it is true. The proclamation of the Mormon elders is that God revealed to founder Joseph Smith that a woman must be married to a Mormon man who holds to the dictates they espouse in order to reach Heaven and God Himself. Could this be true? At All Saints, my parish church in Poplar, I was taught that we have direct communication with God if we so choose. I'm not keen on relying on someone else for the saving of my soul.

But I do seek a good man with a true heart for God Almighty and if I found one in this place called Salt Lake, in the Utah Territory, I would not have to make a decision about whether I believe this or not.

A godly husband. Babes of my own.

Now that we are well on our way towards our destination and the mishaps I envisioned happening while we traveled on the high seas have not transpired, I think of my goal more and more. My excitement grows. I have begun to pray for this husband God will provide me. He will have a warm smile and gentle eyes, will defer to me with kindness, and I therefore will make him a happy home.

My dream does not seem so over-the-top any longer, each day's journey taking me closer still. Dare I but hope...

♦ ♦ ♦

Utah Territory
February 1852

Will Hatcher closed the wooden door to his house and paused, his mood somber. He had wood to chop, cattle to round up. He had newborn calves he needed to keep warm and game to hunt before the winter blast bearing down on them took hold. Instead, what had him strung tighter than a fiddle were the two women he'd left inside; his two wives who couldn't seem to get along together anymore.

Ruth was the wife he'd married first. Some said they'd married late – they'd both been twenty and one. Some said that was the reason Ruth was so stubborn. Had an independent streak.

But Will and Ruth had known each other since they were children; his family and hers growing up together, striving toward the goal of seeing Joseph Smith's visions carried out. Eight-years-old when his parents embraced Mormonism and moved the family from Ohio to Missouri and then on to Illinois, Will knew plural marriage was their way of life; plural marriage was not only expected but necessary: no man was worth his salt if he didn't have wives to have children to solidify his own heavenly kingdom. Ruth grew up same as him. She understood. She'd given her blessing when he married Sarah Ann, eighteen, a year after he married Ruth. Sarah Ann's parents had already passed into the hereafter, so her fifteen-year-old brother, George came to live with them.

They'd all gotten along just fine while in Nauvoo, Illinois with like-minded family and friends, too consumed with carving out life amid strife and struggle to think of much else. Ruth brought forth his firstborn and they'd agreed to name her Sarah Ann after his second wife, 'to make her feel welcome' Ruth said. Not too long after, Ruth birthed Emeline Jane and he'd assured Sarah Ann she'd be with child soon, God willing. Then tragedy struck them all when baby Sarah Ann died. She'd been but two and Ruth had turned inside herself. When they had opportunity to leave for Salt Lake, Will thought it was a blessing in disguise. Word had returned to them two years prior that Brigham Young and his caravan had found the place Joseph Smith referred to as Zion. They'd settled in the Salt Lake Valley of Utah. Will, with his mother, Sally, four brothers and all if their families (the five living children of the fifteen born to Elias and Sally Hatcher), were eager to join them. Will was appointed one of ten wagon-train captains. He was in charge of ten wagons in the hundred-wagon caravan. It was his duty to see the wagons and church members in them arrive safely.

The journey proved harder than anyone realized it would be, more so for his two wives, who, they learned soon after their departure, were both with child.

Ruth birthed Ruthie and Sarah Ann birthed William Jr. days apart and not long after they reached Salt Lake. Amidst the unrelenting hardship and while Will was building his family shelter on the hundred and forty acres he purchased, Ruth bemoaned giving Will a third girl and still grieved for their lost daughter. Sarah Ann added salt to Ruth's wound every chance she got even though she was still weak from carrying his first son, Will Jr. She wasn't much help to Ruth and the multitude of chores. Bitterness and strife set in, leaving Will to mediate. He wasn't patient with such matters, had too much else to occupy his mind. He'd done well providing for them both; working hard, putting good food on their table, a solid roof over their heads. He was carving a piece of land into their future while also working with the elders and bishop to find peaceful resolutions with the natives and a host of other church-related tasks. He also helped his brothers Hovey, Shepard, Joe and Lyman build houses of their own. The four brothers had built another house for their mother on acreage adjoining his own. Coming home to a contentious household after a long day didn't settle well with him.

He now knew plural marriage could have drawbacks; was irritated by the pettiness of it all. He wanted his two wives to stop their bickering.

So far, they weren't listening.

♦ ♦ ♦

When the ship plunged forward again, the girls' cries made my heart plunge as well. The storm had come upon us slowly at first but with increasing intensity over the past day. With each new hour, the severity of our situation grew.

Our captain now shouted orders to draw down the mainsail. We had already scrambled to secure anything that could roll or fly and took to our quarters. Huddling in our small spaces, we listened to the squall batter the hull and the crew try to shout above the howling wind, lashing sea and pitching ship. More often than not their words were swallowed up as I was certain we would all be by the time this night was through. A hurricane, I had overheard the crew murmuring in the early hours before the onslaught. Now there was no end in sight, my prayers to God above frequent and heartfelt as the ship listed heavily, then righted itself, only to list again. Surely one of the swells would tip us completely.

The stench from weak stomachs added to our woes, Ellen along with many others. She moaned as I clung to her, her belly empty now but still roiling, the damp cloth I had placed on her forehead long ago doing nothing to ease her suffering. I had stumbled about in the inky darkness, clinging to anything sturdy, to find bowl and towel and suitable disposal. Others did the same, young helping old and in reverse. We didn't dare attempt to use the chamber pots for risk of worse foulness, and yet the hours stretched on, miserably.

I had not re-examined my decision for this voyage for weeks now, content with our circumstance. Yet, now, once again, I wondered if we had met with folly we could not survive. Why oh, why, had we departed home? Surely God had not led us to the middle of the ocean only to allow us to drown? And yet why should we be spared? Tragedy befell all at times. We were no better, no different. Was the sea going to take our lives and hopes and dreams?

As we pitched forward again, sea water sprayed through the cracks and crevices all around us. I hung on to Ellen and Sarah and Louisa and prayed; prayed for John and Jonathan and Joseph, prayed for our crew and captain. I then prayed for my family and our fellow passengers, and then calmly gave myself over to God's will. What more could we do? At least I knew that if we succumbed, we would have no more suffering in this world.

February 16, 1852

The swells began to lessen gradually and our ship was still upright but I would never again consider her large; not from the middle of a ferocious sea. We began to right what was toppled, surveying the damage, the lost barrels of foodstuffs, cook pots and all else unsecured before the onslaught, and considered ourselves blessed. We were all still alive. Now the hurricane is two weeks behind us and nothing but blue skies have followed, day after day.

We gave thanks to God for sparing us so, and made do with the balance of our supplies amid talk we might put in at the city of New York to replenish what we had lost. The elders persuaded the captain we had enough, wanting to make New Orleans sooner rather than later. We still had to travel up two river ways called the Mississippi and Missouri once we reached New Orleans, all to reach Council Bluffs, Iowa.

Joseph stayed closer to me after the storm, reminding me that he is still but a boy in need of motherly attention. John has also given the girls and I more of his attention and on many a night the family and I gather together for talk, book reading and games.

The stirrings of contentment have settled in around me again, an uncomfortable feeling really, for I am not truly a member of the Sarnge family. And yet the children are like my own; the girls share their innermost secrets with me, their squabbles and disappointments. Jonathan as well. And their father? There are rich talks with John about what our lives can be once we reach our destination. At times I catch him watching me from afar, or notice when he touches my shoulder or smiles my way. Am I foolish to consider he has affection for me?

We keep busy, the girls' and I. Our daily chores include maintaining our sleeping area, laundering and mending our clothes and cooking. I prefer to take our work up to the main deck when possible. There we have the sun on our faces and the camaraderie of our fellow travelers which helps hasten the time to pass. The sightings of porpoise, whales and sea turtles bolsters us as well and the excitement amongst us was palpable today when we glimpsed coastal shoreline.

I can't speak for the others, but I long to feel earth beneath my feet again. The land sighting buoys me even as I know we will follow the shoreline south for hundreds more miles before we turn west around the tip of the area called Florida and into the Gulf waters toward our destination. We have many weeks left onboard ship. I can only pray they go well.

March 26, 1852

"But I don't want to get on another ship so soon," Louisa cries out as the *Kennebec* sails closer into the port of New Orleans. The Sarnge family and I are all standing together on deck, watching eagerly and my first impression is one of relief for the city is substantial, the harbor busy with ships of every size moving to and fro or being loaded or unloaded all along the wharf. In the near distance, I can see an area we've been told is called the French Quarter where there are many balconied houses all in rows, and robust energy from the people moving on the streets. Knowing there are modern conveniences on this side of the world is reassuring.

"Papa, can't we stay for a while?"

Louisa voices my own desire. I long to tarry here.

"I wish we could, Louisa," John says. "But our next ship is sailing as soon as we are all on board. The hurricane put us behind schedule and if we are to reach Council Bluffs on time we must push on."

Ellen leans against me wearily.

"However, I'll see that all the baggage is transferred," John adds. Then to me, "Take the children and walk the streets for an hour or so. Do you see the steamship anchored next to that warehouse?"

I do and I nod.

"That is our steamship, the *Pride of the West*." He glances at his pocket watch. "We should be able to disembark within the hour. Ten o'clock. See to it that you board the *Pride* by noon.

"Oh, thank you Papa!" Louisa hugs her father, as does Ellen and Sarah. Joseph bounces in place as I do inwardly. I am hardly eager for more waterway travel, albeit on a narrower channel with no fierce winds to befall us, but a rocking ship none-the-less.

I steer the children from the *Kennebec* as soon as the ropes are tied and the gangway dropped, leaving John behind. As soon as I plant my feet on the wooden wharf, I breathe easier.

"I still feel like I'm swaying," Sarah says as we walk toward the interior of the city.

"I think we all will for quite some time," I reply.

"Look, Tilly," Joseph says and grabs my arm. "Why are they so dark?"

I had heard of the Negro but had never seen one. Now we see men, women and children with dark skin tone, moving along the roadways, some walking, some in carts and wagons. All going about their daily business. "They are no different from us, Joseph. They just come from a country where everyone has dark skin. It's called Africa. People from many countries have traveled here just like us."

I tip my head as we pass a beautiful young woman with milky brown skin.

Joseph says, "She's pretty."

"Yes, she is."

"Louisa come see!" Ellen exclaims then.

"Dresses!" Louisa smiles.

"Look at that, Joseph," Jonathan adds.

"Is that locomotive a toy?"

The items are in a window display at a general mercantile business. The train is a miniature on a track and spitting steam. Dresses and other garments hang beside and above the train.

"Can we go inside, Tilly? Can we?" Sarah asks.

"We cannot purchase anything. You all understand?"

"We won't ask," Joseph replies.

"Very well. But do not touch anything."

The children race into the store before I can add that they must be quiet. But I cannot fault them for their enthusiasm. The ship awaits all too soon.

◆ ◆ ◆

Joseph is no longer entertained by the loading of supplies and people and cargo. As we stand on the deck of the *Pride*, steam hissing and the ship lurching forward, we silently watch New Orleans fade away. It is replaced by sparsely-inhabited grassland, marsh and vegetation and we are swaying again, trying to gain our footing.

"All right then," I say to the long faces of my charges. "We had a bit of fun but now have things to do. And before we know it, we will be in St. Louis. Girls, lets unpack. John, where are you going to put the stoves? And how long will it be before I can begin preparing our meal?"

"We'll be setting them up at the stern. Hopefully the smoke will drift off the bow. They should be ready within the hour."

The *Pride*, though sturdy, is a smaller vessel than the *Kennebec*, with only a hundred or so passengers aboard. Still, I am already feeling crowded, the size of the ship offering fewer places to roam, fewer places for privacy. And the hiss and spit of the boilers are nosier and closer to us all, the boilers themselves menacing contraptions. It was clear from the moment we boarded that the soot from the black coal used to heat the boilers would impede our food and clothing, and the boiling water contained inside could very well scald someone.

I realize I've already modified my voice so our conversation does not disturb the others and by nightfall I am glad for it and the bit of privacy it brings, shadowing all of us from one another.

My disposition is being stretched. Blessedly, we have new books - Oliver Twist and David Copperfield – to read. And Joseph has a new slingshot as do the other boys his age. They can collect pebbles when we put to shore and shoot them off the bow.

Louisa, Ellen and Sarah will begin knitting new shawls tomorrow and they have learned a new pastime of skipping rope with the other girls.

If only I could have a fresh brewed cup of tea. Tea. With sugar and scones and cream. Alas, our linens and china are packed deep within the bowels of the ship, no use to us still.

Tea.

One day soon.

◆ ◆ ◆

The brick and stone boarding house in St. Louis are a sight for my weary eyes. After twenty days aboard the *Pride,* we've arrived to find St. Louis a city of abundance. Storefronts offer a variety of goods and services, much as was New Orleans. Much to my delight.

And John has promised we will stay for a few days.

Our quarters are along a busy thoroughfare not far from the docks. It is a large estate, purchased and run by the Mormons for the migrating families. We have doors we can close and walls in-between and I so welcome this.

I dare say, were it up to me, I would never board another seafaring vessel again. The weather has grown increasingly colder as we've journeyed north, leaving the warm waters of the gulf and the more southern lands behind. The green marshy landscape is also behind us, the terrain here quite brown and dormant. Frosty mornings are more likely than not, as is an occasional snow.

The Mississippi, as we found, is wide and straightforward, while the Missouri, which we are now on, is narrower with many snaking curves. We had just begun to see ice floes bobbing in the water before we put into port.

"What is that, Papa?" Joseph had asked as he spotted the wedges of frozen water.

"The river upstream is thawing from the winter cold," John explained. "Chunks break off and float downstream from the north. They will melt as the weather warms."

"Is this a danger to us?" I asked in a voice only John could hear.

"It wasn't supposed to be." His brow furrowed as he spoke. "Our delays have pushed us into the spring thaw. We should have been upriver by now."

"Then why are we staying here for a few days? Should we leave right away?" I could feel my own anxiety increasing.

"The ship we had reserved is too poorly outfitted to make the journey. We've been told there is another – the *Saluda* – that can take us but she's still a few days from port" He laid a hand on my arm. "We will wait for her arrival."

I take a calming breathe and nod. At least we will have real beds tonight... and tea at last, despite what the elders say.

CHAPTER 6

Present Day

"That's that then." Granddad's voice cracks, his shoulders hunched as we watch the Salvation Army truck recede down the gravel drive, boxes of Gram's personal possessions stacked inside.

I wipe a tear from my cheek and wrap my arm in his, startled by how frail it feels. I want to do more to ease his heartache.

My Aunt Nell sniffs and wipes her own eyes. "Mom would be glad her things are going to a good cause," she says. My dad's sister and Emory's mother, she and Emory live in Austin together while her divorce is being finalized.

She and Emory stand with us in the yard, watching the retreating truck spew dust. The warm Texas sun is doing nothing to diminish our chill.

"Let's go make some lunch, Dad," Nell adds. She turns toward the house and waits. After a moment Granddad turns as well and they head for the house.

I'm grateful my aunt and cousin are here. Granddad and I had picked our way through Gram's things over the past several days, then Nell had volunteered her and Emory to come help with the last of it.

With their assistance we'd set aside items for special people in Gram's life and waited for the donation truck to arrive.

One of Gram's jewelry boxes is now in my room – a gift to my mom - and her favorite fishing pole waits for my dad. Nell had taken an emerald brooch, Emory an ivory mirror and gold cross.

Before their arrival Granddad had gifted me with a set of Gram's pearl earrings and matching necklace. I'd cried against his shoulder, feeling his hand pat my back in comfort as I'd promised him, I would always treasure them.

"I'll wear them at my own wedding," I'd sobbed, silently wondering if that event would ever happen.

Not long after that Granddad hadn't done too well deciding what else to keep and what to donate, spending more time in his recliner watching old westerns then with us girls.

Sifting through his beloved wife's life's possessions has cost him emotionally, each sorted-through item coming with a memory and then a story and many times, tears.

In the end, he hadn't been able to part with much more than trinkets and clothing – demure and dignified dresses with matching jackets or beaded collars and hand-stitched waistlines, high-heels with bows and lace. I'd found myself envious of the hey-day they had lived in, of the days when manners and morals were common. The contrast to their generation and mine glared at me.

We'd left the family photo albums in Gram's sitting room, my desire to probe Granddad about them, about the woman named Matilda in particular, still on hold since I knew he just wasn't up to answering my questions.

His weariness was more evident when Nell asked him what he wanted to do with Gram's tea service collection. The dozens of tea cups and several tea pots, cream and sugar servers and trays were her pride and joy. Displayed in her glass-enclosed pine hutch in the dining room, there are colorful patterns and styles dating to the turn of the century.

Tea with Gram when I was a little girl had been a special event. She'd hum as she set up a serving tray with flavored teas and a vase of her own fragrant flowers. Emory and I, sometimes my mom and aunt, would sit on the porch with Gram sipping and eating just-baked sugar cookies and watch red cardinal's flutter through the trees while the horses grazed.

Of course, Emory and I always had a doll or two with us. Laughter and roll playing were prevalent. We were all princesses, Gram the kind queen.

"One day y'all can divide her tea sets among the women in the family," Granddad had replied to Nell as he stared at the colorful display, no doubt remembering Gram with a cup in her hand. "Until then they're right where they belong."

I think we all knew he'd meant that 'one day' would be after he had joined Gram in heaven.

"That's fine, Dad," Nell had answered.

I wrap my arm around Emory as we follow Granddad and my aunt back into the house, turning my attention to her. "Want to have lunch next week, go to a movie? My treat."

Emory has her long hair pulled into a ponytail, her calf-length leggings and sleeveless form-fitting top showing off her tall sleek frame. In contrast, I wear an Eagles baseball t-shirt, denim shorts, flip-flops and my mousy-brown hair hangs loose. Maybe I need a make-over.

"One of the waitresses quit yesterday so I'm going to be taking on some double-shifts. I need the hours since I'm still helping mom with the mortgage. The divorce should be final next month. I can't wait. Hopefully the court will force my dad to help financially again. And once all the back and forth negotiations end, I won't need to spend as much time with her. She's just so devastated. And every time they have another mediation session, she has a meltdown because he's being so unreasonable."

I knew my uncle had gone off the mid-life crisis deep-end and moved in with his new girlfriend. "I'm sorry it's that bad, Em," I tell her.

She shrugs. "And then Miller..."

"You mentioned him last week but didn't seem to want to share much."

She lowers her voice and I can tell she doesn't want my aunt to hear anything she says. "It's just because he's forty-two and divorced. We're nothing serious, but Mom doesn't like him. He's the bartender where I work."

Seriously? Emory was in her mid-twenties. I instantaneously don't like the guy either.

"Pick a day that works for you and you can tell me all about it."

"Sounds good."

We enter the kitchen behind my grandfather and aunt. Granddad listlessly takes a seat at the kitchen table while Nell pulls out sandwich fixings and hands a knife and mayo to Emory. While she turns her attention to her task, I sit next to Granddad. "The Aggies game starts in an hour," I say to distract him. "I'll bet Horning has two home runs today. He's hitting the bat well."

He perks up a bit. "Ben thinks he's peaked. Thinks Horning's going to start slumping."

"Ben?" Ben – of course Ben. "Well Ben's wrong. Horning hasn't peaked. You don't think so, do you?"

"I'm with you. He's relaxed. Swinging well. Guess we'll see."

"Yes, I guess we will." I begin hoping Horning will have the best game of his young life. Just to prove Ben wrong.

◆ ◆ ◆

The invitation caught my eye as soon as I entered the kitchen. I set down the bag of groceries I held and saw it on the table – all gold and shimmery, sitting atop the gold-embossed envelop it had come in. The envelope was addressed to Granddad, but he'd obviously left the invite out. For me to see?

The content of scrolled gold print announced the Hill Country Garden Club's 50th Anniversary Gala with Special Tribute to Violet Gatewood.

I blink back tears and re-read the script. Wow, a tribute to Gram. How special is that?

Now that we've completed sorting through Gram's things, I seriously need to think about leaving. But what leaving means is still a mystery. I have my cold boring apartment to look forward to. Or a pricey loft I just can't get excited about. Since neither appeal to me, I put the groceries away and take the invitation outside.

I find Granddad leaning on the wooden fence of the corral watching Glory and Leadfoot romp around the pen. Both horses begin to trot over to where we stand.

"So, this invitation says the Garden Club is going to honor Gram for her contributions over the past quarter century," I say as I step onto the post to pet them both. "That's pretty cool."

"Yep." Leadfoot nudges Granddad between the fence posts.

"You don't sound thrilled about it."

"I'm glad for her."

"But...?" Granddad has always been a man of few words. He extends his hand out for Leadfoot to take the carrot he holds.

"Just not sure I want to attend... you know... without her."

Sadness is written all over him.

"What if I went with you? We went together? I'd like to go."

He briefly glances my way. I see a shimmer in his aged brown eyes. "You'd stay another few weeks? The gala isn't till August."

"I'd stay, if you don't mind a roommate for a while." I wrap my arm around his. "If you haven't noticed, I kinda like this place. And believe me, nothing's pulling me anywhere else."

"It's settled then."

"What's settled?" Ben's voice startles me – doesn't it always? I glance to my right to see him walking toward us from the barn, saddle in hand. It is a warm day and he's ditched his cowboy hat in favor of an Aggie's baseball cap, his jeans for khaki cargo shorts. He looks natural in both boots and the flip flops he wears now.

One more thing he does right.

Just last night, when Granddad and I had been sitting on the porch, he'd told me how he and Ben's grandfather, Oral had become best friends when they were just boys. They'd spent their days helping their fathers plow and plant corn fields, their spare time fishing and climbing trees together. Later they'd joined the Army together and their wives had become friends. After their service days, they'd returned to their adjoining farms and raised their families side by side.

Oral's son was Hamel, Ben's father. Hamel, career Army, had died when the chopper he was piloting went down during a training exercise. Ben had been five-years-old.

Ben's mother Vicki went into a tailspin. She remarried the wrong man. When Ben was nine Ben told his grandfather about the constant fights his mother and step-father had. Soon after Ben and Vicki moved to the ranch. When Oral died Ben inherited his holdings.

"Ben took care of his grandmother, Kate, until she passed, and his mom until she remarried again," Granddad added. "Now Vicki has a good marriage and Ben has two half- brothers."

My opinion of Ben was shifting. I was being forced to concede that not all Millennial men were weak and shallow. Not all of them had an X-box and man-caves. Nor did they all play beer-pong and say 'dude' at the end of every sentence.

Maybe, just maybe, there were a few good ones.

Like Ben.

And maybe that was why he rattled me so.

"What's settled?" he asks again, my senses on high alert as he perches a foot on the fence and lifts the saddle over it.

I wait for Granddad to reply. I don't want to engage Ben in any conversation. But when Granddad remains silent, I finally say, "Our decision to attend the Garden Club Gala. Granddad just received the invitation. They're going to honor Gram."

"Shelley's agreed to stick around and be my date."

I smile at Granddad's terminology.

"Well that sounds like a nice way to spend an evening." Ben claps Granddad on the shoulder. He seems genuinely sincere.

"You want to join us?" Granddad adds, jolting me. "One dance with me and Shelley will be lookin' for a new partner. You up to the task?"

"Granddad, I'm sure Ben— "

"When is it?"

"A Garden Club event really wouldn't be your idea of an— "

"Three weeks from Saturday." Granddad's voice cuts through my words. Neither man is listening to my protest. "Really," I say louder. "I— "

"I'll have to check but I think I can make it."

"It's a black-tie affair," Granddad adds.

"I just had my tux pressed."

His tux pressed? How often does he wear a tux?

He glances at me from the corner of his eye, then adds, "So I guess this means we get to see Shelley all decked out?" A slow smile spreads across his face.

My breath leaves me and I begin to tingle all the way down to my toes. "I—" No other words form in my head.

And then Ben turns his head and stares directly at me, making me forget my attempts to protest, making my inability to breathe seem minor.

Until he winks.

I see the Ben I've always known – the devious Ben, practical teaser Ben – the Ben who will probably stand me up again, stand *us* up.

I take a deep breath, determined to regain my equilibrium. I cross my arms and glare at him.

Even so, I consider his words. I've worn nothing but jeans and uncomplimentary tops ever since my arrival. I rarely add more than a touch of blush or mascara to my face, not really caring how I look since I'm not trying to impress anyone. Right now, I'm at least in a sun dress and sandals but remembering Gram's pretty dresses and accessories I am suddenly self-conscious. I really do need a makeover.

A challenge.

Which means I have some shopping to do.

I notch up my chin in defiance. "I've been known to look halfway decent when I want to," I tell him. Then moving forward, I boldly press my finger to Ben's chest. "I just haven't wanted to. There hasn't been any reason to."

"Oh," Ben returns, that smile widening, "I have no doubt that you can look mighty fine. None at all."

I draw in air again – his behavior making it clear Mr. Perfect isn't having visions of me in a floor-length Gala gown.

CHAPTER 7

April 2, 1852

On the deck of the *Saluda* my skirts billow around me as I hold onto a barrel and shout above the beastly cold wind threatening to topple me.

"Biscuits from last night," I reply to John's question. "They are the only cooked food we have."

"Very well. We will have biscuits then," John shouts back. We have tried to keep a fire lit to cook our cabbage and potatoes but the wind is too fierce on this third day aboard our third ship. "Go below deck and eat there with the children."

I nod, wanting to get off the deck and out of the cold, but knowing it is no better inside. There are too many of us in tight quarters, this steamer smaller than the *Pride*. It is old and dilapidated, permeated with a musty odor that will not dissipate and St. Louis is long behind us.

John – dear, John – was able to secure us berth below, probably by offering extra coin, but as I make my way to the stairs, I am reminded of the others confined on deck, hunkered down now in our severe condition, the wind pressing in on us with numbing force. It is impossible to believe that we are moving upstream at all, and certainly not at a good pace.

"Tilly," Joseph cries as I reach our small, dark area. He hugs me as we both stumble to stay upright. I hug him back and ignore the thunk of another ice floe as it hits the hull.

Then I hear the captain's shout. A frequent occurrence. He never seems well pleased, his barking orders always sending the crew clambering about.

I still question the wisdom of this leg of the journey. Now I am certain we should have waited until spring. Why the elders keep pressing us on, why we were enlisted for a journey during such a difficult weather season, is the mystery. I question why the captain agreed to take us as well. Whispers are many. Voices say he is greedy for our coin, his charges far above what we would have paid another ship. And for a much poorer vessel.

John assures me all will be fine. His kind eyes tell me differently.

I control my fear by thinking of Council Bluffs. Once there, we will blessedly continue our trek across land to the Great Salt Lake Basin. We have a fortnight to reach the others. John has taken on himself the task of seeing to our safe arrival. He regularly converses with the captain and I trust in his decision-making if not the others.

I cannot wait for the day we bid the *Saluda* behind.

I think of my family now more than ever. I suppose it will ever be so during difficulty. But I do so miss Julia's errant tongue, Caroline's vigor and young Rachel's sweetness. I had no inkling how much I would also long for my brothers – all of them, when whilst living amongst them I deplored them terribly. I especially long for my brother Benjamin and fret he will never forgive me for my departure. Joseph is my solace for he reminds me so of Benjamin. I implored Mama, in my last missive, to tell him he was always my favorite, however self-serving of me.

I hug Joseph and refuse to become melancholy, even as my eyes mist. Greater days lay ahead and I will focus on a day not long from now when we will be in a new land where opportunity for men such as John, who have the skills of masonry and ingenuity, will be rewarded. Perhaps, a husband for me as well.

Perhaps John himself.

Sometimes I think I am foolish to consider that might be the circumstance. But then I remind myself that I have seen him cast looks my way. And we have grown close during these past trying months.

So, perhaps it is not farfetched. My cheeks heat as I ruminate.

April 5, 1852

"Ahoy the shore!" John calls to the men gathered on the small wharf as we stand on deck. The bitter wind slaps at us, the crew doing their best to steer the ship toward the small wharf. "Lend us a hand, would you now!"

"Be off! You cannot dock here!" one of the men shouts back. Only then do I notice their firearms; long guns and pistols alike. There are ten men or so. They are guarding the shoreline.

"We mean you no harm! We need to make repairs to the hull." John is the spokesmen for us all. I gather Joseph closer, the girls edging toward me of their own accord. I hold my breath, waiting for the shore-men to reply. We'd received a similarly poor response yesterday when we'd attempted to dock at another town. Our desperation this blisteringly cold morning, with snow falling, has us attempting to do so again.

"Do so further upriver! Take your disease and your heathen beliefs with you!"

I exhale with exhaustion. They fear us we are told, the townsfolk along this river. I see the spite and suspicion on their faces, even from this distance. It is obvious they are not going to let us dock.

We've heard the groups who came through here before us have depleted the area of game, leaving the settlers angry. We've also heard of shipboard diseases such as Cholera.

So far, we've been spared but I do silently wonder if we – the Mormons - are as unstable as they think.

My own parents told me I was being misled.

Since leaving home I have wondered so myself. But alas, I am merely a woman searching for contentment. I am no threat to others.

If there are a few minor things amiss with these Mormon believers, so be it. If they enlarge, I will decide then. I will not walk through life with my eyes closed. Nor be guided by mortal man but by God alone. To date, this new faith is untested. I will carry on until I know for certain.

At present we need shelter from the wind and snow. I have attempted to layer the children's attire to fight off the worst of their numbness and if they can run and play, something lacking onboard, that will help warm them and my heart.

"There is a place just a couple miles further! You can stop there!" shouts another shore-man as the ship turns upriver.

God give us the strength we need to press on.

April 6, 1852

We return to the *Saluda* in much better form just as the shadows grow longer and the cold takes over again.

I am hardly able to contain myself for the wonder of a day on dry land, laughter from the children and the most wonderful new development.

It took another two attempts before we'd been able to put ashore – far from unwelcoming locals. Now all my dear-hearts are exhausted and abed, satisfied and content. And I myself am now able to joyfully ponder on the events of this day as I take pen in hand to share with my family.

Our splendid day was without a bitter breeze and frowning faces in an area where the hilly terrain blocked the wind and the sun shone brightly. We ladies conspired to prepare a warm and filling stew and dumplings, the men hunting the area for several rabbits we spit and roasted while the crew worked on the ship.

Then, after a filling meal, I was quite surprised to have my greatest prayer answered.

A Christian husband to lead and guide me was one purpose for this venture and I am ever-so pleased to announce that I will have one because John Sarnge requested my hand in marriage this day and I gave him an agreeable response.

His question came at the oddest of moments; we were digging, you see, each of us working together on a small pit in the ground to dispose the remains of the rabbits. He stopped mid-shovel, turned to me.

"Matilda, that I could acquire a castle for you, I would. One with servants to do such things as dispose of rabbit bones. You should not be subject to such distastefulness, and yet you do so without complaint. I find myself so enamored by you for so many reasons and I cannot consider allowing someone else to snatch you from the children and me. Would you please, do I dare ask, consider me for your husband?" He pitched the shovel down and his warm hands pressed into my shoulders as he kissed me straight on the lips. I gazed right into his eyes, brilliant green with specks of brown and with his hair overlong – an overdue trim necessary - and falling over his brow, he looked very dashing.

"Yes, John," I said with a rush of air. And then I kissed him back, my limbs all tingly.

I am smiling still.

It is a good match, a fair match, and I cannot wait to become his wife. We have consideration for one another and the children. And I do believe – yes, I do believe I should be very content with Mr. Sarnge.

John rushed me back to our camp, my hand in his, stopping in front of his children. "She said yes," he announced.

"Oh Tilly," Ellen cried.

"I knew she would," Jonathan added with a wide smile.

Joseph and Louisa threw their arms around me and Sarah began to cry.

"You all knew?" I asked, astounded.

"I might have told them my intentions," John replied.

"And we all want you to be our Mama," Sarah added, still crying.

My own tears began to flow. And since then we've learned the captain has the ability to wed us as soon as we choose.

How quickly one's circumstances can change.

April 7, 1852

My dear mother and sisters, Caroline, Julia and Rachel,

Mr. Sarnge and I are to be married in two days' time, on this Good Friday, the ninth of April.

My head is a-swirl.

I have been blessed with a wedding dress, on loan to me by one of the other ladies. It is a glorious gown of fine linen and lace, unpacked for this occasion from one of the many crates below. Mrs. Barnes and Mrs. Lowe have been furiously taking in a few stitches here and there while Mrs. Klemp and Miss Simpson stitch dresses for John's girls.

All the ladies appear to be just as excited as we for a marriage to take place. The event has taken our thoughts from our hardship and given us something to prepare for and look forward to as our ship and crew struggle to push us upriver in this ever-persistent cold. At least the wind has subsided.

My joy would be complete if only you all could be present. I had always planned for you to be with me for such a special day, just as I had planned to be at the weddings of my dear sisters. Alas, I know you will not receive this missive for months to come, months after my nuptials take place, but writing this now brings me comfort. Should I not be able to put ink to paper and communicate with you thus, I would be in such dire straits. I am but glad I brought such a sizeable supply of writing materials with me. I now know I will forever need it. There is always so much to convey. I will make haste to write again soon and share all the details of nine, April, the day marking the death of our Lord and Savior, and now forever the day I wed and commit my life to a man of honor and integrity. If I am not quite in love with John Sarnge, I do love him, and that is, I believe, all important. We will carry on to the Utah territory and make a life together, all seven of us. And I am well pleased by this.

Do think of us with joy upon reading this and have a small celebration.

With affection,

Your daughter and sister, Tilly

CHAPTER 8

Present Day

By noon it struck me that I was having 'one of those days'. I'd turned on my computer only to find it was hiding the wedding vows file I'd saved last night. Then I'd received an email telling me the gown I'd ordered online for the Garden Club Gala was no longer available in my size five. Right after receiving that bit of irritating news, the Denver condo sales rep called to inform me that today was the last day I could lock into the price he had quoted me.

With a sigh, I'd shut my computer down, hoping my file would miraculously reappear when I turned it on again. I'd thanked the sales rep for the forewarning without committing, and decided to head to the Barton Creek shopping center in Austin, determined to find a dress.

Unfortunately, I lose hope after walking through every women's boutique twice. Deflated, I give in to my urge for chocolate, order an iced-mocha that won't look good on my hips, and walk out to the parking lot, hot air blasting me as soon as I leave the building. There is no getting around the fact that Texas is hot in July. Denver, on the other hand, is rarely above the ninety-degree mark. I could back out of the Gala, leave the heat behind and head home. Even if doing so disappointed Granddad.

I enter Gram's Crown Victoria and crank up the air conditioner, contemplating and sipping my mocha when my phone plays "Rock Me Baby". I frown, knowing Steph is calling to give me an earful.

"Hi, Steph." My annoyance is barely concealed.

"Mark said he called you."

"Yes, Mark called and yes I know about the price increase." Mark, the loft salesman, has become one of Steph's 'friends'. "And no, I haven't made a decision yet."

""Come on, Shelley – it's to die for. I don't want you to miss out and the increase is pretty steep. What are you waiting for?"

When I was a kid, I was certain I wanted to be a professional artist when I grew up. Maybe live in Paris or Italy, paint beautiful scenes of beaches and meadows. My mom bought me my first oil-painting kit when I was seven, and took me to art museums for inspiration. As an only child, solitude and quiet were normal. Then in high school I saw Kate Hudson in "How to Lose a Guy in Ten Days". That was it – I was hooked; the high-profile ad executive life was what I wanted.

Reality was somewhat different. I graduated at the height of a recession, when companies were cutting back on their advertising budget. My glamourous ad agency position fizzled.

Making a living writing wedding vows wasn't glamourous either. But it had practically fallen into my lap. Gave me the freedom to spend time with Granddad and the currency to shop for the drop-dead gorgeous gown I wanted so much to find - to knock Ben's socks off even if I wasn't admitting it.

But writing wedding vows wasn't something I wanted to do for the rest of my life.

Maybe Steph was right, and I should buy the loft and settle into the lifestyle Steph and Linda loved so much.

But, I conclude, as she waits for my reply, I don't want to. It's not the something better I'm seeking.

"I don't think I'm interested in the loft anymore," I finally tell her. "I really haven't given it much thought for weeks. If I'd wanted to live there, I'd have been anxious to buy it and move in."

Steph is silent. Then, "What about your apartment?"

"I don't want to live there either. So, I'll probably put my things in storage and stay at one of those weekly hotels for a while. I'll tour the condo again when I get home and pay the increase if I decide it's the right place."

"You're making a mistake," my friend says.

"I don't think so." I feel an instant release of tension, sip my mocha and promise myself I will run an extra mile tonight after the heat subsides.

By the time I pull up to the ranch I've decided to invite Emory to go shopping with me at the Georgetown Square where I've heard there are some great shops. I park and grab the bag with the one and only item I'd purchased from the back seat. I still had another week before the Gala and at least I'd found a shiny pair of Jimmy Choo's. I'm confident the dress will follow.

Heading for the house I notice two people in the paddock with Malibu. My mood shifts even more – from dejected, then hopeful, to shamed.

I pause and watch Carmen, the mother of Angie, as she leads Malibu around the pen, Angie atop her. Angie is thirteen and has Down Syndrome. Carmen brings Angie to the ranch twice a week to ride Malibu. When I'd first met them, Carmen explained how therapeutic the riding sessions were for Angie. I'd noted the patience Carmen had as she walks beside the horse, watchful her daughter doesn't fall, and Angie's apparent joy as she laughs and pats Malibu's neck.

My day's annoyances have been trivial compared to the daily challenges Carmen and Angie face.

I make a quick decision to join them.

"Hi, there." I brush a strand of hair from my perspiring brow as I approach them. "How's Malibu behaving today?"

Carmen turns my way. She is a woman in her mid-fifties, her brown hair graying, her face etched with lines. She and her husband have two adult sons. Angie is one of those 'unexpected blessings'.

"Malibu is my horse," Angie says. She is short and plump with a cherubic face and perpetual smile.

"She sure is," I confirm.

"She's always as gentle as can be," Carmen adds. Holding the reins, she pulls Malibu in a slow wide circle. "We so appreciate Carl letting us ride her."

"Oh, Malibu loves it, don't you girl? Besides, its great exercise for her." Malibu was one of the oldest horses on the ranch.

"I love Malibu." Angie wraps her arms around the horse's neck.

"I was wondering if you have time to stay for a glass of iced-tea when you're through?" I probe Carmen. "I was just going to make a pitcher."

Carmen smiles. "It sure is warm today. That would be nice. We'd love to."

"Can I pour?" Angie claps her hands together and smiles brightly.

"You can be the princess of the day. And the princess of the day is the princess in charge of pouring," I tell her as her eyes widen. To Carmen I add, "I'll be waiting on the porch. Take your time."

In the kitchen, I begin a search through Gram's ware, wanting something better than the everyday pitcher Granddad and I regularly use. I find a pretty decanter with a floral print, matching glasses on another shelf. Gram has several trays and cute sugar bowls and silver sugar cube tongs. She also has all those beautiful tea cups just sitting in their place in the cupboard. In a moment of emotional inspiration, I decide I will honor her by having tea in one cup every morning for the rest of my stay.

I return outside just as Carmen and Angie are walking out of the barn. As we sip sweet tea and eat lemon cookies, I say, "You know, Carmen, I wouldn't mind leading Malibu for you. I could take care of Angie if you'd like."

Carmen looks at me with weariness. "Oh, I wouldn't bother you— "

"It wouldn't be a bother," I interrupt, serious. "I'd really be happy to help. I could take your place one afternoon a week. Give you time to run errands or go shopping? Would that be okay, Angie? Can I spend some time with you?"

"Sure."

Carmen sets her glass down and puts her hands in her lap. "Are you sure?" she asks me.

"Very."

When I see her shoulders sag, I realize how tired she is. And my spirits lift, knowing I can help her. I haven't done enough of that in my life.

♦ ♦ ♦

The porch shades me the following morning as I walk outside, one of Gram's pretty tea cups in hand, to see my Aunt's SUV approaching the house.

I like my aunt. She's a computer expert working for Dell, but she's a country girl at heart.

"Hey, Aunt Nell," I offer as she closes her car door and strides toward the porch.

"Morning, Shelley." She climbs the porch steps dressed in cargo shorts and a tank top. "Warm morning," she adds, sinking into one of the chairs. "Is your granddad in the barn?"

"Yep."

"I'll sit a spell and wait for him. What do you have there? One of Gram's tea cups? Are you having tea?"

"I am. Would you like a cup? I decided just yesterday to use one of Gram's tea cups every day for as long as I'm here."

Nell stares at the cup I hold. "Mom sure loved her tea sets, didn't she? She would have tea with a friend or two nearly every week. And I would have tea all the time when I was a little girl. I was with her when she bought some of her tea sets. In fact, I gave her many of the cups. Me and your dad and Granddad. Over the years. For birthday presents and

Christmas gifts. Then you and Emory came along, and she put on all those little girl tea parties. Remember those?"

"I could never forget. Princess parties, she called them. I had one yesterday with Carmen and Angie."

Nell smiles. "Good memories. I'm glad you're using these now. I'll join you soon and show you which one's are the oldest."

"I'd love that."

"Right now, I have Emory's birthday present to pick up. Did Granddad tell you he was going with me?"

"He did. Here he comes now. I think he's as excited about the puppy as he was about Leadfoot."

Granddad approaches as fast as his eighty-five-year old legs will allow him, hands in his jean pockets, hat perched on his head.

"I picked out this puppy a week after he was born. He's eight weeks old now. I already regret all the work he's going to cause us but Emory really wants a dog."

"She'll love him."

"And she needs that security right now. She might be turning twenty-six but she's missing her dad. I think that's why she's dating older men."

I'm surprised when my aunt mentions Miller. "We've discussed that, Emory and I. Hopefully this phase will pass."

"And quickly," Nell adds with a sigh and turns toward my grandfather. "Hey Dad, you ready?"

Granddad gives Nell a kiss on the cheek. "Let's go pick up the newest member of the family."

I smile, pleased he really is excited.

He then turns to me. "You coming along?"

"Oh... well... I wasn't planning on it."

"Sure," Aunt Nell says. "Come on. Join us. The more the merrier."

Weren't puppies everyone's favorite thing? How can I resist? "Okay. Let me put this cup inside. I'll be right back."

A few minutes later we are seated in Nell's SUV heading back to the highway, dog crate in the back waiting for Emory's gift, when I say, "So where are we headed to pick up this puppy?"

Granddad and Nell share a glance and I have a sudden feeling I should know, as well as a sudden feeling I'm not going to like the answer.

"Oh, just Ben's," my aunt replies, hands on the steering wheel. "I thought you knew it was his litter."

"Nope," I reply, hoping my voice sounds normal. "I had no idea. But then, I don't know why I would. Ben and I don't talk much."

I ignore Granddad tapping his fingers on the arm rest, instead adding to myself, *Okay*. I haven't been to Ben's ranch yet. So, I am more than willing to ride along. More than willing to feed my curiosity. Wouldn't it tell me a lot about the man? Yes, indeed it would.

CHAPTER 9

April 9, 1852

Can it be true? In one hour's time, I will wed John.

The girls and I are fluttering about with last minute details, Joseph running from one end of the ship to the other with excitement. Now he tells me his father is on deck, Jonathan with him. He is all neat and pressed, Joseph says, better than he's ever seen him. He tells me I'm pretty in my borrowed dress, a dress of ivory that is just a shy too short and fails to cover the toes of my boots. Never-the-less it makes me feel special. I smile broadly and ruffle my boy's head just before he races from view. I hope he carries to John word that I look pretty as well.

"Hurry!" Louisa says as Ellen and Sarah attempt to finish tying a ribbon in her hair.

"Hold still, then," Ellen scolds.

"There, all done," Sarah adds.

Louisa looks at me. "You are lovely," I tell her. And she is in the rose and white paisley smock she wears.

Her embrace takes my breath. Then she too races away, anxious to see her Papa.

Ellen and Sarah and I are silent. They are lovely, too.

"Go join your father," I say with so much love in my heart I can barely speak. I accept their hugs and watch them walk away. In just a few minutes I will be their mother. They are my heart and I am ever so thankful-

The roar reaches my ears first. I look up, alert. A moment later I am blown off my feet with other flying debris. I tumble through the air, hit the icy river water hard. I try to draw in breath, but water fills my lungs instead. And then I am sinking... sinking...

April 12, 1852

"Matilda? Matilda? Are you still awake?"

"Read it back to me, please. From the beginning." My voice is weak and raspy to my ears. My lips feel numb as I try to speak. I can barely move in the bed I am confined to, my limbs weak, my abrasions painful, but I need to concentrate for just a while longer.

"Certainly," the woman beside me offers. She puts her hand gently on my arm:

To: Mr. Miles Wyeman and Mrs. Carolyn Wyeman
London, England
From: Nurse Blanche Filmore,
Lexington Charity Hospital
Lexington, Missouri

Dear Mr. and Mrs. Wyeman,

It is with great sadness that I am writing this letter for your daughter Matilda, who cannot at present, do so herself. You see, I'm afraid Miss Wyeman was gravely injured on 9 April when, at midday, prior to the commencement of her own wedding ceremony, the steamship Saluda exploded.

Miss Wyeman, although injured, was one of the spared, because you see, more than a hundred others lost their lives. Miss Wyeman's fiancée, John Sarnge and his young son Joseph were two of the casualties.

Miss Wyeman, we've learned from all accounts, was blown from the ship into the cold water along with many others. Travelers on another steamer, who were witnesses to the explosion and aftermath, promptly began rescue attempts.

Mr. Sarnge's other four children have various injuries. The girl Louisa is severely scalded on her legs and presently under hospital care as well.

I am assisting with the wounded, Miss Wyeman among my patients. She requested I write and tell you of the tragedy.

An investigation has begun into the steamship's explosion but to date evidence points to the boilers being dry and the captain attempting to proceed around a bend amid heavy ice floes blocking passage. The captain along with his crew, were also killed.

Miss Wyeman wishes me to convey to you that her injuries will heal. She is being tended to with great care and will remain here for quite some time. She will write as soon as she is able. Until then, she asks for your prayers and covets her memories of you and your family.

Yours,

Miss Blanche Filmore

May 2, 1852

I ease myself to the side of the bed with care, my contusions still healing. I am grateful I can at last move on my own even though my heart is so wretchedly broken and bruised I'm paralyzed with grief.

I'm convinced I will remain so forevermore.

I still cannot reconcile what took place, my mind reliving the garish scene as it unfolded with vivid detail and yet still refusing to acknowledge its reality.

John dead?

My precious Joseph dead?

How can this be so?

I had just said good-bye to the girls when I
was blown off my feet.

The next thing I remember is hitting fiercely cold water and sinking
fast, my borrowed wedding dress weighing me down. I had no breath
inside me as I sank. Then I bumped into something. I turned to see another
human being with unseeing eyes. My panic multiplied and I pushed myself
away from the horror and surfaced long enough to draw air. I realized
then that the more I flailed the worse my situation would be so I quit my
action and took hold of a large plank of wood, one of many bobbing around
and into me. I remember nothing more save for being hoisted into a
wooden boat sometime later. I was rolled to the floor where I lay,
exhausted, unable to move, knowing I was going to freeze to death within
minutes.

When I woke in the infirmary, I was told two days had passed.

Now I know if not for my rescuers who risked their own lives to save
me and others none of us would have survived.

And yet my dearests John and Joseph are lost.

I now cherish my last memories with Joseph; the morning when he was
racing around, the prior night when he was bidding me goodnight.
Walking away with his father, he turned back to face me, his small hand
in John's. "I cannot wait for you to be my mama," he'd said. I then knelt
before him, ever so pleased and I told him so. He'd smiled and John had
led them away.

I am never to see them again.

Now the *Saluda* is destroyed, most of our possessions with her. And all
these weeks later, I'm told sweet Joseph's body has still not been
recovered. We have given up such hope.

John was laid to rest in a mass grave, no hope for me to rise from my
bed to be on hand. Jonathan, his physical injuries few, was there alone to
witness and say goodbye. He is struggling with the horrid visions he saw

and his sadness, and yet I see such resolve in him. His father would be proud.

The girls are all wounded to varying degrees, Louisa by far the most. I could not, to my utter misery, comfort her for the first several days after our fate. I am now by her side as much as my ability allows. She is sedated most of the time, for if she is not, she cries out from the agony of her scalded legs. It is most distressing to see her thus, and yet she will heal, I'm told. It is to what degree that is uncertain. The physicians cannot tell us if she will be able to walk again.

Several such physicians answered the call to assist at this hotel turned into a temporary hospital in the town of Lexington. All came from the greater distance and larger town of St. Louis and beyond. As one would expect chaos was the initial result after the explosion. The townsfolk, I've learned, were at a complete loss as to what to do with all the maimed and dead. There are near a hundred deceased and so many of them friends I had made in the course of our voyage. Thankfully for us the residents here have been kind-hearted and compassionate. They have rallied to our aide. Sarah and Ellen have been taken in by one caring host family, Jonathan by another. Their injuries not requiring hospitalization, they are recovering from abrasions and bruises and what a blessing it is to know they are well tended while I am incapacitated.

They look to me now, as I improve, to determine a course for us all. Yet all I know for now is that our duration here will be several months. Louisa is nowhere close to being able to travel, nor I as of yet. I am told I will have a place to stay once I have no more need of this hospital and while we continue to tend my sweet girl.

What will we do then? Go on to Utah? Do I take the children? Return them to England? We have not the funds for a journey back, nor have any of us any desire to board another ship.

John has already paid for our full passage to Salt Lake. He would want us to continue on, I suppose, though an attempt must be made to contact his family. Since all of his belongings were lost, I must rely upon my own family to notify his. I have no street addresses for his parents or siblings. Should my parents succeed in contacting them and they wish the children returned I will need assistance from them to do so.

These are the dilemmas swirling in my head, so in shock am I still. All my hopes and thoughts for a life with John are now so abruptly ended.

The Lord alone is my strength now. If not for Him, I would surely curl into a tight ball and thus remain. I can only rely on Him now to see us through, and am grateful I that now. I must care for John's children above all else. How could I not, and how else can I best honor him?

Oh, how I wish that we had never begun this journey. Yet it is ever too late – utterly so – to turn back.

CHAPTER 10

August 12, 1852

"Yes, with great trepidation I have decided we will continue on to Utah. Louisa and I have healed enough to travel again and I've pushed off this decision for as long as possible, weighing the difficulties we will face, the thought of the unknowns. I have no means to stay here; that is the hard truth."

I set down my empty tea cup and look into Blanche's kind eyes. She and I have become friends and I am ever grateful to her for the care she gave me until just recently. "I called a meeting with Jonathan and the girls – the most difficult meeting I have ever had, and through our tears we discussed our situation. "We cannot wait any longer to hear from your grandparents," I'd told them. "We can no longer remain here on the charity of others. We really have no choice but to move on and your father has made a way for that by pre-paying for our journey." Ellen had burst into sobs, saying. "I don't want to leave. I don't want to travel any longer."

"I know, dearest," I'd told her. And the Dowlins want her to stay. They want both Ellen and Sarah to live with them as their adopted daughters and have been so good to them during these past months. I left the decision up to each girl, confidant they love them as their own.

"I'm staying with you, Tilly," Sarah had cried, hugging me tightly, and as I hugged her back, I gazed with tear-filled eyes at her sister.

"We will stay in touch," I'd told Ellen. "We will write often and perhaps visit one another at some point."

Ellen nodded vigorously, her face streaked and red.

"Oh Matilda," Blanche sniffed. "I don't envy you at all." She refilled my tea cup with warm brew and sat back in the brocade chair. The two of us were in the parlor of her home in Lexington.

"Ellen will do well here with this new family, and though I am wretchedly saddened by her decision, I believe she has made the best choice. More than ever I wish I had counsel from my parents and the children's grandparents before this decision was my own to make. But we leave with the other *Saluda* survivors who have also healed enough to push on. For John's sake and dream I will honor him this way. Then, Blanche, should we not find things to our liking, I will do all to return us to England."

"I'm certain you will. And your travels forward this time will be by land?"

"None of us is willing to journey by steamship. A decision that will make our journey longer, but I am hopeful moving on will assist Jonathan in his recovery. He has grown restless in these last days. No doubt he feels concern and responsibility for his sisters and me, and yet his loss is nearly greater than ours in that he lost father and brother."

"It is. And tragic that looters stole so many of the trunks and barrels floating in the river after the explosion."

"Fortunately, there were also honest souls who fended some away so some of our possessions were recovered. We will have some our housewares and linens. It still distresses me to know John was blown ashore and in death, as he lay on the ground, his purse robbed of all."

"So much has been brought to light about the ship and her captain since the explosion."

"As I suspected even prior to our tragedy, the *Saluda* was not seaworthy for such a voyage. Neither was her captain an upright individual. The newspaper reported that this same ship sank a few years ago, only to be salvaged and poorly refitted. It is not so strange then that the man died with his ship, which sank not ten minutes after her boilers blew. Such unspeakable grief could have been avoided." I bow my head, feeling tearful again, then take a steadying breath. "We depart in two days. I'm anxious but bolstered by Elder Kelsey, who by all rights should have been in Utah by now but remained with us. I admire his determination to see us all safely to our destination and if I was not completely assured of his decision-making prior to nine April, I am at this time and believe him sincere. He has promised the animals and equipment John purchased will be waiting for us in Council Bluffs."

"That is exemplary."

"Between Jonathan, Sarah and I, surely, we will be able to lead the oxen," I chuckle. "Louisa will ride in the wagon, her legs still unsteady, her scars heartbreaking, and yet her smile returning. I am ever grateful they are in my life and I pray without ceasing that I am up to the challenge God has bestowed upon me. I have no great confidence in my abilities, merely a need to press toward a grander day. Once again, I will strive to do so with good cheer, my sweet Joseph's smile ever present in my mind."

"You will do fine, Tilly. I know you will."

I rise from my chair, leaving the tea Blanche has poured. "I have asked God if Joseph suffered and He has assured me in the calmness of my heart that he did not. I cradle that knowledge and will hold it close always. And you, dear Blanche, for all your care. I have not much left save that."

CHAPTER 11

Present Day

My senses sharpen as we turn up Ben's long gravel drive. I can feel my heart rate increase, am unnerved by the tug of war between my brain and body.

It's just Ben, I say internally, trying to harness my unwanted reaction. But *it's Ben*, my insides argue back. The image of his slow grin and all-encompassing gaze when he'd teased me about the Garden Club Gala override my reason.

Nell pulls the car to a halt in front of a sprawling log-siding house that could be on the cover of *Better Homes and Garden*. Two gabled dormers shape the front exterior above the wrap-around porch, sandstone pillars standing sentinel at the corners. A manicured hedge of green boxwoods surrounds the front of the porch and two large shady oaks border the sandstone walkway.

I'm thoroughly impressed as we exit the car and I see Ben descend the porch stairs to the walkway.

I take a calming breath.

"Shelley," he says to me after he greets Nell and Granddad. "Glad you could make it."

I try to reply, falter and am relieved when he adds, "So, let's go see that pup. I think Sadie and Hick are ready to be empty-nesters again. We sent two pups to new homes yesterday and three go tomorrow."

Ben leads the way towards a large log-siding barn. I follow along, steadying myself by looking at anything except Ben. I notice two other large metal buildings a distance away, a paddock in-between them, a parking lot with several cars beside the farthest building and a few horses and people moving around.

At the barn entrance, Ben pauses to let us enter first. Granddad and Nell move forward and I feel Ben's hand press into the small of my back as I follow. The simple touch sends a shiver through my frame and I hope no one notices my intake of breath or the goosebumps that rise on my arms.

"Something wrong?" Ben says close to my ear. Panicked, I pretend I don't hear him and surge forward. Nell is already lifting a puppy into her arms while other furry, whimpering pups scamper around a hay-filled stall and mom, who must be Sadie, stands nearby, tail wagging. Another adult dog – I'm guessing Hick – lays in a corner, unconcerned by all the commotion.

"Oh my gosh." I'm mauled by two adorable pups who jump onto my feet and try to climb my legs, so I bend down and pet both, then another who dodges under my hand.

"Aren't they precious?" Nell says, petting the furry pup she holds. "This is Samson. Unless Emory wants to rename him."

"She's going to love him."

Ben scoops a puppy off the floor and places all ten pounds of soft brown fur into granddad's arms. "You know, Carl, this little guy is the last of the litter and he still needs a home. Wouldn't it be great if he could see his brother once in a while?"

Ben then looks at me and adds with a grin, "You've got room for a pup, Carl. And Shelley could help you. He'd be great around the ranch."

I can't react fast enough. *This* was the Ben I knew. Underhanded, conniving, sly, shrewd, cunning.

No, no, no, no, I want to say. But before I can voice any opposition, Aunt Nell chimes in with "That's a great idea, Ben." Emory's puppy wiggles in her arms.

"What do you think, Dad? Shelley can help with him while she's here and Gail after Shelley leaves. This pup would be a good companion for you."

"And I'm sure your granddaughter would love having him," Ben adds – staring at me with a grin and a wink.

Not *this* granddaughter, I want to shout. But I could see he had a plan. If I complained about taking the puppy home, he could call me a spoiler, dog-hater, or worse – he'd turn Granddad against me.

"He sure is cute," Granddad says as the pup licks his face, so I am lost anyway. But I make sure my gaze says what my words can't.

And I watch his smile widen. He is toying with me.

He takes the puppy from Grandad and hands him to me as my glare increases. The pup licks my face and begins to whine, his tail wagging faster than his little hind end can keep up with.

"You are going to pay for this one day," I manage to say.

"I hope so," Ben replies, causing my heart to hitch.

Flustered, I break eye contact with him and move closer to granddad so he can pet the fluffy ball of fur we have just inherited. "I guess we're going to need a few things for him," I groan.

"How about some sweet tea before you leave?" Ben's offer does nothing to ease my ire. But Nell accepts quickly and we leave the puppies behind to trek back to the house, as I consider how I will get Ben back for complicating my life with a living, breathing dog I must now care for.

I follow my Grandfather into a wide foyer, to see an open interior of tall wood-beam ceilings, earth tone walls, multi-hued rugs, rich leather furniture and a ceiling-high split-log hearth. Ben leads us towards the kitchen where a pitcher of iced tea and several glasses sit on a marbled granite breakfast bar. Modern appliances and rich cabinets add to the décor, as does a large dining area with a long, rough-hewn wood table and twelve matching high-back chairs.

Masculine in theory, Ben's home is also warm and comfy and welcoming. How I wished it had been the opposite.

I just can't win with him.

He is just as wily and scheming as he was when we were kids. He is also, as hard as it is for me to admit, the upstanding man everyone thinks he is.

I conclude this even before finding out what the other outbuildings on his property are for. But after we have our tea and retrieve the pups for the rambunctious ride home, and leave Ben and Sadie and Hick, I ask about them.

"That's the area where the veterans come to learn about ranching," Aunt Nell explains. "You know, wounded warriors. Ben started a non-profit program here to help retrain them for civilian life. Some have lost one, two or three limbs and have many other lasting injuries. They are taught to work with the horses and cattle."

"Ben's grandfather and father both served in the military," Granddad adds while the puppies' mew and play in the crate beside me. "Ben planned to join as well. But his mother, Vicki, pleaded with him not to. She'd already lost her husband and said she wouldn't be able to stand losing him, too. Ben honored her request and instead devotes his time assisting men and women who did serve. Everything is free to the vets, sponsored by deep-purse cattlemen and Hill Country ranchers."

I could no longer deny that the torturous kid I once knew had changed. He was still too good at teasing me, too good at getting under my skin. But Ben was admirable as well. There is no dirt to find on him because none exists.

He makes time to play chess with an old man, he coaches kids in more than just baseball – and he supports our veterans.

He's the kind of guy I have always wanted to fall in love with.

And just maybe, already have.

◆ ◆ ◆

I lead Malibu around the pen an afternoon a week later while Angie balances on the horse. The paddock has puddles from a morning downpour, my boots and Malibu's hoofs are coated with mud, but Angie is enjoying her ride and Carmen had been able to leave to run errands with a bounce in her step.

"You'll need a good cleaning up," I say to Malibu quietly and rub her neck. "But I know you don't mind helping out any more than I do."

Malibu whinnies as if she understands me and agrees. She turns her head with me when I hear another horse approaching at a gallop. Granddad has gone into town to watch the Eagles play so I'm surprised to see Ben pulling his horse to a halt.

"Hi, Ben!" Angie calls, waving her hand.

"Hi, Angie," Ben returns. "Having fun?"

"Angie loves Malibu!" the girl replies with a bright smile.

"What's wrong?" I ask. Something must be wrong. Ben must know Granddad isn't here. My phone is in the house so I would have missed a call if Granddad had tried to reach me. Did something happen to him? I calmly lead Malibu and Angie toward the fence even though my heart is racing. "Why aren't you coaching the game?"

"Nothing's wrong. No need to worry." Ben appears relaxed on the back of his horse. The black has a shiny coat and beautiful mane and Ben pats his neck. "I had to attend a meeting in Austin and couldn't get back in time." He stays atop the horse, looking down at me. "Carl texted me a few minutes ago. We won six to three." So, he *did* know Granddad wasn't here.

"Oh, good. But then why are you here?" I walk Malibu back into the center of the pen, willing my heart to stop pumping so hard.

"Does something have to be wrong for me to visit?" he says from behind me.

I'm not sure how to reply. *Yes, since Granddad isn't here. No, not if Granddad were here.* I haven't seen Ben since we brought Brutus home last week - although after the first night of his whimpers and whines (until, of course, I'd put him in bed with me) we'd considered renaming him something less ferocious.

Brutus is now a permanent fixture at Granddad's feet in the morning and recliner after supper. He's also my sleeping companion at night.

He is the love of our lives all of a sudden; a great companion for Granddad I didn't realize he needed. We'd spent a full day buying everything a puppy could want – and a few to help us keep our sanity while he learned some manners – the latter not happening as quickly as I want it to.

"What can I do for you then?" I compromise. Surely Granddad will be here soon.

"Sherlock needed a run. And I needed to drop off some papers for Carl," Ben replies. I circle Malibu around, a bit deflated that he wasn't calling just to see me. Brutus wasn't the only thing keeping me up at night. Thoughts about Ben were inflicting their own havoc.

"Just leave them on the kitchen table."

"I thought I'd hang around until Carl got home if that's okay. And see how Brutus is coming along."

"Sure. Brutus is in his kennel right now but you can go see him. Just don't let him out here. He's too good at spooking the horses."

Ben slides a leg over Sherlock's saddle and plants his boot on the ground. "I'll go break him out of jail. Is his leash by his kennel?"

"Yeah."

He leads Sherlock to the fencepost and leaves him loosely roped, then heads towards the house.

I watch him, still edgy, uncomfortable. Glad I have an unobserved and unobstructed view of him at last. Damn the man.

Malibu must feel my anxiety because she tugs at her bridle. "Easy girl," I say and return my attention to her and Angie. "How you doing, Angie?"

"Good. Ben is nice."

"Yes. Ben is nice."

Too nice.

He disappears into the house and returns to the porch with Brutus in his arms, the pup pawing him excitedly. He secures Brutus' leash while on the porch and lets Brutus bound down the steps, keeping a safe distance from the paddock.

"Brutus!" Angie calls. "Can I play with Brutus! Angie wants to play with Brutus!"

"Let's take Malibu back to the barn and then you can play with Brutus. Okay?"

"Okay."

"Let's get you out of this muddy mess," I say to Malibu.

I lead the horse and the girl out of the paddock, pass Sherlock and head back to the barn. I tie Malibu to the stall post and help Angie dismount and remove her helmet.

Angie begins to run back toward Ben and Brutus and I follow.

Luckily, Ben has Brutus on a patch of green grass that is puddle and mud free. I smile as she giggles with abandon and hugs Brutus. I wish I could feel that free with my expressions.

Ben moves closer to me, shadowing the sun from my eyes as we watch the girl and dog play. His nearness does anything but cool me down.

"I'm going to bring Angie some iced tea. Are you thirsty?" I shield my eyes from the sun and look up at him.

Ben faces me. "I'm parched," he says. Boldly.

I take a step backward, nearly tripping over my own feet. "Y-you watch Angie then. I'll be right back."

By the time I enter the house I'm wondering if the impressions I'm getting from him could be real.

But by the time I return with a tray of tea Granddad is there and he and Ben are in deep discussion about the Eagles game. Ben doesn't even look my way when I hand him a glass of tea.

Obviously, they weren't real.

♦ ♦ ♦

"Granddad, who is this woman?"

Granddad is playing tug-of-war with Brutus on the front porch. His chuckle is nice to hear, a sign he's beginning to heal. So, I sense I can ask him some of the questions I have.

I sit down on the rocker beside him and point to one photo. "I have some questions about these pictures in Gram's album. I thought you could help me identify them. Like this one."

He glances at the sepia-toned print I put before him, looks at me briefly and returns his attention to Brutus. "Didn't your dad ever show you his copy of that picture?" he asks.

"Not that I remember. My dad has a copy of this photo?"

"Sure. It's a shot of his great-great grandmother. Gram's grandmother. Matilda Wyeman." He leans back in the swing as Brutus begins to chase his tail. "She's the one who started it all."

"Started what all? You mean she's the one we're named after? The first girls in each generation?"

"Sure. Your mom wasn't so set on such an old-fashioned name for you, as I recall. But she came around when she heard Matilda's story. And your dad agreed to make your first name Rachel. My Nell is Matilda Rachel and Gram's sister was, too. And their aunt was the namesake of the first Matilda. She was one courageous woman."

"Really?" I finger the photo. "Now you have me more than a little curious. I was going to wait and ask my dad some of my questions but do you mind filling me in?"

"Suppose not. Matilda Wyeman was the first immigrant from England. In the 1850's I think."

The photo appears to be from the turn of the century. "Isn't that interesting."

"My family's been here since the early 1700's. There's a few good stories to tell about them as well but Gram's grandmother – well now – that's a whopper. I'll have to scold your dad for not passing that on to you."

"I will too, but in the meanwhile, tell me about her."

"Better yet, let's go find her diaries. She journaled about all of it."

The hair on my neck tingles. "Gram has her diaries?"

"Somewhere. Let's check the bookshelves."

CHAPTER 12

August 26, 1852

"Well, now. What do you say, Dearhearts? Are we up to the challenge?"

Jonathan, Sarah and Louisa eye me with reservation as we stare at the oxen before us.

We had arrived in Council Bluffs yesterday, having traveled for two weeks and across two-hundred-miles from Lexington by way of stagecoach. Now we have just been shown our new covered wagons (they will do nicely) and the beasts who will pull them. I appraise each two-thousand-pound animal with fear and trembling as they munch grass in the pen that holds them.

How, I wonder, will I ever survive this?

Louisa tilts her head as one snorts loudly. "Can we name them?"

"I don't see why not. Shall we consider names while we learn how to harness them?"

"I don't want to touch them," Sarah says.

I do not either, I want to tell her. Instead I say, "And so you shall not." I know full well she will have to at some stage, but at present I will give her leave. "You and Louisa stay here. Jonathan?"

Jonathan's nod is tentative. "All set," he replies.

I shift my gaze to the animals' keeper, Mr. Lynch. He is already in the pen. Standing beside the docile creatures, his head is mere inches above the oxen's back. He has a whip in hand, and has already informed us he will teach us all we need to know in order to make them do our bidding on the thirteen-hundred-mile journey to Salt Lake City. Our wagon train leaves in three days.

I take a deep breath and open the latch on the pen's gate, stepping inside. "Let's proceed, sir."

September 1, 1852

I try to keep my protest silent as I slowly lower my body onto the pallet. Louisa is already asleep, but restlessly so, the heat of the day lingering into the night, keeping the inside of the wagon steamy. She stirs when I lay beside her, issuing a subtle cry of distress. She is as miserable as I am.

"Can't we turn back, Tilly? *Please!*" she'd begged me earlier today as the oxen pulled and the wagon swayed, and our joints ached from days perched on the uncomfortable high seat.

My shoulders and backside protested without respite.

"Louisa, we've come this far. We'll arrive before you know it and then you'll see what a grand plan your Papa had for us." I'd said the words, similar to others I've said on this journey, but knew in my heart my girl wasn't hearing me.

We are in the middle of nowhere, surrounded by unending miles of wilderness and only days into this expedition. It is dark now, quiet, the train of wagons immobile for a few brief hours. Jonathan and Sarah are in the wagon beside ours, the two of them just as worn through. Jonathan will be woken at three o'clock to begin a two-hour watch over the oxen and cows. I will take my own shift tomorrow night. Others are in charge of finding wood, hunting, and still others for keeping an eye out for marauders.

At dawn, we will all rise and begin another grueling day of travel west. We will eat quickly, take down our camp and stow our supplies. Once the teams are hitched, we'll follow the lead riders who have scouted our path through terrain that has already been stripped bare.

I hear a coyote in the distance as I try to relax. It is soon followed by another and yet another until a rifle shot pierces the night and only the ricochet remains.

Louisa sits upright.

"It's alright, sweet. Everything is alright."

She looks at me before her eyes close and she lays back down. She begins to sob.

I do as well.

September 20, 1852

The scouts spotted Fort Laramie this warm morning, the trading post more than five-hundred miles from Council Bluffs that is to be our resting place.

I was so relieved to hear the news I hugged Louisa tight. "You see, we have made it."

Weary and dusty, I have difficulty believing it myself. Our best days since leaving Council Bluffs saw twenty miles of rutted bone-jarring trail behind us; our worst no more than two or three. Some days we maneuvered steep inclines and crevices, others we crossed marshy and swollen riverbeds, pressed through soaking rains, biting wind, thick, sucking mud and swarming insects.

Oppressive heat sapped us. After fierce rains, lightning strikes and roars of thunder, mud-caked wagon wheels refused to turn until scraped clean. Worse were the mud-mired ruts and working the oxen and wagons out of them. The stinky beasts have minds of their own and do not budge until I smack their hides and loudly implore them to do so.

It is grossly against my nature.

And we still have five-hundred miles to go.

By noon we could see the buildings of the fort and soon after Louisa nudges my arm. "Look, Tilly."

As we followed the other wagons to a well-worn area by the winding North Platte River, I saw what she saw: the red-skinned men, bare-chested and with head-dresses of feathers and animal-skin pants. We had seen a few along the trail, always from a distance – they as wary of us as it appeared, we are of them. But today there were many of them – women and children as well, camped outside the fort gates. They had erected tents made of animal skins and secured with long poles. Firepits were outside, women tending them. Some of the men were on horseback, others walking into and out of the fort's gate.

"We were told they would be here, remember?" I say to her. "They are natives from the Lakota, Cheyenne and Arapaho tribes. They trade their furs and meat with the captain of the fort for supplies they need for their people."

I've also heard that many of them no longer have tolerance for us just as those along the Mississippi and Missouri rivers did not. We, I've seen firsthand, have stripped their land, have not been good stewards, have taken what once was theirs.

"Perhaps we will meet a few while we are here. Right now, I am eager to park this wagon, aren't you?" And air-dry the musty bedding and swing wide the canvas flap in hopes the heat will escape.

Louisa merely nods, her gaze still trained on the Indians.

She, more than the others, did not want to leave London for this new world. And she has suffered so horribly.

I wonder now if she had forethought of what would befall us if we chose this path. It is disturbing to think she would still be whole had we never left, her father and brother alive, and I rather think she will blame John as she ages.

Dear John would have never undertaken this journey had he known the cost. I will have to tell her so.

Once she is older. Once this journey is long behind us.

Until then I keep from her the stories I've heard of other trains ahead of us – of snowy passes choking off forward progress, of outbreaks of cholera and influenza, of deaths and disillusionment and mass gravesites.

Our train is plagued by no such illnesses, but rather coughs and fatigue. Our losses have been in cattle when they become weary and collapse. Some days the scouts can find no water, others no meat to hunt. But overall, we manage.

Prayer sustains me. Prayer and the calming words written in Psalms and Proverbs. The elders, after leaving Lexington in Missouri, began teaching us from the book Joseph Smith penned after receiving his visions. I rather prefer the Bible, a lifetime of teaching along with it, invoking Christ's name with every amen. I believe I always will no matter what I'm being taught now.

Did John know Joseph Smith's visions were not just of a Utopia on earth but of a belief apart from Christ altogether? Could it be that our migration is all for naught and the futility of man is to always suffer from a wandering spirit?

The people in this wagon train our good-minded. But are they gullible?

I am hundreds of miles away from knowing if there is a place of this God-fearing people I'm told about. Perhaps there, I'll find others who struggle with the same concerns I have. No tea? Christ not God's one and only Son? A woman needing to marry a man in order to get to heaven herself?

It all rankles me.

But first, I must concentrate on gaining stability. Perhaps I can work as a school mistress. Or wait tables at the public inn. Finding a husband who will accept three orphaned children and myself; no great prize any of us, will be difficult. If I give thought to this for too long, I realize the impossibility of it and yet...

We have made it thus far.

We have many more days and nights where we must find food and warmth and cross rivers and nurse wounds. But today I smile and begin to hear the hum of people as the wagons come to a circled halt.

It is time for Louisa and I to find wood for a fire and bring up water from the river. Jonathan can fish here; Sarah can wash our apparel. Then I will begin a pot of turnips and once our bellies are full, we will explore the fort.

For the next two days we will rest.

Ah, but should I have known I would be making this journey without John.

Me, Tilly Wyeman.

I am no longer a citified lady for certain, but have learned to be decisive and determined; to fend and tend and do so well.

Had I a choice?

September 22, 1852

I poked my head from the wagon's interior when I heard the voice.

"Hello," said a woman standing outside. "Are you Matilda Wyeman? I have a post for you, if so. From Lexington."

Chills running through my frame I hurried forward, descending the wagon stairs and dropping to the ground. "I am," I said, barely containing myself. "Matilda."

"Mary Carver," the woman replied. She was clothed in dungarees and spurs over her boots, a plaid shirt and floppy leather hat. "A friend of Blanche Filmore. Blanche knew I was traveling to Oregon. She entrusted this letter to me."

Miss Carver extended the letter my way and I gasped.

With shaking hands, I accepted it and stared at the familiar script of my mother.

"Mama," I choked out. "Thank you, dear Jesus. Thank you." I could not – did not try to contain myself as I tore open the post. I began to read before remembering the woman who had delivered it. "Forgive me," I chuckled. "I'm so thrilled to have this. You have no idea. How can I thank you? I would offer you tea but I have none."

Mary Carver waved my words away. "I can see you've waited a long while to hear from your mother."

"But how did you find me?" The letter was addressed to the Lexington hospital.

"My companions and I left Lexington three weeks after you did. There are just ten of us – all on horseback, so it was likely we'd catch up to your wagon somewhere along the way."

"I can't thank you enough."

"Your excitement is enough." She began to walk away, back toward the fort's interior.

"Please join the children and me for supper, Miss Carver. The least I can do is prepare you a meal. Jonathan is hunting right now. We might have meat."

"That's kind of you. I'll do that."

I told Mary Carver when to return but before she had left my view, I'd already refocused my attention to Mama's post. I pressed the parchment to my nose, inhaling the welcome scent that still lingered there. Then scanning the contents first, I now know Papa is still quite well, Mama also, and yet they are heartbroken with distress for me. All of my siblings are safe and sound at her writing.

Once I satisfied myself with this knowledge, I read the missive again, slowly, absorbing every word.

♦ ♦ ♦

That evening, Mary Carver with us, we enjoyed the squirrel Jonathan had trapped along with beans and corn I'd acquired from the fort.

94

I concentrated on braiding Sarah's long hair, the campfire glowing around us, and said, "And Mama says my dear sister Rachel has a beau. Rachel is still young and somewhat headstrong, so I have some concern here. I must ask Mama if she believes Mr. Thomas Lancelett is worthy of her. Rachel," I continued, "is still working with Papa in his tailor shop, so I do pray Mr. Lancelett has the means to provide for her if things progress between them. And Julia, my youngest sister at eighteen, is still restless, sullen at times, Mama says. She continues to feel her lot in life is inferior. She has a misguided dream of being swept away by a wealthy nobleman."

"I do too," Sarah says, leaning against me.

"Well you and Julia are both beauties," I added. "And Louisa." I smile at Sarah's sister across the fire. "But I dare say, that might be a tad foolish to hope for.

"Now, Caroline, my sister closest to me in age, is content to remain with Mama and Papa. Perhaps that will change one day and she will find a beau, too. She is but twenty. But I can see her remaining with my parents throughout her days."

"What of James?" Jonathan asked. If he was unhappy with listening to the news I shared, he was showing no signs.

"Ahh, my brother James. Well, he and his wife Ann seem to be doing well with their London pub, although Mama and Papa still despair that they truly own such an establishment."

"I remember when you took me there on our way to the milliners," Jonathan added.

"I dare say I did not take you inside." I would have never done so. James' pub was usually filled with raucous men behaving badly.

"I peeked in from the carriage." Jonathan's sheepish smile brought one to my face as well.

"I had to deliver him a package from Mama that day or I would never have ventured there with you."

"Who else did your Mama write about?" Louisa asked then.

Unfortunately, I couldn't tell the children any pertinent news of their own family. Mama was still trying to locate them. "My brother John. He has truly decided to sign on with the P&O Freight Company and venture to Australia. This saddens me."

"Australia!" Johnathan sits up straighter. "Perhaps I'll go there one day. I can meet up with him."

"Don't go, Jon," Louisa says with a pout.

We are all silent for a moment as Jonathan's words lead us to remember his father, brother and sister.

I clear my throat. "John has never been content being a butcher and yet I considered his talk of leaving just that. I pray my own departure has had no bearing in his decision. Mama fears my younger brothers Joseph and Benjamin will follow John although their words are to the contrary. They are still impressionable, merely sixteen and fourteen years respectively. They will find their way in due time; hopefully in England."

"And you here with us," Louisa says to her brother.

"I'm not going anywhere, Lou," Jonathan tells her.

Later, when we are all bedding down and Miss Mary Carver has left us, I again hold Mama's letter to my nose, her scent reassuring to me. The parchment is a tangible and calming thing and I remind myself she is but three months travel away. She and everyone in England. I can reverse course and return if I find there is truly the need. I will find a way if to that end I must.

Alas, for now I take comfort in the news of home, thanking God for His mercies.

I know one more moon and I'll discover the truth. Discover if I will then mount a return to England or make my home in Utah. My anxiousness and excitement return now that we have come so far. Taking these few days to rest, resupply and repair has given us new strength. Ahead are some forty thousand Mormon saints who have gone before us. Surely if they all made the pilgrimage, we shall be able to as well. And surely if they remain, there is something to remain there for.

I draw on this as I listen to the night sounds and the girl's sleeping. Fear of how I will survive with three children to care for plagues me.

Now though, I am content. I can still hear Mama's voice saying, "Always remember we will be here if you need to return." I will never forget them, and because of them I can continue on.

CHAPTER 13

Present Day

I found my dress for the Garden Club Gala at a shop in the Georgetown Square. The square is a popular destination for everyone in the hill country, complete with its historical courthouse, Texas flare and hospitality.

"I'm glad you and your mom are coming with us to the Gala," I said as we strolled through one antique shop. "Granddad wrangled Ben into coming, too, you know. I'd be pretty uncomfortable if it was just us three."

"Mom said he was coming. If you're not happy, why are you looking for a gown that will dazzle him?" Emory nudged me.

"I'm not. Well, maybe I am. A girl's gotta do her best to tantalize. Not that I'd ever consider having a thing with him. I'm not even convinced he knows I'm alive. But the last few weeks..."

"He's made some comments?"

"Yeah." With more than his words, I added to myself.

After the day with Angie and Brutus in the yard Ben had returned the following morning to invite me to hear a therapist give a talk at his ranch.

"I'm holding it next Tuesday," he'd explained. "Since you've taken on working with Angie, I thought you might be interested."

"Thanks," I'd replied from the porch. He was riding Sherlock again, looking fit and comfortable in the saddle, his hat shading his chiseled face and eyes. Making me *un*comfortable. "I'll consider it."

But truth be told, walking Angie's horse was one thing, but immersing myself into the world of genetics was beyond my comfort zone.

And, truth be told, I didn't want to risk being close to Ben, either.

He was messing with my head.

Suddenly warm, I startle when Emory says, "What about this one?" She has stopped in front of a dress rack and lifted one gown from the rack.

My eyes widen. "This better fit."

◆ ◆ ◆

Granddad had hired a limousine service, so our drive to the Gala is in style. The driver picked up Em and Aunt Nell first. After Granddad and I enter the car, the driver treats us all to a glass of champagne. Then we make our way downtown to the swank Starlight Hotel.

I see Ben as we approach the ballroom entrance; all six-foot-tailored inch of him. Half-wondering if he was going to stand us up – stand Granddad up – I'd been nervous when granddad had said Ben would meet us at the hotel. My nerves don't settle now that I've seen him.

He shakes granddad's hand, gives my aunt a kiss on the cheek, then does the same to Em. When he leans towards me and lingers a second longer than necessary, my heart accelerates.

I can smell his subtle citrusy aftershave, I can feel his close proximity. He exudes pure masculinity, his muscles corded beneath the black jacket he wears. He clasps my arms with his hands, pressing in gently, and touches his mouth to my cheek – just for a moment – just long enough to send sparks streaking through my bloodstream.

He steps back and releases me as he clears his throat, his gaze never meeting mine as he says, "You all look nice tonight."

Nice?

"You do too, Ben," Aunt Nell smiles.

"Our table is near the podium," he then adds.

I feel surreal as we follow Ben into the crowded, brightly lit ballroom. Along the way friends of Gram's see us, turn or stand to shake Granddad's hand, say a few words.

There are already three people seated at our eight-person round table when we arrive. It is elegantly covered with crystal glasses and china-ware, a large multi-colored flower arrangement as the centerpiece. A woman stands and hugs Granddad.

"Good evening, Carl," she smiles. She is middle-aged and wears a corsage of fresh roses. "It's good to see you. I'm so glad you decided to come."

Granddad shrugs. "It's good to see you too, Catherine." He turns to us and adds, "You all met Catherine at Gram's service. She's the Garden Club president this year."

"And this is my husband, Stan, and son, Stanley," Catherine replies.

We are introduced to the other table guests and then we all take our seats. I'm placed between Granddad and Ben, Emory in-between Ben and Stanley.

Em immediately asks if I want something to drink and leaves to find the bar. Catherine engages Granddad in small talk with her husband and Aunt Nell, leaving Ben and I to nod and say things like 'really?' and 'how nice'.

When Em returns, I sip my Cabernet and listen as she asks Ben if he's going to the Aggies versus Longhorns football game at Arlington Stadium this fall. The game is one of the premiere sporting events of the year in Texas. Ben is an Aggie alumni and Em a Longhorn.

"I'm planning on it. You?"

I feel out-of-place, like a third or fifth wheel. Ben's arm brushes mine when he moves, keeping me off-balance, keeping my senses on high alert.

I'm glad when Catherine finally goes to the podium, settles the crowd and welcomes everyone. She announces dinner will be served, followed by the presentations and dancing. A pastor from one of the local churches says grace and then the salads are being served.

Ben is quiet, concentrating on his food. I ask Granddad if he wants something other than iced water but he declines. He picks at his salad, then his plate of braised beef and red potatoes.

I know he'd prefer to be home listening to the Rangers or watching a western. I pat his hand in reassurance.

When Catherine once again heads for the podium I hear Granddad sigh. Then she is announcing what a wonderful year the Hill Country Garden Club has had and how many awards the members won in the competitions they entered.

"And, sadly, we lost two of our members this year, as well. Bob Mears was a member for fifteen years and won many awards with his hybrid Springtime Daffodil." She takes a plaque from inside the podium. "His wife Paula will accept this plaque in recognition of his contributions."

Paula Mears makes her way to the podium and accepts the plaque as everyone applauds. After she returns to her seat Catherine continues.

"We also lost one of our oldest and longest-serving members. Violet Gatewood was one of my closest friends and a member of this club for more than twenty-five years. She was president of this club for five years, took first place more times than we could count for her lilies and roses. It is my proud honor to recognize her tonight and with us is her husband, Carl, who will accept this award."

Granddad stands as everyone else does as well and the applause begins. His shoulders are low as he makes his way up the steps to the podium and he and Catherine hug again. When he takes the plaque, the applause grows louder and I see him sniff.

Oh, Granddad, my heart cries out.

He leaves the podium quickly and takes his seat just as quickly. He stares at the plaque in his hands as Catherine continues her program.

"What does it say?" I whisper to him, leaning close.

He hands me the plaque, his jaw tight.

"Look how nice this is." I see Gram's name and a rose beneath it, with words about her tenure and service. "Isn't that nice?" I add to Granddad while passing the plaque to Ben.

"Yep," Granddad replies.

The pain in his voice is heartbreaking. I'm glad I'm here with him but I wish none of us were and I don't know what to say to help ease his sorrow.

Ben hands the plaque to Emory and leans close to me, saying to Granddad, "That's a nice tribute to Violet, but I bet she'd frown at all the fuss."

"Yep," he says again.

"And frown at you," Ben adds. I snap my gaze his way, surprised by his chastisement, then look to Granddad to see he is looking at Ben, too. His gaze has sharpened and he sits up straighter.

"Suppose you're right."

"Thanks," I whisper to Ben for managing to shake Granddad free of his melancholy.

"And now," Catherine says once more from the podium, "the band will play *Moonlight Serenade*, one of Violet's favorite songs. And joining Carl on the dance floor will be his daughter, Nell Gatewood-Simpson."

Granddad rises again and leads Aunt Nell to the dance floor as everyone claps. Then Catherine and Stan are joining them, and Stanley asks Emory to dance. Stanley is in his mid-twenties, nice-looking and they have kept up a stream of conversation.

Suddenly it is just Ben and I at the table and my unease returns as time clicks by and Ben does not ask me to dance.

When the silence is screaming at me, I don't even bother to excuse myself. I stand, place my napkin on my plate and walk away.

The sting of his rejection hits me hard. Brings back the day he'd stood me up when I was fifteen. I retreat to the powder-room. In front of the mirror near a pair of posh sofas, I adjust the spaghetti straps of my gown

– the drop-dead gorgeous midnight blue silk that Ben said I looked 'nice' in. I thought I looked a lot more than 'nice'.

The jerk.

The braindead redneck.

I begin to touch-up my make-up while I berate myself for wanting him to notice me. For wanting him to ask me to dance. When was I going to admit Ben was always going to let me down?

Taking a deep breath, I try to regain my equilibrium. I console myself with the fact that, at least now, I know Ben has flaws. It is a small solace after nearly putting him on a pedestal like everyone else. But it is something. And I remind myself he is here to support Granddad, not me.

Still smarting from his indifference, I leave the powder room. I head back to the ballroom, deciding to find someone who *wants* to be around me. Among the predominantly older crowd of garden-clubbers there are a handful of younger men. And since I'm not looking for a lifelong commitment, just a bit of fun – a few dances, few compliments, few sparks – I decide to mingle.

It is then that Ben startles me.

"Carl scolded me," he says, approaching from my side. As other guests move around us and as the band plays Sinatra's *Strangers in the Night*, I pick up my pace. "I'm supposed to ask you to dance," he adds.

His comment is nothing less than degrading.

"I think that ship sailed," I reply with nonchalance I don't feel. "We'll just tell Granddad it was my choice so you can save face."

I keep moving, but he swings in front of me. "Well just one dance then," he says as I nearly bump into him. He takes my hand before I can protest.

I refuse to be led and tug my hand free. When Ben turns back to face me, I smile brightly, assuming Granddad is watching.

"You're going to make me grovel, aren't you?" Ben smiles back.

"That's the last thing I think I'll ever see," I reply. Not Mr. Perfect.

"Would it help if I asked with a please?"

"Not likely."

"Then how 'bout just to make an old man happy?"

"I thought that's what this night was all about to begin with. I'm only here for him."

"Then dance with me."

I consider pulling away but feel the gazes of Gram's friends and my family following me. I allow Ben to maneuver us through the crowd to the dance floor and then he faces me, his other hand wrapping around my waist.

"Let's make this quick and— "

"You look incredible, by the way," he interrupts as the band starts playing Patsy Cline's *Crazy*. The lyrics are too apropos. "All decked out. Not that I had any doubts you would not look incredible but it's nice to see I was right."

His words astonish me. "Smooth," I toss back.

"You don't think I'm sincere?"

"Like I said, that ship has sailed." There'd been plenty of opportunity for compliments long before now.

"I've messed this up, haven't I?" Ben's hand tightens on my waist and he spins me.

"There was nothing to mess up, so I don't know what you mean." Refusing to meet Ben's gaze, I search for my grandfather instead and see him at the table tapping his fingers to the beat of the song.

"Okay."

"Okay."

"But you do look great."

"Well, thanks. Thank you." I'd wanted that compliment, had longed for it. But now it's tainted. Still, seeing Granddad relaxed calms me and I add, "You look nice yourself." Nice wasn't the word. He looked scrumptious in his tux, all shoulders and five o'clock shadow, dark hair falling over his brow. Just standing as close as I am to him now, inside the circle of his arms, sends more shockwaves through my system.

How can that be when he's been so rude?

I feel his thumb on my waist begin to move back and forth. Surely Ben doesn't realize he's doing this. With someone else I'd assume the motion was a pass – with Ben I consider it just a reflex.

"So, has the slower pace here caught up with you yet?" he asks.

I try to concentrate on his small talk, not his thumb. "I love the ranch. Always have. And I've enjoyed having this time with Granddad. I'm not sure I think the pace here is slower, just different. There is always something going on."

"Guess you could say that. But not like city life."

I shrug. "I haven't experienced any withdrawals."

Ben leads me easily. When the song ends, I try to pull away but another ballad takes its place and Ben keeps me firmly anchored in his arms.

"So, tell me more about this business of yours. Do you enjoy writing wedding vows?"

I shrug. I'm not interested in talking about my business but at least it's a safe topic. "It pays the bills. It was something I fell into unexpectedly and it's lucrative." I tell him about helping write a friend's vows and his suggestion I make a business out of it.

"And the grooms? Are they pretty oddball?"

I chuckle. "That's a good term for them. Most of them. They wait until the last minute to think about vows. Then they panic when they don't have a clue what to write."

"I understand that. Men don't think ahead. It's not in our DNA."

"Fair enough. But then they shouldn't promise something original. There are standard vows available."

"The ol' till death do us part?"

"Yes." I try to keep my cynicism out of my voice.

Chances Are continues to play in the background as Ben adds, "I should hire you to write my wedding vows while you're here. Not that I have a bride yet. For my future bride. You know, get them out of the way so I'm not a last-minute groom, too."

I swallow hard. "Well sure. I mean, if you already know what you want to say."

"Oh, I know exactly what I want to say, what I want her, my bride, to know."

"Really?"

"Sure. I just don't know how to frame it all, I guess. Make it flow."

"Yeah, that's where I come in." I lower my head briefly, my disappointment acute. Then deciding I'm being an idiot, I notch up my chin. "I won't be here much longer, so you better make an appointment with me soon."

"I thought you weren't having withdrawals."

"I'm not. But, well, I think Granddad's doing just fine now, and I... I'm buying a house."

"A house?"

"Yeah. A loft really. In Denver. And well, I think it's just what I'm looking for." The song ends and this time I pull away before Ben has the chance. "Thanks for the dance. You can tell Granddad you've done your duty."

I walk away before he can reply, needing distance and air. And a good slap upside my head. It really is time for me to return home.

CHAPTER 14

Far back in the line of wagons, the murmurs make their way down to us, gaining momentum and volume as they carry on the biting wind.

"Let me down, Tilly!" Louisa says. "Let me down so I can run ahead and see."

We are in a narrow gorge surrounded by high rocky cliffs and a forest of scrub oak and pine trees. The wagons stretch ahead of us and behind us, impossible to see around the one in front of us. I tug on the team, slowing them enough for Louisa to jump from the high seat.

"Don't trip!" I call to her as she races away, skirting the wagon in front of us.

"Is it true?" Sarah calls from the wagon behind. "Have we reached the summit?" The wagon ahead of me stops, so I bring ours to a halt behind it. Quickly securing the reins, I climb down the high seat. I position myself so I can see Sarah and Jonathan behind me. Jonathan halts his own team and he and Sarah join me.

"Can it be true?" Sarah says again.

"We can only hope," I answer and we begin to follow the line of others forward.

Soon we can hear shouts of excitement and my heart lurches. I pick up my pace.

"Tilly!" Louisa shouts as we near an ever-growing crowd. "Tilly look!"

I scan the crowd for her, see her pointing and run to join her. "Look!" she says again and as I do, I realize the trees have given way and we are perched on a cliff.

And below us is a wide valley.

"The Salt Lake Basin," someone says.

Mountains tinged with rich autumn reds and oranges rise up from the other side of us but I stare below – at buildings and roads.

I blink as tears pool in my eyes and my throat swells.

John, I silently whisper. *We made it.*

"I wish Papa were here," Louisa says and takes my hand.

"And Joseph and Ellen," Sarah adds.

I draw her close and hug both girls while I gaze at Jonathan. He smiles sadly.

"We were told it would take us two days to descend into the basin once we reached this point," he reminds us.

"Yes," I reply.

And then, I add silently, I will know if what I've been told is true.

◆ ◆ ◆

We reach the bottom of the pass with bruised bodies and frigid noses, but also with wide smiles and joy. Even the oxen, their pace steadfast, seem to know their journey is nearly over.

We follow, as always, the wagons in front of us, until the path becomes more of a rutted road, puddled from last night's freezing rain.

Soon buildings become visible, small houses with pitched roofs set in rows. People begin to wave and follow our train, until we are in the center of town, a garrison of sorts, with a few main street buildings of wood and brick. The wagons are circled and halted, and just as quickly some of our train-members are reunited with family who have come on previous trains.

I sit atop my wagon and watch them embrace, happy for them, but it is then, having arrived at long last, that my newfound hope begins to fade once more, slowly at first, as if my brain does not want to believe what I am seeing.

I cannot mince words: this 'Paradise' is not a fine shiny city but rather a large, mud-packed area with makeshift tents and a few buildings. I notice a mercantile. I also notice a jail. Laundry flutters outside the tents on strung rope, wooded boards create an unbalanced walkway from one area to the other, horses and donkeys mull about untethered.

"Miss Wyeman."

When my name is spoken, I focus and see Elder Kelsey standing beside my wagon. "This is Mr. and Mrs. Dawson."

"I'm pleased to meet you," I say and disembark the high seat.

"You and the children will be staying with the Dawson's until more permanent lodging can be found," Kelsey adds. Louisa hugs my side and I sense Sarah and Jonathan have joined us.

"We have three children of our own, so space will be tight, but we'll manage," Mrs. Dawson says, taking my hand. "Welcome to Zion."

"The Dawson's are previously from Nauvoo, Illinois," Kelsey continues. "They were with Joseph Smith on the night he was killed and all the saints rousted away."

"In the dead of night, we began our trek here, with nothing more than our lives," adds Mrs. Dawson.

"How much space do you have?" I say, realizing I must sound rude. I glance again at the homes set away from the main street. They appear to be very small.

"We have one bedroom and a loft," Mr. Dawson answers. His hat is in his hand and his eyes are downcast. I'm convinced he's rather unhappy about taking us in.

"And a barn," adds Mrs. Dawson. "The boys can sleep out there."

Until a cold freeze? I want to ask. Then what? I've learned winter is nearly upon us, a winter that lasts months and is very cold.

"It will have to do for now." Elder Kelsey scratches the back of his head.

I grumble inwardly, I'm ashamed to admit. I had ever so envisioned a sparkling city with modern conveniences and all manner of new inventions to make life easier. Instead, there are the makings of such, the noise of hammers and saws and many wagons piled high with cut timber and construction supplies.

"As long as this is very temporary," I say to Elder Kelsey. But somehow, I know better. Especially when his eyes won't meet mine. If nothing else, I have the wagons. The children and I can live in them if need be – until what; Winter is over and we can begin to return home?

I lead the oxen on foot as we follow the Dawson's from the town center to Temple Road. There area is nicer here, cleaner. We come to a large modern building.

"What is that?" I ask as Mrs. Dawson walks with me.

"Why, the State House. It's where President Young meets with his council. And there, next to it, is his home. We call it the Beehive. See the top? It looks like a beehive."

I keep walking, past the State House, to the home Mrs. Dawson speaks of. It is not a simple structure like the others. It is a large beautiful mansion one would see in London.

"Mr. Young is very important," Mrs. Dawson states.

I though he was a servant of God, I say inwardly. "Why is there a jail?" I ask her.

"Pardon?"

"A jail. I saw the jail and yet I was told all the men here are god-fearing and sinless."

"Oh. Well. There's no such thing, my dear."

CHAPTER 15

Utah Territory - 1853

William Hatcher flicked the reins of his team of horses, his mood as foul as the overcast skies. There was no doubt about it: life had been harder ever since he'd moved his family to Utah. And it didn't appear life would be getting easier any time soon.

Not that Will was one to fuss about hardship – back-breaking labor he knew too well. It wasn't the land he'd been unable to tame – it had been his own household.

Ruth had left him last year. She'd taken baby Miriam with her, leaving Emeline and Ruthie with him. And now Sarah was dead. She'd never regained her strength after the birth of Will Jr.

It was difficult for him to believe that in seven short years he'd married twice, had five children, lost both wives and a daughter and was now caring for his other children on his own.

Nothing in his beliefs and teachings had prepared him for *this*.

He glanced downward to where his children sat beside him, Emeline the oldest at four and pups Will Jr. and Ruthie. Since Sarah's death last month his mother and other women in his ward had assisted with caretaking and meals. He'd had no choice but to accept their help. But it didn't sit well with him. He never shied from assisting others when there was need, but it was one thing to give and another to take. It humbled a man, to be sure and perhaps Will needed a bit of that. Some said he was prideful, opinionated. He'd just thought he was doing what was best for all concerned.

Ruth found him difficult. Too difficult, he realized now. That's why she'd left. She was already re-married to Will Covert now.

Sarah, God rest her soul, hadn't found Will difficult. She'd understood him better than most; his dedication to the faith, his need for adventure, his passion to conquer the impossible. To that end he'd taken his responsibilities seriously – God and family. He put food on the table, provided shelter, honored the church's teachings and enjoyed wrestling with a task till complete. He'd been acknowledged as a leader, been given tasks other men failed at. It was an honor and a privilege for Will to be recognized. Why hadn't Ruth understood that, been proud and stood by him? And why had Sarah died? She'd been but twenty. She'd wanted a child badly. Signs had been that she'd lost one or two. Then Will Jr. had been born and she was content. If only she'd healed properly.

He'd just had a meeting with the bishop about his situation. Monroe was sympathetic to his plight; Will needed to work the fields, no time to care for youngins'. The man pledged their wives would continue to help with the task of child care and since his children were mere tots that would be for a long time.

But he could hear the placating in the bishop's voice, the tone that said he had more important things to tend to. And Will knew help from others wasn't the best long-term solution for him and his children. No, what was best was another wife. There was no other choice. This time though, he'd be a bit different. He'd learned from his past mistakes and had matured a bit. This time, he pledged to himself and God, he'd be a bit easier to get along with.

Once he found her.

♦ ♦ ♦

July, 1853

My dear sister Rachel,

How excited I am to have a letter from you inside Mama's packet. I can hear your enthusiasm for Mr. Lancelett in every word and am thrilled you have found such a caring prospect. If not for Mama's grand endorsement I would caution you, as should an older sister, but alas, she, our Mama, is very taken with Thomas, and so then am I.

I wish you only the best.

As to my own travails, I endure. I would return home in a heartbeat if not for the children and their refusal to accompany me. They want no part of another months'-long journey, even though their grandparents have requested it. However, I am anxious to change our circumstances – Jonathan, Louisa, Sarah, and mine own. We are still with the Dawson family. Elder Kelsey saw to it that another two rooms were added to their home, but it is still their home, and not easy doing so when I have dreamed of nothing but my own for many years. For the children, learning to carry on without their father, brother and sister is no less challenging. Yet it has been more than a year now since our tragedy took John, Joseph and Ellen, and since the elders have failed to assist us as they promised – and my patience at an end – I have begun to inquire in all manner of ways for a position or circumstance more to my liking. I've made it known I am good with needle, tending children, horticulture (I do so remember and miss Father's gardens), cooking for large gatherings (having so many siblings did require such talent, did it not?), and all else God has gifted me with. I daresay I can even handle a team of beastly oxen now.

To my reward, one of the ladies informed me that her husband viewed a post in the newspaper that might interest me. An audacious post truly, by a man in need of a wife. I procured the paper, needing to verify for myself and there it was, from one William Hatcher. He, it appears, is just as frustrated with the church as I am with their false promises. Setting aside my many misgivings, I did not delay in asking Mr. Dawson for an introduction. He, in turn, has asked Mr. Hatcher to visit.

I will send you word after our meeting. Please pray for us.
Your loving sister,
Tilly

CHAPTER 16

Present Day

During the week after the Garden Club Gala I make my plans to leave.

Granddad seems resigned, understanding, saying, "Never thought you'd stay this long but I sure am glad for it."

"Why don't you come with me and visit mom and dad for a bit?" I suggest. But he is leading Leadfoot at the time and I already know his answer. He needs his horses and they need him. And now he has Brutus.

Saying good-bye to Carmen and Angie is difficult, Emory more so. We've become close, my cousin and I. She enjoys hearing what I've read in Matilda's diaries as much as I do. There are still a few of Gram's tea cups I haven't used yet, but I promise myself I'll visit Granddad every few months and begin my ritual again.

I call my parents, make arrangements to visit them the following Sunday so I can ask my dad the questions I've been storing up. And I call Mark, the condo rep, and make an appointment to see it one more time. I've told Stephanie not to get her hopes up, but maybe I'll fall in love.

And enjoy my old friends again; my old life.

Purpose and direction calm me. Take my mind off Ben.

I am polite when he's around, but have reverted to avoiding him again.

On my final day in Texas, I make Granddad his favorite breakfast of biscuits and gravy, head to the afternoon Eagles game with him and once home take Chester out for our final ride.

The summer sun is hot, the heat index hotter. It is a typical Texas summer day. And I will miss it; the balmy nights, the cicada's cadence and songbirds whistling from the oak trees.

I tell Chester as much, tell him how much I'll miss him as well. I even ask him to forgive me.

"I know. I'm being foolishly sentimental."

His whinny tells me he understands. He's better than a two-hundred-dollar-an-hour therapist.

I give him his head and he leads me through the meadow of knee-high grass towards a copse of shady trees and the river below. I dismount and pull a carrot from my pocket, holding it open for him to take.

We head for home soon after, but I can't help but glance around me, wondering if Ben is going to suddenly surprise me, like he used to as a boy.

But there is no one around – just me and Chester.

"Let's go, boy. I have an early flight."

CHAPTER 17

July, 1853

When he looked at me it was as if I could see into his bruised soul.

I wasn't expecting to feel much of anything, let alone flustered. We had a mutual need, Mr. Hatcher and I. That would have been enough. But as a rush of warmth ran across my skin, I hoped he could not see it. Like a debutante, I felt my pulse dancing. I had to lower my gaze and scold myself.

Taking a deep breath, I cautioned myself *not* to be enamored. Merely pleased. Even as I watched the precious way his babes clung to him. It made my heart near burst.

The potential for a merge rang in my ears.

Mr. William Hatcher might do nicely.

He twirled his hat in his hands as his children wrapped themselves around his dungaree-clad legs, peeking around them to get a glimpse of me before darting behind again.

He is fair in appearance, a similar age to me, his brown hair slicked back, his attire clean and pressed if a bit thread-bare.

I'd heard he came from good pedigree, from one of the first families to join the church. His father Elias was a personal associate of Joseph Smith, highly regarded within that circle of confidantes. The Hatcher family migrated from Ohio to Illinois with the earliest members. Mr. Hatcher was a mere lad of seven when his parents decided to follow Mr. Smith and his teachings.

He introduced himself with a nod and good day and introduced me to his tikes - two young girls and a boy who are meek and frightened and if for no other reason but that they need a mother, I would consider marriage to their father.

As the babes clung to him, it told me that he has affectionate toward them, when he ruffled their heads it was confirmation. Emeline Jane is his eldest, a beauty of four years. Ruthie is not three. They are the children of William and his first wife, Ruth. Will is his son of two years with his second wife, Sarah Ann. I have since learned William and Ruth had two other daughters as well. Ruth has infant Miriam with her but another, Sarah Ann, passed at the tender age of three. I'm told his two wives (married to both at the same time and something I must reconcile) were good friends until the younger Sarah Ann's death and the older Sarah Ann's delivery of young Will. According to Mrs. Dawson, who heard it from Mrs. Mays, who knows Mrs. Sally Hatcher, William's mother, young Will's birth led to Ruth's discontent. She left Mr. Hatcher soon after, left her two oldest daughters with him. She then married Mr. Covert and they live nearby.

I am as smitten with Mr. Hatcher's children as I am with my own orphan waifs.

Sweet Louisa made attempts to engage the babes and soon won over their smiles and trust as she began to play pebbles with them. And upon glancing at their father, I saw that he was pleased by Louisa's friendliness.

"Shall we discuss our situation?" I said to him then, my own voice sounding foreign to my ears.

He nodded and we left the children to play, walking a distance from the Dawson's home so we could talk in private.

"It appears we're both in the same circumstances," he said.

"It does."

"I don't mean to sound unfeeling but my young'un's need a mother," he continued.

"Isn't there another woman here that would suit you?"

"A few have responded to the paper ad. But when they find out I have three children and Sarah Ann's fifteen-year-old brother, George to tend, they get skittish."

"George lives with you as well?"

"He's a big help to me in the fields."

"Mr. Dawson told me he explained my situation to you."

"Three orphans. I understand."

"And you'd be willing, should we... that is if we were to..."

"I have a good 'stead a few miles outside of town. An apple orchard just planted, a house with two rooms. I'd add another. They'd be welcome. Mother Sally lives next to us, my brother Lyman on the other side of her. I'll take proper care of you and yours and you do the same." He turned to face me, this rather nervous, rather stiff and formal man. "How about a trial run?"

"I need to talk this over with my children," I told him. "Can I give you an answer tomorrow?"

"Fair enough."

Hours later we had made our decision, Jonathan, Sarah, Louisa and I. Jonathan rode out to Mr. Hatcher's home the next morning to give it to him.

If he were not of good reputation, if I were not certain he is a good and devoted man, convinced in his ways and convicted by his faith, I would not consider such a trial run. On the other hand, I will need to point out some of the conflicting teachings we surely have.

But we are willing to take a chance. Jonathan has already told me he will not stay with us much longer. He is restless and talks of journeying to Australia to find my brothers, or west and north, to the Oregon Territory. He is old enough to decide and wise above his years due to our past travails, so I will not dissuade him although my heart hurts when I consider it. Yet Sarah and Louisa need stability now – stability Mr. Hatcher offers.

They protest immensely when I broach the subject of returning to England. And so, I am hopeful for us – hopeful my own life is about to begin anew, even as I have learned to temper excitement. Things dire can befall us at any given moment.

At least I – we, Mr. Hatcher and I – will be of service to one another for however long.

We are both increasingly aware that church leaders who promised so much to us have delivered so little.

Do I regret this quest? I will not lie. I do.

We were fools for believing the false teachers.

September 18, 1853

"There now, feel better?"

I wipe the dusty tears from Will Jr.'s face as he nods and scoots down from the chair, charging through the front door and back outside before I can caution him to keep his distance from the goose who took a nip at his earlobe. The dreadful thing has made itself comfortable in our yard, returning no matter how many times I shoo it away. If it's honking were not irritating enough, it's droppings are, adding to my chores as I clean up the mess several times a day.

It's as mulish as William can be and I declare, after living with the man for a few months now, I must admit the workings of his mind do not always settle well with me.

He, as I surmised, is a righteous man, devoted and true to us these past months. I so enjoy having my "own" home. Most barren upon our arrival, with only the minimal of necessities for food and sleep and all else. But I have, with William's provision and permission, filled in all the emptiness. We, the girls and I (and Will Jr.), are delightfully busy from morning till night, tending our small home which now consists of two bedrooms (one for me, Sarah, Louisa, Emeline and Ruthie and one for William, George, Jonathan and Will Jr.), and the main room.

In the main room, we gather. It has a stove, shelving, a table and six chairs, and two rockers. William, I am proud to say, made the furniture. He is quite talented. Of course, he accepts Jonathan's and George's assistance, teaching them fine skills.

The stove keeps us sufficiently warm during our meals. We've no need for extra heat at night but know soon enough, when winter sets in, we will need heated stones for our pallets.

Soon we will need more chairs, as well. Emeline is getting too large for my lap, as is Ruthie for Sarah's, and Will Jr. for William's.

The babes grow like weeds. As does our vegetable garden. I cannot harvest fast enough before more carrots and potatoes, leeks and onions appear. And our chickens are healthy and always underfoot. It is Sarah and Ruthie's chore to collect eggs each morning. In turn, Louisa helps me knead bread, and we all take turns churning butter. I covet our evenings when we spin yarn and stitch and mend new shirts and dresses.

While we maintain the house - things I have always dreamed of doing for my very own family - Jonathan and George help William in the fields. William's apple orchard sees no real fruit yet, the trees being too young. But in another season, we might be blessed so.

William has plans for many other avenues of support. He plans to build on a cellar for storing apple cider and cheese. He is very industrious and townsmen regularly journey here to probe him for his information and ideas. He designs tools to help harvest and till and all manner of invention. He regularly modifies his designs - all etchings on paper thus far. He does so in the evenings while we sit for a while, exhaustion from a day long with chores finally at an end.

I present a pleasant table for him. It is my pride and joy to do so. The new cloth I stitched covers the rough wood, and with the remnants of the silver and china and crystal restored to me from the *Saluda*, we have added to it. I arrange it for our 'family' every morning and evening. Mama would be proud to know her teachings are being put to use. It pleases me to think of her and Papa, as well as my siblings during this time. The best time of my day is when we too, crowd around the table and are boisterous with talk and laughter as we sit together.

All-in-all I am content with things and William himself. We talk at length and I find his company enjoyable. We have similar desire for family and a common bond created by our endurance and stories from crossing the plains. I have not allowed my warm feelings for him to cloud my judgement but must say, I would be hard-pressed to live elsewhere now. I have taken his children to bosom and love them fair to distraction. Emeline is pure joy, as is sweet Ruthie and the rapscallion Will. Sarah and Louisa adore them as well and assist me greatly. We all have created a warm and comfortable home together.

When the children are abed and quiet fills the room, we read together. I have been able to share with him the biblical references that point to God's son, such as in the book of John, chapter fourteen, verse six.

In his fair-minded way, he gives this consideration. He also voices his opinion about other church matters and the territorial government.

I find him balanced in his thoughts.

All but one.

The issue that rumbles my spirit to its core.

To rationalize, I must consider William's family and upbringing. He was born in the wilderness of Ohio territory but his family did not remain in this outpost long. It seems his father Elias Hatcher had meager means and the family traveled continually throughout the area to hunt and find work. Elias and Sally were bowed down by the weight of life and eleven children. And then they heard Joseph Smith preaching one night. Needless to say, they believed him and were compelled to join his movement. Their plight remained hard until an uprising against fellow believers in Missouri hastened Mr. Elias Hatcher to Missouri to help. When the uprising was suppressed, he was recognized by Joseph Smith. He returned home, gathered the family and moved to Illinois where other fellow believers were settling. William was eight then. Sadly, his father died soon after from the influenza. Several of his siblings also died, including all of his sisters. Left were his mother and five brothers. Hovey and Shepard are William's elder brothers, Lyman and Joseph his younger brothers.

William remained in Illinois until three years ago when he was twenty and two – and *all* of Smith's teachings are engrained in him - he knows nothing else.

One such proclamation is that of plural marriage. Mr. Smith saw in his visions that a man should have multiple wives for the celestial heaven; the more wives, the more children he begot, and therefore the larger his celestial kingdom. Now the practice has been propagated by president Brigham Young. I knew William had previously had two wives. One would think, after the disaster of those two co-unions he would not be so inclined to repeat.

There one would be wrong.

Last week he took my hand as we were walking in the orchard and as I was awash with joy from the contact, he said, "I've asked you to marry me, Tilly. How much longer are you going to make me stir?"

I wanted to tell him I was inclined. "Until your position changes on plural marriage," I said instead.

"Now who's being stubborn?" he replied.

As a member of this religion, I have tried to obey its teachings. My attempts have been half-hearted since leaving Lexington, since realizing Christ is not their savior, that Salt Lake is not the Utopia promised. And this particular dictate is just as repugnant.

"Did not Abraham suffer when he took Hagar?" I reminded him. We had just read about Abraham and Sarah and Sarah's maid Hagar in the book of Genesis. God specifically told Abraham not to have more than one wife.

Had my fiancé John Sarnge lived I would never have faced this dilemma. John preferred one wife only.

In my mind, the practice suits self-serving men of a wandering nature. And yet William, though bruised by his first two marriages, will not rule it out.

I fear I would not make a good plural wife and yet other women are doing so. What then should I do?

"And if I pledge not to look for another wife, but take one only if the bishop requests?" he offered.

He was giving as much as he could and I knew it. "I'll consider, William," I replied, and felt the tug he had on my heart tighten. I am, at last, content with life and yet... I am now at a serious crossroads.

CHAPTER 18

Present Day

I wake and reach my hand out to pet Brutus, and realize he isn't there.

My bedside clock says it's five-thirty - but Granddad isn't walking down the hall to the kitchen and the smell of coffee isn't reaching my nose.

Dejected, I blink and realize I'm back in Denver. I stare at the pictureless white walls of my bedroom. Dust particles spin in the air, visible from a slit in the aluminum blinds that allows the exterior corridor light to shine through. I remind myself I'd never meant to stay in the one-bedroom unit in the mega-complex beyond my one-year lease, so why decorate.

I toss my comforter aside, planting my feet on the floor. My suitcases lay open there. Having no motivation to unpack, I step around them, through the door into the living room where more staleness hits my eyes. Dull-white apartment-grade paint stretches into the small kitchen. A chipped and scarred white Formica countertop holds my toaster and Keurig.

I brew a single K-cup as I hear my neighbor's television begin to blare. Oprah's voice drowns out the traffic rumbling by from the interstate.

My breakfast blend helps clear the fog in my brain and the sadness in my heart.

I need a plan - need to decide what I really want.

I know it isn't this apartment.

◆ ◆ ◆

On Sunday afternoon, I greet my mom in her entryway with a heartfelt hug. She's petite, shorter than I am, her hair nicely styled, her shape nicely rounded.

She takes a step back, her hands on my arms and asks,

"Anything wrong?"

"I just missed you," I admit.

"Well I'm glad you're home. You need to fill us in. Tell us how your granddad is doing."

We make our way through the living area, furnished with simple oak tables, a couple of recliners. The interior is dated but clean, the kitchen walls the same yellow they were when I was a teenager. I'd love it if Mom changed out the old linoleum for some nice travertine, but I keep my opinion to myself and follow her to the backyard. I can already smell the lilac bushes and Dad seems quite content sitting in his lounge chair in the middle of the patio, book in hand.

"Hey, Dad."

"How's my girl?" I lean over him for a brief hug. I inhale the fresh scent of his shirt, remembering how Mom always threw a freshener towel in with our laundry. It's a good memory.

"Work is busy." I'm not going to bore them with the details about my personal life.

"How's Granddad?" he sets down the book and sits up.

I take the seat beside him and fill them in on Granddad and the ranch. I do so without interjecting any of the raw emotion the subject brings me. "All-in-all I think he's doing pretty good. Brutus and Leadfoot help."

"Thanks for going out there, honey. It meant a lot to me."

"You're welcome, Dad. I'm really glad I went."

"But. . .?" My mom eyes me.

"But what?"

"I can tell something's wrong. Spill."

"Wrong?" How could she tell?

"Off."

"You're too perceptive, Mom. I just miss the place. I want some roots. I've been looking at properties this week and trying to figure out if I want a city house, a country ranchette, or what."

"Well, why didn't you tell me you were looking at places? I'd have joined you."

"I have another appointment tomorrow with this realtor. Are you working?"

"Not any longer. I'll take the day off. Meet for coffee first?"

"I'd love that."

My dad rises from his chair. "Can we eat now?"

"It's all ready," Mom says.

"And while we're eating," I add, "I have some questions for you. Questions about Gram and Granddad, about you and your childhood. And about my great-great-great-great grandmother Matilda."

"Whoa." Dad wraps his arm around me as we walk into the house. "Where'd all this come from?"

"Going through Gram's stuff. And learning about her and the family. Let's say I have a newfound fascination. It's been kind of fun. And it hit me that I don't know why I was named Rachel Matilda. So, let's start there. What can you tell me about Matilda Wyeman?"

CHAPTER 19

November 26, 1853

I think I always knew I would marry him in spite of my concerns.

Thus, being so, I sought peace from the Lord and have gained it. He is ever so faithful in allaying my fears and frustrations. So, in the end, my decision is rather easy. I determine I trust William. Simply that. He has proven himself and I know he will care for me. Our differences will curtail over time, and if, in the future, other wives arrive, I will confront it then. This being so, I once again find myself affianced and William Hatcher and I will marry in a week's time.

I am blessed.

Excited once again.

Eager for the future.

Life is about compromise, is it not, my papa always told me. I was willing to settle with Mr. Sarnge (it seems a lifetime ago) and to gain the greater I will not be obstinate.

Instead, I marry William for several reasons: pointedly, where else would I go? It is winter again here and the passes are closed. Already frigid we have had a fierce snow of several inches and a few smatterings as well. The beauty has quite worn off; it will be many months before we enjoy a warm blast of air again.

I marry him foremost because I believe I am in love with him. He is so different from John, truly a man of the earth who possesses great determination to carve a place for us. John would have done no less but in a much different way.

I marry him because I think we can have a life together and I am not willing to begin anew, seeking to find another. I long for another babe in my arms – my foster tikes all grow like weeds and I am not getting any younger. A babe of my own is what I want. And I marry him because I have claimed this place for my own. My home, my family. I will not allow fear to push me away.

I can only submit prayer for all of us here. Pray that William will see the light. And should I falter in this, my second attempt for hearth and home, I will, I vow, return to England. Defeated, yes, but no less grateful for the opportunity I was afforded. And should I return then I will cry on my mama's shoulder as she welcomes me. For in that, I know she will.

December 6, 1853

Dearest family,

I am a bride, married two days hence.

How I wish you could have been present for the occasion and I cannot help but admit I thought of John Sarnge and the ceremony that was to have taken place on the day the Saluda exploded, changing the course of my life forever. But I am blessed to have new friends here – so many women I have come to know and care for – as well as William's daughters and son. They are now my very own step-children, whom I dearly love. Other witnesses were members of William's family. His mother, Sally, was present, as were brothers, Lyman and Shepard, and their families. They have been kind to me. William has since taken to having everyone to our home on Sundays after church service for dinner. It makes for quite a gathering. Shepard and his two wives Lucinda and Eliza have seven children thus far.

William, George and Jonathan added a third bedroom in anticipation of our wedding. Now William and I share our own and our 'family' is adjusting.

We are settled in for winter. William is busy as ever in the early evening with his tool sketches and plans for spring. George and Jonathan listen and offer suggestions, which William considers. The three are good companions.

Sarah, Louisa and I are ever busy, our home full and boisterous and I believe, at last, I have found the richness I was seeking. God has indeed made my crooked path straight.

My appreciation, family mine, for all your prayers and understanding.

That I would hear from you all soon and know that you are well.

Your loving daughter and sister,

Tilly

May 29, 1855

He is two days old and I am still marveling at him – this new son of mine. He suckles well, has a lusty cry and a firm hold on my finger already. William told me I could name this firstborn between us so I chose George Miles after my own dear brother and papa. William has already kindly delivered to the post my letter to my family announcing George's arrival. How I wish I could see their smiles when they read the news.

On this warm spring day, I sit on the porch and rock my boy, marveling at the new life all around me. It is in the meadow, in the air and in my own arms.

Such God-given abundance is overwhelming.

January 24, 1857

Another son just yesterday, he, this precious boy, given the name Joseph after the child of my heart who I lost on the *Saluda*. Young George, a handful now at one and three months, is quite taken with his brother and my joy continues.

I am so blessed.

February 23, 1857

Our lives all changed irrevocably today when my William wed Janet Blaunt.

I smiled when he brought her home, welcomed her in and will try beyond all good measure to accept this new chapter. William did not look for this wife, as promised. Janet was pressed upon him by the bishop, she in need of a husband much the way I was in need of one; alone and destitute. How then could I not be understanding? In difference to me, William did request my permission and so I gave it. I will not tell him that I hesitated. Even if Janet is not the sister-wife I would have chosen for us both. She is younger than me by five years so perhaps in time we will bond. William has arranged for her to have a residence closer to town so we will not see each other much. For now, I will embrace her and hope for the best.

But is it wrong of me to already miss William's uninterrupted attentions?

I am consoled by the letter I received from my sister Rachel. She was delivered safely of her second child, son Thomas. Her first – my namesake Matilda Jane – is now nearly two. How I wish we could all be together.

Perhaps in the coming years we will all set eyes upon one another again.

April, 26, 1858

Janet delivered William a daughter, Jeanette. I suppose I am to be happy. Instead, I am rather numb. I keep my mind from wandering to a place that will serve me no good purpose. Instead, I swaddle the babe and deliver her to the arms of her mother.

July 26, 1858

I rocked Ruthie long into the night, long after she had passed from this world into God's arms. Emeline wept herself to sleep curled beside me and only after William had carried her to her bed and returned to gently take Ruthie from me, did I relinquish her. I still cannot reconcile that she was well and running through the meadow just last week. The fever took to her and would not relent.

November 24, 1858

I longed for a daughter this time, one I would name Rachel Ruth after my own dear sister and sweet stepdaughter. James was delivered to me instead, just yesterday. He stole my heart with his first squall and made Emeline smile.

Miriam, who came to live with us when Ruthie died, has been a solace to Emeline these past months. And to me. Now, with James, perhaps the morose of these winter months will slide more quickly by.

June 12, 1859

William has taken another wife. Another Sarah Ann. This Sarah Ann is with child by another man and needed refuge. The bishop brought her plight to our attention and William and I both agreed we could assist. Sarah Ann also has several other children by her first marriage. She brings with her a daughter Josephine who at ten is Emeline's age. Three other children remain with their father. An older woman, she appears defeated. I in turn, took her by the hand and steered her toward the firelit hearth.

William will make her and her children a home nearby.

Heaven help us all.

August 20, 1859

Janet delivered William a son, Robert. He is a stout boy. He'll thrive well. But Janet avoids both William's gaze and my own as we sing Robert's praises.

December 18, 1859

Sarah Ann brought forth Mary Ann. William has given the child his surname. Sarah Ann cries against my bosom as I rock her and the child in my arms.

July 17, 1860

My Benjamin arrived this morning, another fine son and I do believe William is well-pleased. I had once again decided this child would be a girl but alas, a daughter was not meant to be, and I welcome my Ben.

It is hard to even remember when I was without a babe on my hip. When I pined for a child of my own and fretted I would never know such pleasure. A little girl, if there is a next time, would be the ultimate blessing of all, but I would never dare plead such selfish desire to our great Lord when He has already given me so much. Four sons in five years with my William; I am humbled by such gifts.

More grand news is that our own dear Sarah Sarnge is betrothed. William and I approve of John Martin but I will miss her sorely once she is wed. I so wish her brother Jonathan were still here for the occasion but we received word from him last month that he has arrived safely in Oregon. We wish him all good things.

George Baldwin has also moved on, taking work as a helper on another farm, although we still see him on Sundays. I think he felt swallowed up by young children once Jonathan left.

The rest of my babes thrive well. Now that Louisa has married Martin Harris, I rely more on Emeline and Miriam to help me. They are the daughters of my heart, the daughters God has chosen to bestow upon me, though not of my own womb. They are good girls in my current time of need, with James just walking and Joseph always under foot. George is now out and about with his older half-brother Will Jr., they with William in the fields or workshop William built.

We have been blessed with a warm spring and William is hopeful our fall harvest will be plentiful. He is pleased with this new son, yet I fear the weight of so many children and wives wear on him. We see the others on occasion and all of us attempt to be cordial to one another. Only in private do I admit I am more than concerned with the way things are now. Sarah Ann is a nice woman but I don't believe she is truly content here. Nor is Janet, if I discern things well. William has done his best to accommodate this burgeoning family, but I am still not persuaded plural marriage is God's design for us. Too many women vying for one man's attentions bodes no good thing. And too many mouths to feed for one man does not either.

The sisters defer to me, I being the first wife. But I ask little of them and always with a smile. Yet I can still sense their contempt, mild, I will admit, but there non-the-less. I think there is discontent that they did not come first, as I might be in their place. I pray they are the last wives William accepts, but now that the door has been opened... I can tell you plural marriage did not take with Lyman, William's brother. He married three women this past year – two on the same day. Now two have already left him. Both were carrying his child. Only Mary has remained and she and Lyman have decided to relocate to an area called California. Pluralism does not exist there.

If I am not mistaken my sister-wives will leave William one day as well. They may have no choice if the federal government leaders have their way. We hear rumors some are pressing for its abolishment.

Only time will tell what becomes of this practice. And I would go mad if I dwelt on it all, so I focus on my own contented life; my babes, my home and my fullness. As long as they thrive, I thrive.

May it ever be so.

I do fret for my family far away. Mama has had no news from my brothers Joe and Ben since they sailed to Australia to meet up with John more than a year ago. Mama, in her last letter, admitted her fear for their safety. She also relayed that my dear sister Julia is still causing her sorrow. She married Mr. Sims without Mama and Papa's blessing, he an older, twice-married man already. They believe he is no good for her and will lead her to further ruin. How I wish she would respond to the posts I send her.

Thankfully, Caroline and her husband, Mr. Reed, remain nearby. They and their young daughter Caroline Susan are a blessing to Mama and Papa.

Rachel and her family as well, and James, at least, continues to do well in London with his pub, however distasteful the venture is.

I, being such a distance away, can only pray for all. I do so diligently and with honor that God hears my supplication. He has been ever faithful to me thus far.

September 5, 1860

William's eldest brother Hovey has been called to the San Bernardino area in California territory. President Young selected Hovey and a group of others to assist those who have had little luck with the crops they have tried to grow there.

We have not been called on such a mission but President Young is pressing more and more of us in this way. He does so because of the growing unrest in the eastern states and the talk of secession if the southern states refuse to abolish the system of enslaving black human beings. President Young wants us to be self-sufficient for our daily needs.

To have no need of supplies from the east and Europe. To that end, he is attempting to establish new mills and crop fields, asking followers to stead further south and north on new terrain outside the Great Salt Lake basin.

William is preparing us for such an event. We have heard of some of the hardships our friends face on these missions, and I can declare I have become accustomed to my quaint home and our bountiful supplies here because of the hard work and diligence of my husband. I would be hard-pressed to begin anew, especially with all the children.

Never-the-less, we desire, William and I, to assist in this effort as much as we can. We wish Hovey God's speed and wait to hear of his efforts. They will help with our own decision when and if we are called.

January 2, 1861

Janet has left us (William), taking with her Jeanette and Robert. I was convinced she would not remain long but neither did I realize if a sister-wife leaves, she can also take her children. Ruth did not do so, choosing to leave Emeline and Ruthie and then Miriam with William.

William has not discussed the loss of his children but I can sense he is as distraught as I in losing his babes. More so, the strangest occurrence about this all is that Janet went straightaway to Sarah Ann's previous husband. They have married, he being years older than she. Her marriage to William has been canceled. No divorce decree has been issued, as was the eventuality of William's first marriage to Ruth. Our bishop has assured us none is needed. Sarah Ann remains and we have settled in for the season. Sarah Ann is quiet on the issue of her sister-wife leaving to marry her former husband. I am perplexed, yet at this point the issue is neither here nor there. It is done.

CHAPTER 20

November, 1861

My beloved family,

I write to you with urgency, knowing this might be the last missive you receive from me for quite a long while. As I have written in the past, our leaders have attempted to make us self-sufficient and to that end have sent friends and family afield to plant, harvest and build. Last month was our turn to be called to a place called Toquerville, south of us some hours. William, though he could have refused, has decided we will go. We have been warned of the harsh conditions there. Many who have gone before us have returned in defeat. Our task will be to tame a rocky soil, mitigate a river that floods regularly and plant and harvest cotton. We are told there is little lumber in the region, the summers hot. We will be many miles from the nearest outpost of St. George and though others before us have had success with the natives in the region (indeed Toquer is the name of the tribal chief in the area), there have still been raids upon settlers.

We will need to rely on all of our resources to see us through, and yet I believe William is more than up to the task to keep us safe and sound. I am of the opinion this is also his attempt to satisfy himself with all things about our church. There is growing unrest in him as we both read the Bible regularly. He sees the differences between Christianity and Mormonism and is conflicted. After a caravan of pilgrims headed to Oregon were slaughtered, rumor abounded that it was not Indians who did the deed but rather Mormon men. William knows some of these men, has heard them bragging about their deeds, one of them a cousin of his. He is heartsick to think they took the lives of women and children, looted all and placed blame on the tribes. Now there is a federal investigation into what is being called the Mountain Meadow Massacre. When he went to the bishop with his suspicions, he was told to keep quiet.

William does not keep quiet well.

Our mission to Toquerville is to garner for certain whether our leaders are to be trusted. To that end, William is selling our land here. He is the last of his brothers to do so. Lyman has gone to Watsonville, California, Hovey is in San Bernardino, California and Shepard is in Missouri. I fear my mother-in-law, Sally, will not last long after we are gone. She is of poor health now.

William has decided we will take three wagons and oxen and provisions to keep us for a two-year period. We have cows and horses as well. The boys (Will Jr., George, Joseph, James and Ben) as well as Emeline and Miriam, will go with us. To my surprise Sarah Ann, Josephine and Mary Ann will go as well.

We go with many other families, more than two-hundred in all, and will attempt to relieve the others who have gone before us. I'm told they are weary from their endless and defeating work.

We will need to make do in the elements when we arrive until William can build us a cabin. There is little timber, we understand the wagons will be our shelter for the winter and perhaps beyond. I have no small concern with leaving on our quest just as winter arrives but am told the climate south is not as harsh as it is here.

And so, my dear family, knowing there is little possibility any posts I write will find their way to you, I do not want you to fret should you not hear from me. I will keep them at the ready should someone trustworthy pass our way, and know that my greatest sorrow in our move is the understanding I will not hear from any of you either. News from home has always strengthened me.

In closing, know that all my boys are sturdy and stout and eager for this adventure. I would not risk them otherwise. Nor would I attempt such a journey with a man less qualified than mine own.

Alas, remain well, my family. I could not bear to hear otherwise when this all ends.

I send you all my love for all eternity,
Daughter and sister,
Tilly

CHAPTER 21

November 1862
Toquerville, Utah Territory

William wipes my drenched brow in the pre-dawn light as my stomach continues to roil and I wait for another convulsion to further empty its contents.

I'd awoke only moments ago, hastening out of the wagon I shared with my three youngest sons, my protesting stomach determined to upend.

Of course, I succeeded in waking all.

Ben, two, now protests along with my stomach, his squalls annoying James, who at four, is shouting for Ben to be quiet. Joseph, five, shouts at James for shouting at Ben. Unable to intervene, I kneel among the black boulders and thistles that plague this terrain, allowing myself to be ill again. I can only listen to my boys' cranky behavior; they as withered as I am of this barren, miserable place.

And now my stomach has confirmed what I already knew – another child grows inside me. An early spring babe she will be – my lass.

If we were still in Salt Lake, I would welcome the news, but here – in Toquerville – I cannot muster much enthusiasm.

"Shush down!" William admonishes the boys as he pulls my hair from my face and presses the towel to my brow again. "Will, tend to your brothers."

I hear more than see Will Jr., now eleven, drop to the ground, George, seven, behind him. I can only groan as they chuckle at my discomfort.

They, along with William were asleep in our second wagon until my body rebelled.

Sarah Ann, Mary Ann, three, Josephine and Emeline, both twelve, and Miriam, ten, are still tucked inside the recently completed dugout. This is the eight-foot-deep, twenty-foot-long, eight-foot-wide shelter William dug in the hillside beside our wagons. Hopefully the disturbance outside will not rouse them, too.

I take the cloth he has and wipe my mouth as he rubs my back. As my morning sickness ebbs, I look at him and I see my concern mirrored in his own eyes. Granted, we knew the task we had been given here would be difficult, the task we willingly accepted. But a year into it we now know how naïve we were, and therefore our leaders, in thinking we could discipline this land. It is so very bleak. The earth is a red clay called adobe. It is dry and crumbly, littered by large and small black stones. Nothing planted in it thrives. Though the winter is mild here – snow rare – what rain does fall quickly runs off instead of into the soil. All of our attempts to plant cotton have been met with defeat. All my attempts to clear land and plant corn and greens to sustain our family have met the same fate.

We are no closer to taming this land than we were the day we arrived.

William is not one to accept defeat; he works tirelessly with the other men to produce crop. What is impossible to plan for is the sudden flash floods coming down the hillsides, or the prolonged heat that withers all. Keeping livestock from our own small water source is also an on-going task. Unfortunately, those who tried to stead this area before us found out that cows and pigs carry vermin humans cannot tolerate. After much tragedy they realized using the same water the animals used was a sure way to a quick death. We do our utmost to keep the cattle out of the river and boil our water but Ague is still rampant here, dysentery in every campsite.

We have been spared – thank God – but danger rides on the wind. Bee stings are an everyday occurrence, as are ant bites, sunburn, and thorns the locals call goat-heads. They sting to the quick. George was kicked by a neighbor's mule last month, his ribs still bruised to this day. James has an itchy rash on his legs that my ointments do not help.

I long for the normalcy of the life we left behind.

If not for William's forethought and dedication to us we would have suffered more. We have our wagons and the warmth therein. We now have the dugout. With no nearby wood source, adobe stone was our best material to build with. For months we have all been collecting stone while William and Will Jr. dug the massive hole. William then began placing the stones around the structure, until he'd created a dome.

The dugout now serves as our home of sorts, providing shelter and storage.

But I'm not thrilled to think I might be giving birth in it.

"Can you make it back to the wagon?" William asks me.

I nod and he helps me stand. He leads me to the wagon where the boys are all lined up, watching us.

"Take the boys to the other wagon," William says to Will. "And mind yourselves," he admonishes to them all. "I'll stay here with your mother for a while."

"Yes, sir."

"Go back to sleep," I say, hoping they will do so, knowing they will not. Then I turn my attention toward climbing into the wagon and laying down.

William follows me, and as I sigh, he tucks a blanket under my chin. "The babe will come in the spring?" he asks.

I place my hand on my now-quiet stomach. I've never been ill before – not with one of my boys. "She. She will come in the spring," I tell him.

I see a glisten in his eyes as he brushes his finger against my cheek. "Then it will be a fine spring, Tilly," he replies.

I swallow the lump in my throat. "Yes. With Sarah Ann carrying your child as well, you will have two more children come spring. Your kingdom enlarges even here." The bitter words cause him to pull back. I promptly want to retract them. Instead, I turn aside from his gaze, my silent prayers shouting into the heavens.

CHAPTER 22

Present Day

I avoid Stephanie and Linda, concentrating on house-hunting and family research. But with my apartment walls creeping in on me, I finally take Steph's call and agree to meet both my friends at the movie theater.

"That was hilarious," she says afterwards, as we walk through the crowded parking lot towards our cars. The air is crisp, a prelude to the coming winter. Steph and Linda don't seem impacted, but I'm already hugging my arms.

"Pretty good acting, huh?" Linda's bracelets tinkle as she reaches into her purse for her car keys. "I've never really liked Katherine Heigl much, but she was funny in this film."

"I'll take Chris Hemsworth any day. He's to die for." Steph runs her hand through her short, spiky hair. Today it's a mere three shades of brown. Last year she'd tinged it purple, the year prior, stark black. "What'd you think, Shell?"

"An easy way to spend a couple hours, I guess. I liked the plot. I just don't get why these directors have to make things so graphic and crude. It would have been funny enough without the language or the sex scenes." The romantic-comedy was about a burned-out female attorney who takes a job as a Zumba instructor on a cruise ship, only to discover her old flame is the captain.

"Yeah but those two sure knew how to lock lips, didn't they?"

They did, I grumble to myself. Which made me long for the same thing. Put thoughts of Ben in my mind. "They were just acting, remember?"

"Hey, let's head over to *The Chop House* and have a drink. The Avs game should be ending. Maybe some of the team will show up and we can get in on some of that lip-locking." Linda presses down on her car key and her engine starts.

"I thought you decided to swear off pro-players for a while?" I search through my purse for my own car keys.

"That was last week."

"Can't we go someplace nice and quiet and just talk?"

"Talk about what? I'd rather go dancing. There's a new club— "

"The Xanadu."

I'm glad I've driven my own car. "You two go on without me." I shouldn't be disappointed but I am.

"Come on, Shell. It's not like you've got anything better to do. I mean you're not moving in to a great new loft or going out on a hot date."

"You're right, Steph," I say a bit too irritably. "Although I did look at the loft again just yesterday. I've permanently scratched it from my potential list. As for a hot date, that depends on what you mean." I didn't add that doing some family research was more stimulating than going to another night club. I quickly unlock my door. "Have fun, you two."

I'm able to leave before they protest. But as I pull out of the parking lot, I drive towards the one-way streets of Lower Downtown, Denver. I do so just to see if something in me wants to revisit the place; to bar hop and man hunt. People are out and about, walking up and down the avenues, sitting at outdoor cafes, riding the 16th Street Mall by light-rail. I drive by a few clubs, see the lines of patrons waiting to get in, the bouncers standing at attention, hear the boom of a bass inside.

Maybe I'm not stirred to enter because I don't have the right person with me. Someone I could trust. Someone whom I wasn't worried was going to assault me, drug me, use me and dump me.

But I didn't. And it wasn't likely I ever would.

So, I keep right on driving.

Nearing home, I pull into a fast-food parking lot, deciding a naked-burrito will help bury my angst.

I'm standing in line, waiting to order when I hear someone call my name. Hoping I'm hearing things, I ignore the voice, but I casually turn to see the guy I once thought might be my lifelong partner. He's making a small scene as he stumbles from his table to where I stand.

"Shelley!"

"Carter."

Carter was in my life for two years. Right after college graduation Carter had been the one to call it quits, telling me he was looking for someone who would complement him better.

Complement him better? I hadn't known what he meant and refused to dwell on it.

Now he hugs me tight, rattling me, before he starts with that small talk ex's make. "Wow, you look great. "How've you been?"

The food-line moves around us as I assess his successful-looking self. I wish I looked just as successful. Unfortunately, my hair is in a ponytail and I'm wearing movie theater comfort clothes; leggings and a baggy shirt.

The ultimate comes when he tugs me towards his table. "I have some people I want you to meet," he tells me.

And then I immediately understand what he'd meant all those years ago when I see a woman with sultry skin. Carter is blond and she is dark. Carter is rough-around-the-edges and she is sleek.

"My wife, Shauna." His smile is wide as he introduces us. "And this is Leah." He lifts a toddler from her booster seat.

She is perfect, gorgeous, adorable, with beans and rice all over her face. Shauna and Leah complement him well.

I decide not to order my burrito, especially after we all promise to keep in touch, to get together. We never will of course. And I can't leave fast enough.

At home, I close the door and lean against it.

Then I wind my way to the kitchen, grab the quart of Snickers' ice cream stashed in my freezer. I curl up on the couch, turn on *Pride and Prejudice* and eat the entire quart.

♦ ♦ ♦

The next morning, after jogging off the ice cream calories and my depression at a local park, I'm thinking about Emory just before she calls. A few days ago, she'd told me she'd broke off her relationship with Miller.

"Hey, Em," I say as I take her call, hope she isn't going to tell me she's decided to give Miller another chance. I have sweat running down my face. I towel the moisture and take a seat on the park bench. "You must have read my mind. I was just thinking about you. What are you doing this morning?"

"I'm at Granddad's. I brought Samson over to play with Brutus. I'm going to text you some pictures. They are so cute together."

I exhale, glad she hasn't mentioned Miller. Then my emotions shift. "Don't be so cruel." I pat the new moisture on my brow. "You know how much seeing them will hurt me."

"That's what I'm hoping. Then maybe you'll come back. You haven't exactly found what you're looking for there, have you?"

No. No I hadn't. "Not yet. But I'm still touring houses with a realtor. I'm focusing on houses with a few acres now."

"Then why haven't you found the right one?"

"Maybe because I don't know what the right one looks like?"

"I think you do. It's Granddad's ranch. He says to tell you Chester is waiting for you. And we all miss you."

"That's not fair." My heart cracks. "Tell him I said thank you. And give him my love." And hug Brutus, I want to add, but that would have made me start weeping.

"I will. So, he tells me you were using Gram's tea cups, like one every day. What gives with that?"

147

I explain my ritual. "It was just my sentimental way to honor Gram."

"I love that idea. I think I'll do the same."

"Great."

"Okay, I'm sending a couple pics now. They are getting so big."

I groan. And when I view the photos, I can't stop my tears. The two puppy brothers are rolling around on the grass playing together. Just the way Ben had wanted them to.

We hang up minutes later, after Em confirms Miller is in the past and her parents' divorce is final. And then she sends me a picture of herself with one of Gram's teacups in hand.

I am a blubbering mess on the park bench, no closer to 'finding' what I'm looking for in life than I was when I left for Texas months ago. Except that Emory is right; everything about Granddad's ranch – the area, the people, the horses and terrain and lifestyle – is exactly what I want.

Except Ben is there, too. Unavoidable.

Why should that matter?

CHAPTER 23

April 18, 1863

The squall is music to my ears. Strong and fierce it is, this precious daughter God blessed me with today.

My own Rachel at last, I hold her to my chest as Emmeline helps me gently bathe the filmy birth muck from her eyes and nose.

"Miriam," I say to my step-daughter. She has just witnessed her first birth. Her eyes are still wide with awe. "Run and tell your Papa," I smile. "He's waited long enough."

"I can hold her when I get back?" Miriam asks.

"Yes, you may." My voice is weak as I sink into the stacked pillows and soft linens, spent from giving birth.

As she races up the dugout stairs into the light of day, I place my knuckle against Rachel's mouth and she begins to suckle, her cries silenced. "You did well, Em," I say to Emmeline who is still beside me. "Thank you. Without Sarah Ann to help you were the only one I could rely on."

"I'm glad you had me watch Sarah Ann deliver Elias last week or I wouldn't have been much help."

"We would have managed." I say this without much conviction as even now I hear Sarah Ann's labored cough from the other side of the room. She is struggling to recover from her son's birth. I might have to nurse two babes' if her milk doesn't produce soon.

But for now, I close my eyes, Rachel's mews lulling me.

September 10, 1863

"There! See it? She smiled again." Miriam is perched on a boulder. She holds Rachel on her lap while I weed the patch of red-clay earth I'm attempting to grow corn in. The weeds have no problem sprouting in this miserable soil, while the corn...

I stretch my back and give my attention to my daughters just as Rachel smiles again. "Well then, I guess she did."

"I taught her," Miriam says. "I smile at her all the time."

My feet carry me toward the girls and I brush a strand of Miriam's braided hair back in place. "You're a very good big sister."

As if concurring, Rachel smiles again.

She then coughs.

October 3, 1863

"Let me take her for a while."

I'd felt the wagon shift from William's weight, blinked when the back-canvas flap rose to allow the daylight in, and saw him peer inside. I continue to rock Rachel, humming to her when she stirs, trying to keep her sedate so her hacking won't begin again.

She and I are alone in the wagon. It is warm inside, free from the dust and damp and mold that plagues the dugout. I'd scampered the boys out days ago, given William charge to find them new beds while I tended their sister. Given him charge to feed and clothe and tend them all until Rachel was well.

"I'm fine," I whisper, though I am not.

She is not.

"Let me relieve you," William tries again. "I know you're exhausted. I wish I had a rocking chair for you instead of that hard bench."

I do, too. If so, we would be in civilization. If so, I would not need it and my daughter would not be ill.

"You're just as tired." I don't ask about the boys or the cotton crop or supper. I don't want to know.

"How is she?" His voice is weary-laden.

"Her shivers have calmed." I don't add that her fever has not. Nor her cough, and that she is too weak to suckle my teat. I regularly soak a clean rag with my milk and press it into her mouth instead, hoping...

"Tilly—"

"Go back to the others. Tell my children I love them."

The wagon's flap drops in place, daylight with it. I am plunged into darkness.

October 4, 1863

I sit on the hard wagon bench, motionless, as William scoops Rachel from my arms and lays her atop the pink blanket I had knitted for her before she was born.

He slowly, carefully, begins to wrap her still body inside the material, then lastly covers her unbreathing nose, unseeing blue eyes, sealing her from my sight.

He lifts her into his arms, takes hold of my arm and I allow him to steer me toward the canvas door. He jumps from the back, Rachel undisturbed, then helps me down.

I pause, reach for my daughter, then stop myself. She is not there, I say silently. She is safe in God's arms, waiting for me in heaven.

William takes my arm again and leads me to the back of the dugout where he has made a deep hole in the harsh red earth I loathe so much. I'm listlessly aware of my other children standing nearby, watching me, watching William.

I hear their sniffles, hear Miriam's sobs.

I want to reach out and comfort her – comfort them all - but I have no strength. William slips down into the hole, places Rachel at the bottom, the pink blanket softening the red clay. When he climbs out, Rachel is left there. He grabs the shovel leaning against the dugout.

"William!" I cry out. "Wait!" Perhaps if I remove the blanket, she will open her eyes, breath again.

"Tilly." His voice is calm though his hands shake as he faces me. Will Jr. stands beside him, shovel in hand, waiting. "She's at rest, wife."

Sorrow sparkles in his eyes.

Emmeline moves beside me, draws me close and I nod, defeated. Then one shovel of red clay splashes atop the blanket. Its followed by another and another until the blanket disappears.

I draw in a breath I might never exhale.

William drops the shovel and withdraws a knife from his belt. He turns toward the dugout, chooses an adobe stone above Rachel's grave and begins to etch into it. When he stands back minutes later, I see the cross he has carved.

As tears run unchecked from my eyes, I exhale.

Come spring I will plant flowers atop my daughter's barren grave. I will water them with fresh tears. As for now, I thank God for my brief time with my daughter, knowing my heart will be forever crushed.

CHAPTER 24

March 6, 1864

William finishes harnessing the horse to the wagon and turns to face me, the march wind whipping around us, playing havoc with my skirts. A trace of frost still coats the cold ground, adding to my disquiet.

"I wish I didn't have to leave like this," he says.

"I know." I do. Truly. But his words do little to calm my spirit. "I've tried every herb poultice I know of and nothing has helped Sarah Ann's cough. Now that her breathing is raspy, she needs to go back to Salt Lake before it's too late."

"And you're sure you want Mary Ann and Elias to stay here with you?"

"They would merely slow you down." As we all would if we packed up and left this horrid place. "Besides, with Josephine and Emeline going along, there is no room. I'll have Will Jr. and Miriam to help me with all the others." I was more concerned about Emmeline begging to go with her father than I was about keeping Sarah Ann's two children. Em had become restless of late and I feared she'd refuse to return here. Not that I could blame her. "Besides, we need supplies. I'm as weary of dandelion roots and gamey rabbit as anyone. You have my list? Don't forget the molasses."

William taps his coat pocket. "It'll stay right here."

"You won't be wearing a coat by the time you return." I wasn't expecting to see them again until the heat of July at the earliest.

"I'll keep it safe."

I turn toward the dugout. "I'll get Sarah Ann ready."

August 24, 1864

There is a reverberation between my ears that has not ceased.

No matter how many times William has explained himself since his return last week, how many times he seeks me out for forgiveness or absolution or whatever it is he is seeking, I cannot get past the noise.

I sweep away dirt and dust. I scrub and mend and tend and darn and cook and everyone presses for my attention -but I cannot hear them.

I am provoked.

After days of trying to come to terms with all the news he brought back with him, that is the word I have attached to this emotion. More than betrayed. More than disappointed.

Provoked.

So provoked.

Is it not sufficient that I have given all to this quest? To this church, this mission... this man?

I am bound to this life in so many ways; bound by my children, my God, my own commitment.

How then, can I go on here? When my husband tells me he has married Josephine. Josephine, who is Sarah Ann's daughter. Josephine, who is fifteen – the same age as his own daughter Emeline.

"I felt I had no choice." He has said this repeatedly and every time I recoil from him. He says it again now, as we stand between two rows of withering corn stalks, having no other place for such private talk. "Sarah Ann worsened days after we left. We made it as far as Lehi before she passed. After we buried her, Josephine, Emeline and I moved on."

"And met the man from Norway. Yes, you've said."

"He asked us for a lift and by the time we got to Salt Lake he and Emeline were asking to get married."

"But she is only fifteen," I shout at him.

"And strong willed. Determined. I saw no way to stop her."

I snicker as he continues, my disdain unchecked.

"I tried to find Josephine's father but found he had left for Idaho."

"And so, your solution is to marry her? The same day your daughter marries the Norwegian Christopher Jacobs? And he thirty-years her senior as you are to Josephine?"

"What were my choices?"

I did not know. I did not care.

Heavy with a child that I would deliver within the month, still mourning the loss of my Rachel, and having been left alone in a desert that is hell on earth for five months, I just did not care any longer.

"She will be the last, Tilly. I swear it."

"This is supposed to soothe me?" For the first time in years I consider returning to England. How am I to do so with a newborn and all his brothers for I would not leave them?

"Living in a real house again will help, won't it? I did bring back all the supplies to build it."

"Which means we will stay here."

"Not much longer."

I cross my arms, walling myself off from him.

"You'll see, Tilly. I'll make things right."

I wish I could believe him. But he has led me far afield from the life I desired. A life for a simple home and family of my own. A man right with God and his Savior.

Instead I am married to a man who has had four past wives and two current ones and thirteen offspring. My new child – a boy if I'm right, who I will name Samuel - will add to that count. More should his child-bride breed.

I would change so much... and yet... I would really only change one thing: my daughter's death.

And so, as he speaks, I wish I could hear him. But the roar between my ears is too loud.

155

November 9, 1865

There is a boulder I go to now, for quiet and privacy. It sits above the house William built for us, overlooking the valley. It is large, protruding from the mountain. I can see our house, the children playing, even William and Will in the west fields with the other men, plowing and seeding for the next withered crop.

There is a breeze today, but the weather is mild so I trek up the hill and sit down to read my sister Rachel's letter.

It is the second letter I have received from her now that the war between the northern and southern states has subsided. The first shared the good news that she is expecting again and Caroline delivered twins in May.

Today's news tells me my mama is gone.

"She died in her sleep after feeling tired and going to bed." Rachel wrote.

Oh Mama.

It lessens my sorrow to know Papa is well and that Rachel and Thomas are caring for him, but in my mind's eye my mama is still young – too young to have passed on. It does not seem possible that I have been away from them for thirteen years.

I will write back tonight, relaying that William finished our house last month. It has stout wood walls and a thatched roof, is warm inside and large enough for us all. I will also write that Emeline has moved on from Mr. Jacobs, much to my relief. In Emeline's letter to me she said she realized early on what a mistake she had made. I am grateful no children were born to them and glad she will stay in Salt Lake with her mother.

Rachel does not mention any of my brothers, gone these many years now, so I will ask her if there is news of them. I can only pray they did not all meet with tragedy themselves but rather allowed their mama to know they were well before she passed.

And Julia? She has never reached out to me. Has she them?

I am comforted to know Papa has Rachel, her husband Thomas, daughter Matilda Jane, and sons Thomas and Miles. He also has Caroline and her husband George, and their children George, Susan, Charles and Mary.

I wish I had them, too.

I will tell them so in my letter.

What I will not tell them is Josephine will give William his fourteenth child before the new year.

I cannot.

August, 1866

It is difficult maintaining my composure while settling Ben, Elias and Sam down for a midday nap.

As soon as I can, I slip from the house. I leave Josephine and her daughter, Olive, to themselves.

I skirt Miriam and Mary Ann without a word. They continue to skip rope while I make my way to the back of the dugout, to Rachel's grave.

I grab the hoe leaning against the dugout and ignore the splintering wood that tears into my hand. Instead, I attack the weeds, ever attempting to choke out the flowers.

Tears begin to roll down my cheeks, unchecked, dripping onto my hands.

Today's news is too cruel. A continuum of grief that never ends.

"And dear sister, I must tell you that Caroline's husband and son took ill in February."

The words Rachel had written in her latest letter, a letter I'd read just an hour ago, play in my mind.

"Both succumbed after every attempt to save them. Caroline and her other children have moved in with Papa and me. She is still so distraught I must tend them all."

"Why the tears, wife?"

William's voice startles me and I flinch. He'd been repairing one of the wagon's wheels, last I'd seen him. Will Jr., George, Joe and James are down by the riverbed shooting slingshots, so I thought I'd be alone.

I sniff, wipe my tears and keep hoeing. "Word from my family." I tell him the sad news. "Now Rachel's husband, Thomas has taken a two-year commission with the P&O Line as a ship's steward in order to support them all."

"I'm sorry for their sufferings."

"Yes." My throat is swollen, gravelly.

He grabs the hoe and stills it. Stills me. I look at him, something rare these days. There is too much between us now.

"And what else is troubling you?" he asks.

"These weeds," I say, casting my eyes downward. I tug on the hoe, tug it from his grip.

William takes the hoe from my hands and sets it against the dugout. "And this place?"

"Yes."

"And this life?"

"Need you ask?"

He takes my hand in his. I allow it, though I'm not sure why.

"Come with me."

I walk with him, realize that he is taking me toward the hill behind the house. We climb the well-worn path there to my boulder, a path he has never ventured with me before.

The day is warm with a layer of clouds that block the sun as he says, "Sit for a spell," and sits on the boulder first. I sit beside him, keeping a distance between us. He moves closer until his leg touches my skirts.

"We've been here for five years."

Five years too long, I want to remark. I keep silent.

"We've given our best. Cotton does not like this soil."

"Nor do I."

William takes my hand. I start to pull away. I place no blame on him for our hardships here. But I have not pardoned him for taking Josephine as his wife. Still, I reconsider and leave my hand in his.

"We will only stay one more year."

"What?" I breathlessly mutter the word.

"There is a valley not eighty miles north of here that is fertile and green. We passed it on our way here. It's been on my mind ever since. On my trip to St. George last month I met a few people who have settled there. They say it's a good place."

"A good place. What about our mission here?"

"Do we stay forever because our church leaders won't listen to the truth? We have told them cotton will not grow here. We will make one last attempt in the spring. But I won't spend the rest of our money on a failed venture.

"I'll buy another parcel of land. Plant another apple orchard instead. There are trees along the mountain ridge for a new house and furniture."

"You don't have to convince me."

"And I think we can take some of our tithe and send it to your family."

"William, truly? The church will not be pleased."

His response is a shrug.

I squeeze his hand. I then gaze down at the valley, the girls still playing near the house, the boys running around near the river. I look towards the dugout and Rachel's grave. I will have to leave her behind.

CHAPTER 25

Present Day

Returning to Granddad's is an easy decision.

This time I drive my car, the backseat loaded with most of my meager worldly goods – including a supply of watercolor paints and an easel.

My dad had helped me move my bedroom and living room set into storage, then I'd said good-bye to him and my mom, the Rockies, the noisy freeway-close apartment, cold winters and Steph and Linda.

I hadn't decided if I would permanently stay in Texas, but for the time being I knew it was the right place for me. I couldn't wait to see Chester and Angie and Carmen. I was even looking forward to collecting eggs.

I could also do family research easier from Granddad's. Matilda Wyeman's journals were there, and I hadn't even begun to explore the attic for artifacts about her and other family members. With the summer heat beginning to subside, exploring the attic would be possible soon.

I told myself I was no longer concerned about seeing Ben. I would just steer clear of him, pretend nothing had happened the night of the Gala. Pretend I hadn't started to fall for him.

I was ready to move forward - hang out with Emory more, go to a few Honky Tonks - meet a cowboy or two, and stop judging any potential new boyfriends based on clients who couldn't write their own wedding vows.

It is hot when I arrive – still humid and damp this early September day. All along my route I had viewed the changing terrain – the brown summer meadows in southern Colorado, barren desert in northern New Mexico, small ranch towns in west Texas.

Now mossy lushness surrounds me, trees and flowering shrubs in full bloom, green grass high in the fields, corn stalks tall and ready for harvest.

Granddad greets me in the yard. I hug him longer than I should, sniff and hear him do the same before he makes way for Brutus to jump up and nearly knock me over.

"Hey, boy!" I kneel down, hug Brutus close, feel his tongue licking my face.

And feel joy for the first time in a long time.

I pick up where I'd left off the following morning, rising at five without the alarm clock telling me I have to. I eagerly greet Leadfoot, Glory, and the rest of the horses, and Chester with a promise for an afternoon ride, before gathering eggs and feeding the chickens. Emory and Samson arrive near eight, and as the dogs' romp in the yard, she and I enjoy a pot of tea and Gram's tea things on the porch before she heads off to work.

With the corn ready for harvest, at lunch Granddad and I go over the details together. I learn Ben will be on hand when the Co-op combine arrives next week to begin plowing the fields. Granddad, Ben and I will rotate shifts while the combine plows, helping where needed.

That afternoon I see Carmen and Angie coming out of the barn, Malibu in tow.

"What took you so long to get back here?" Carmen asks.

"You say that as if you knew I'd return." I open the paddock gate for her.

"I had my suspicions," she says with a mischievous smile.

"I wish you'd shared them," I smile back. "I'm free Thursday."

"Then I think I have errands to run."

I close the gate behind the mother and daughter and step onto the fence, watching them. "You know Carmen, if Angie has friends who would like to ride, you're more than welcome to invite them and their parents to come over." I say this as inspiration strikes. If Ben can develop a program for wounded vets, why couldn't we organize one for kids with Down's?

161

"Its pretty obvious horse therapy is helpful. Maybe we could create a support group."

Carmen pats Malibu's nose as she faces me. "Wow, Shelley, that's awfully generous of you."

"Think about it?"

"I will. Thanks."

I'm still thinking about the new program when I hear, "Welcome home."

My stomach tightens as I turn to see Ben walking towards me. Sherlock is tied near the water trough. But I can't believe I didn't hear them approach.

Ben places one booted-foot on the fence rail and swings the other over the top of the fence, planting his backside.

"Hi Ben!" Angie calls.

He waves and smiles. Then he focuses on me.

It's obvious he is not concerned with keeping any distance from me. When my heart hiccups I try not to frown.

"Granddad just went into the house to turn on the Ranger's game," I say, hoping Ben will go join him. The Rangers were tied for the American lead. A win against the A's today would get them home-field advantage for the playoffs.

"I was watching at home. Rangers are down six to one so mind if I keep you company instead?"

A hundred replies enter my brain – everything from 'not at all' and 'you wouldn't want to get cooties' to 'sure thing, Big Boy' and 'beat it, Buster." I settle for: "Um, I guess so. Actually, Carmen and I were just talking about something I could discuss with you."

"That's funny. I have something I wanted to discuss with you, too. You first."

I swallow my hesitation to engage him in small talk for the good of something more important. "Can you give me some pointers on how you started your program to help the veterans?"

His gaze still pierces me, keeping me edgy. "Sure. Any particular reason why?"

"I'm thinking of starting something here. A program for kids with Down's Syndrome. Broadening what Carmen and Angie have."

"That's admirable."

I shrug. "Not really."

"Okay. Well..." I listen as he begins to give me insight on how to start a horse therapy program. After a while I realize I'm more interested in what he is saying than worried about interacting with him. For the first time, I am more conscious about the topic than averting my gaze from his moving lips or focusing on the way he tips his hat back on his brow. My body relaxes, my perspiration subsiding. "Thanks for the input," I finally say. "That was really insightful. It certainly doesn't sound as easy as I'd hoped, but I think we could pull it off."

"I can tell you I don't regret one day. Not when I see the impact the program has on individual lives. Neither will you."

"That's encouraging."

I turn to watch Carmen and Angie, excited by this new endeavor. Then I remember Ben had alluded to wanting to discuss something with me as well.

When he doesn't, my discomfort returns and I decide it's time to leave. I jump down from the fence. "I'll go tell Granddad you're here."

"Before you go..." He swings his leg back over the fence but remains perched on high, staring down at me. "I have a friend who's starring in a play at the Palace Theater in Georgetown this weekend. She's bugging me to go and well I was wondering if you'd go with me. We could catch some dinner first."

Ben was asking me out? Like in, the two of us?

Or was this a female friend? Someone who'd set her sights on him. Or maybe someone he wanted to stir to jealousy.

"When is this play?" I fumble for time, pretend I need more information before I flat out tell him no.

"Saturday night. I could pick you up at five. You'll like the Palace. It's an old movie house, seats a couple hundred. And the Wildfire has some good dishes."

"Sounds great but I—"

"You're going to turn down a date with me?"

"A date?"

"Well isn't that what it's called when a guy asks a girl out?"

Adrenaline shoots through my body. I swallow as I try to squelch the chemical reaction. How can I be so steamy inside when all I want is to appear cool and collected?

I take a calming breath. "I'm not interested, Ben. I'm guessing you're looking to get your friend's attention, or looking to get her attention off you. Neither reason gives me incentive. We've been pretty disastrous together over the years. Let's just leave things as they are. I'll stay out of your way and, please, stay out of mine." I begin to walk towards the barn. Chester and I have a real date.

I hear him jump down from the fence. "Whoa, whoa, whoa." His hand grasps my arm and gently spins me. His gaze is intense. "I sure bungled that, didn't I? Seems to be a theme with me. But I have no ulterior motive here, Shelley. I was just asking you out. You. And me. Mandy is an old friend. Yeah, we dated once, in high school. She's married now. Has a son. She dabbles in small-town productions a couple times a year and I just thought... well I was actually looking for an excuse. I wanted a do-over."

His height shades the sun from my eyes. I am well-aware of his hands on my arms, the just-enough pressure to hold me in place but not man-handle me. I could easily step away from him. I don't. "A do-over?"

"I need – want - to make up for my ornery behavior at the Garden Club Gala."

"That again?" I keep my gaze on his, confidence giving me courage. Not easy when he's looking right back and the depth of his gaze threatens to pull me closer. "You already did. There's no need for a retake or a do-over. It's pretty apparent we – you and me - just need to maintain our distance. I really want to live here right now. So, for Granddad's sake let's just do our best to get along and forget— "

"I don't want to forget."

His softened tone and words nearly buckle my knees. He moves one hand from my arm to my hand. I inhale, finally understanding how serious he is.

His thumb begins to move slowly over my skin, sending my senses into dangerous territory. "Are you going to make me grovel?"

I look down at our hands – a mistake – as his thumb continues to move sensuously along the back of my hand. "What's your motivation here, Ben?" I manage.

His gaze zeroing in, he takes a step closer. "Maybe," he says, his voice low and gravelly, "Maybe I'm finally giving into the attraction I've felt for you since the first day we met."

♦ ♦ ♦

It is three in the morning when I trek up the narrow attic stairs, flashlight in hand.

My mind has been racing ever since Ben's declaration, replaying his words over and over again.

And my response.

"You're going to have to convince me," I'd said.

"I'm looking forward to it," he'd answered. His grin had softened me enough to agree to go out with him.

I'd been spinning ever since.

With the impossibility of finding sleep, I'd left Brutus snoozing on my bed, deciding to at least be productive.

The attic door creaks open with a good shove. I've been inside years ago, know there are old lamps and a few over-stuffed chairs and tables inside. As I shine the light into the dusty interior, I can also see an old mannequin with a wool scarf around her neck, two tall stacks of shoe boxes and a few packing boxes scattered around. The side walls are only about four-feet high, the ceiling arched in the middle to about six-feet. Everything is dated, from the fifties era paisley curtains sitting on a table-top to the twenties Singer sewing machine in a beautiful but scarred wood cabinet. I wonder what that cabinet would look like restored.

I move to a sixties-era floor lamp and flip the switch, seeing dust particles dancing in the beam.

Then, as my eyes adjust, I scan the room for the cedar chest Granddad said was up here. I soon spy it under the only window in the room and weave through a wooden rocker, plant stand and brocade loveseat until I'm standing in front of it.

A crazy sort of reverence falls over me; I can almost feel that I am about to discover some vital information, some long lost information about our family. Something I was meant to find.

With excitement, I kneel down and open the lid. The chest is filled with loose papers and photographs, photo albums and stacks of unseen items below. I lift the first item on the top of one stack; it is my dad's school report card from 1967. So maybe there will be some not-so-spectacular finds as well; this is going to be a longer night than I had hoped.

CHAPTER 26

It is extraordinary how God restores the soul, how time lessens despair.

I look upon the valley spread out below me and breathe easy, the sight grand to my eyes and my spirit.

Our home sits above it, a mountain range behind. Our valley is green and vast and ripe. We have rain and the soil absorbs it; we plant crops and watch them sprout.

We left Toquerville behind and moved to Beaver City in October of 1867, delayed a few months while we waited for Thomas to be born. He my seventh child, sixth son.

Today his wobbly legs carry him towards the apple orchard where his father and older siblings water the trees.

As I watch from the porch, enjoying a cup of strong, sweet tea with my friend Margaret, I am content.

Miriam married Thomas Wilkerson early last year. She lives nearby and gave birth to Wallace in February. And Emeline is also here now, with her new husband Neri. She gave birth to Luella, our first grandchild, April of last year.

Our household is still full. Will Jr., eighteen, is still with us, as are my own six sons and their half-siblings, Mary Ann and Elias.

The house William and the older boys worked hard to build us is finer than anything I could have asked for. It has a grand fireplace and the most wonderful porch that gives me the view of my valley and our orchard.

What a grand day it was when we sold the wagons. I have vowed never to sleep in one again, but I thank John Sarnge for his forethought in purchasing them all those years ago.

Thankfully, I have my husband to myself now. Josephine was disgruntled from the beginning, and who could blame her? She struck out on her own not long after we arrived here, leaving Olive with her sister Angeline. William is content to leave Olive with her aunt but he provides for her needs and we see her on occasion.

William's union with Josephine nearly broke me.

Most of us have come to realize that plural marriage is an atrocious ideal, one the federal government is attempting to outlaw. For Brigham Young to promote it still, is a disgrace. I would give him a piece of mind should I ever meet him.

William now turns his nose when the elders teach on the subject. Too many women and children have suffered because of it.

Margaret Farworth is one such woman and I am glad I can offer her a respite on this warm afternoon. Her two-year old daughter, Mary Elizabeth, is in her lap and she is swollen with her sixth child at the young age of twenty-nine. I took an instant liking to her when I met her at the mercantile not long after we moved here.

And sorrow for her.

Her weariness shows in her gaunt cheeks.

Her husband has three other wives. He lives with his first wife and Margaret lives alone – unless he chooses to visit – outside town nearly seven miles. The cabin Philo built for her is lacking in everything that would call it a home.

"When will the trees begin to bear fruit?" Margaret asks as Thomas reaches William and he is scooped up into his arms.

I refill Margaret's tea cup with fresh black tea Rachel regularly sends me from home, relishing my defiance in this simple but strong act against our elders. Margaret seems to be enjoying hers as much as I am.

"We are hoping for next season," I answer Margaret. "I'll bring you a pie from our first harvest."

"Apple pie. What a treat that will be."

"Then I'll make you two."

"We'll eat every crumb."

Margaret rouses herself a few minutes later, saying she must get home before dark. She has left her older children alone and frets for them.

I promise a visit before she births her babe and watch her depart in the buckboard before turning my attention back to the orchard and my own brood.

Tomorrow William and the older boys will ride up the canyon about ten miles to our saw mill. Will Jr., George, Joseph, James and Ben will go with him, while Elias, Samuel and Thomas stay with me. William and the boys will stay for a week or more, sawing, stripping and carting down the wood for houses and furniture. William has become a masterful furniture maker. We have a barn for all his projects.

The hardship of Toquerville behind us, I have still vowed to always have food a-plenty for us all. I bake and preserve more than we'll ever need, just to be safe.

Life here is as it should be. I have finally forgiven my husband for his transgression. How could I not if I'm ever to get him to see how Christ forgives us? He is asking me questions about this again. Curious to understand the free gift of grace we receive when we believe in God's Son. This is the greatest contrast to what we are taught in our Mormon church. They teach we can only gain access to Heaven through our works. The scriptures tell us differently.

Beyond wanting William to understand this, I lack nothing now that we are in Beaver.

Save for my sweet daughter Rachel.

The sadness of leaving her behind still plagues me.

My solace is in knowing I will be with her when I depart this life. Another burdensome teaching of our church is that we must be 'sealed' to anyone we wish to be with in heaven. We must journey to the Salt Lake temple and fill out paperwork to do so.

I fretted about this after Rachel's death. But, once again, the Bible counseled me differently. God's yoke is light. He does not require such absurdity.

I check to see that Thomas is still with William and his siblings, say a short prayer for Margaret, then head inside to prepare supper, knowing I am blessed.

CHAPTER 27

Present Day

"This is amazing," Emory says from her position on the attic wood floor.

"Isn't it?" I agree. I'm sitting beside her, rummaging through another box Granddad has just brought up from his bedroom closet while Em sifts through the items I'd found in the cedar chest. There are lace handkerchiefs, bronze statuettes and a stack of yellowed letters. Em lifts one from the pile and opens it. "This one is dated December 10, 1870. The address is 7 Nelson St in Southampton, England. *My dear sister Matilda,*" she reads. "*I received your letter with joy and have sent it off to James to see. He is still in London and doing quite well having bought a lot of property over the past few years. I hear from him once a month for he allows me a pound each time for father's keep. As to Sister Julia, she is still in London as well. I never hear from her for I have nothing to do with her. I am sorry to say she has taken to drink very hard. We have never heard anything about the boys in Australia.*

Father is still alive and well but, of course, feeble. He will be seventy-nine in February. As to Caroline, she has taken position with the P&O Freight Company as a ship steward. My own husband assisted her in acquiring the post. Thomas has been gone for four years now but will be home in March. Caroline has been gone for two years now, traveling to India and back. I have got all the children with me. I do not believe Caroline ever fully recovered from the deaths of her husband and three children. Her position has benefited her and provided for her remaining two babes. It is a rather bleak life I lead without any save Papa and the children as companions.

I should like very much to have your likenesses and I hope that you will forward them if you possibly can. Please do not keep me so long without a reply as last time.

I hope this will find you all in good health, as I am happy to say, it leaves us at present. We all send our kind love and wish you a Merry Christmas and Happy New Year.

I must conclude now and remain your affectionate sister, Rachel.

Emory looks at me. "This is fascinating." She opens another. "November 24, 1872. *Dear Matilda, I received your kind and very welcome letter quite safe. I was very much pleased to hear from you once more and that your family are all well and doing so well. My dear sister, I am happy to say this leaves me and my family quite well at present, thank God.*

You wish to know where the boys are but that is still out of my power to tell you. But I can tell you, dear sister, that poor James died the 7th of last January, and that is the last of our brothers that I know anything about. I miss him very much. For the last five years he has allowed me compensation for father's keep, but since his death I have had the burden myself. I must tell you that poor father is very feeble now, as he will be eighty-two soon, if he is spared.

Caroline has gone to India once more, signing on for three years. She is on the ship Behived and transports through the Suez Canal. I still have her children and my own as my husband is on the ship Simlia.

Dear sister, I believe we still have got three brothers alive but we never hear anything of them. Jonathan's son, Jon, and daughter, Mary, are both married and each have two children. Jon went to work in Bombay for three years and he gets twenty pounds per month. We heard through him that Jonathan is still alive with Benjamin and Joseph in Australia but we don't know where.

Alas, James left his wife well provided for with all his properties. But it was all left to her as long as she lives. So, what will become of it all after her death I cannot tell you, but she has nothing for father. She sent a letter to me when the breath of James was going from him and I took the first train. I went up on Sunday morning but when I got there he was already gone. I was there a fort-night till after the funeral. So, my dear sister, when all was done and the will read, all was left to her till her death. I have decided to go to London to see her and know what is in her will.

Dear sister, do not fail in replying soon and I will continue to send all the news as I have it. Enclosed is a portrait of James' grave, which I hope you will get quite safe.

We all send our kindest love to you and your husband and your family and please accept the same from your affectionate sister, Rachel."

Emory leans back and sighs. "Australia, India. Don't you just love how they write?"

"Here's another one from Rachel dated three years later. August 29, 1875. The address is different. 46 Hack Road, Victoria Docks, London. *Dear Sister Matilda,*" I read aloud. "*No doubt you think me very unkind for not answering your last letter. You must forgive me as I have been ever so busy since relocating us all to London. The P&O ships are all sailing from here now so, my dear sister, I took over the running of a lodging house and I am doing very well. Should it be twice as large I could always have it full. I found this necessary since James' death and my Thomas and Caroline's prolonged absence. We see them on occasion when they return for a brief time and then put to sea again. To that end, I am happy to say father continues to do quite well here, thank God, (if spared he will see his 85th year in February), and all our children. I must also tell you that Caroline took leave to journey to Australia last November for news of our brothers. She made all the inquiries she could but did not see any of them. But about two months after, we received a letter from our dear brother Benjamin and do so now every few months. He sends regards, is ever so well and married. I must tell you, dear sister that he sent me four pounds for father's keep.*

Benjamin is a guard on the mail train running from Melbourne to Geelong, and he tells us Jonathan is keeping a hotel in the middle of the forest and Joseph is still there as well. So, my dear sister, I sent him out your address. I trust you have had a letter from him before now. If not, I have enclosed his address. I trust you will write him as I am sure he will be well pleased to hear from you.

Oh, how I should like for us all to meet again once more.

Jonathan's son Jon went out to Australia and saw his father and the woman that he lives with. But she soon cleared out when she learned who he was. In my last letter from Ben, he told me that Jonathan and this woman had two children. Young Jon found Ben first and he and Jon went to visit Jonathan. When they opened the door, he had no idea that it was his own son, and when they went in young Jon talked to his father for about two hours, in good sound talk. But he could not or would not answer Jon's questions that he asked of him. On my last letter from Ben, he tells me that Jonathan then sold all and left and now no one knows where he went off to. I hope he found that young Jon is a credit to him for he is.

And now dear sister, I have a new letter from Ben's wife telling me he is doing poorly. He is not expected to live from the first of June. She is going to write by the next mail to let me know how he is and I long to receive it.

I conclude now, busy with duties, sending our kindest love to you and your husband and your family. Please accept the same from your affectionate sister, Rachel."

"Caroline must have been very adventurous, don't you think?" Em says. "To be able to go to Australia on her own like that? I'd love to retrace her steps one day. Go to Bombay and the outback."

"Rachel appears to have been the homebody."

"Yeah. She took care of the kids and her dad and then a boarding house. Very industrious. And the sisters were so concerned about their brothers."

"Here's one more letter from her. May 8, 1880. Five years have passed. She's writing to both Matilda and William in this one. *My Dear Sister and Brother, I am pleased to say that I received your kind and welcome letters and portraits quite safe. I was very pleased to hear from you, and to hear that all are quite well, but my dear sister when your letter and likenesses came, I was in a very great deal of trouble. My husband was lying quite sick and we did not expect him to live, but thank God, he is spared. He has gotten quite well again, even able to return to work. But my dear sister, I am very sorry to tell you that our dear sister Caroline is dead."*

"What?" Emory shouts in disbelief. "Not Caroline."

"She has been dead for two years the 11th of this month. She died on her way from Bombay to England three days after sailing from Bombay, and was buried at sea," I continue. *"So, the poor dear never had any one of her family near her to do anything for her. When I heard my heart near broke. Furthermore, her passing left her two children quite destitute. They continued to live with me."*

"That's tragic," Em interrupts again.

"And now I am very pleased to say that her daughter Susan got married at our house about four months after her mother's death. She was with child soon thereafter. That was last Christmas, twelve months, and now I am pleased to tell you she has got a very fine lass. Her brother George went away today to New Yourk (I am not sure of this spelling) on a P&O ship and I am so glad he is able to work. He is seventeen years old and I have had him since he was three and his sister was five.

Now my dear sister, I must tell you that father is still alive and quite well. Ninety he will be next February. He gets about as well as ever, only very feeble. And my dear sister, I must tell you a bit about my own family. In the first place I am pleased to tell you that they are all quite well. My second son Miles has been out to Australia to see Benjamin but he only got to see his wife for Benjamin was out. His wife was a very nice woman and made much of him. My oldest son has just come down from Australia to Bombay so I am in hopes he has seen Ben but I shant know for another fortnight. I am also pleased to say I expect my husband home next week.

Now my dear sister I must also tell you that my daughter – your namesake – was married the 15th of December and is getting on very nicely. She has got a splendid home so I have had quite a bit to do to help her with her things, getting them ready and putting her home to rights. Her husband's family keep the old Netly Abbey. There are only two sons. My Tilly is married to one and he is the Chief Steward on one of the P&O Company ships. His brother is a head waiter on another.

My dear sister, I went over to James's wife yesterday to see her and she sends her kindest love to you. So, my dear sister, I think I have told you all about the family at present. I am happy to say that all that is left is quite well. Trusting this will find you and all your family quite well. I was very pleased with the portraits, and I hope you will favor me with the others as convenient.

So, with kindest love from all to all, I remain your ever-loving sister, Rachel

P.S. You shall have a piece of Tilly's cake next letter, but she is staying down with her husband's friends and won't be home till the end of the month. So now I must say goodbye and God bless you all. Trusting to hear from you soon. R"

"Matilda's namesake. Like you. Poor Caroline."

"I wonder how Rachel sent a piece of cake clear across the sea. Was it edible?"

"I don't think I would have tried it even if it were. Okay, there's one more letter here." Emory opens it. "And look, it's from Benjamin. November 13, 1882, Shaftesbury Villa, Addington Road Bow, London, England. *My Dear Sister, No doubt you will be surprised to receive this letter from me. I have arrived in England from Victoria, Australia. Me and my wife are at Rachel's today. I have come home for my health, which, please God, will improve. I saw your last letter and now I write a few lines to let you know I am still alive. I was glad to hear all was well with you. We would be very glad to see you but to venture west is beyond my time and purse.*

I am here – come home – for a twelve month leave. I have been 27 years on the government railways at Melbourne. We went to Southampton to see our nephew Jon who is quite well and we will go on Wednesday next to see our sister Julia. I should very much like to see you and your family, not forgetting your husband.

My coming home is like the dead coming to life again, after over 30 years. Our dear father is still alive and well. He is 92 years now. Rachel has had a great handful with him. He goes out by himself and tumbles down and hurts himself.

We start for Australia next April. Please write before so.

With all kind love to you all, from your affectionate brother,

Benjamin Francis Wyeman."

"Wow. Matilda's journals made reference to her brothers going missing. No one in England knew if they made it to Australia."

"Can you imagine never hearing from someone you love again?" Emory is sitting with her legs crossed, her tall, lanky body protruding at all angles. "Like having a sea captain for a husband and watching him sail away, knowing he might never return? Or a husband in the service? At war? Before texting? Before Skype?"

"We can't go without our cellphones for a second."

"It would be nice to try. But it's also nice that we don't have to." Em untangles herself and stands. She carefully re-inserts the last letter into the envelop it was in. "I feel like I know these people so much now."

"And look at this." I brush dust from the jacket of a small leather-bound book and read "Journal of William Hatcher," out loud.

"Grandma Matilda's husband? Our forth-great grandfather?"

"Yes," I whisper almost reverently. Goosebumps rise on my skin.

"Come on. Let's go make ourselves a cup of tea. I want to read this."

I rise from the floor, eager to discover what is inside. And sharing a cup of tea with my cousin is the perfect way to do it.

We tuck the letters back into the trunk along with the other items that were inside. I carry the journal as we head toward the attic door. We pass the sewing machine cabinet as we go and I say, "Hey Em, have you ever restored a piece of furniture?"

CHAPTER 28

August 1883
Beaver, Utah

"Looks like last night's rain will help plenty." Will fisted a clump of dirt and let it filter through his fingers. Slowly, his sixty-year-old body protesting, he rose from his hunched position. "The moisture's good. If we get some sunshine now, we'll have another decent harvest."

Thomas, his youngest child at sixteen and the only boy still living at home with him and Tilly, plucked an apple from one branch and took a bite. "Juicy and sweet."

Will nodded, pleased. He gazed out at the apple grove stretching acre after acre down the hillside. As much as he didn't cotton to superstition, he wasn't opposed to believing in signs either; a prosperous harvest was a good sign – assurance he was making the right decisions. Assurance there were blessings in the here and now, not just eternity in heaven.

It soothed him to know the Almighty showed mercy despite his past mistakes.

Those he'd made aplenty.

He'd begun making amends for them years ago. He'd started by leaving Toquerville.

But it hadn't been easy coming to the conclusion that he'd been taught wrong and lived wrong most of his life.

That hadn't come until February 10, 1878.

After finally realizing the Bible was the true source to learn about God. Rejecting the Book of Mormon, done with years of clashing with church leaders, making excuses for them, battling them and his own doubts and suspicions.

On that day, he'd ceased to be a Latter-Day Saint. He'd made official on paper what he'd already known in his heart.

First, he'd scrawled his intentions in the church rolls. Then he'd signed excommunication papers for good measure. Next, he'd recorded the date in his journal. He wanted all his offspring, current and future, to see and know. Make sure they had no doubt that he was leaving the Mormon church.

He knew his decision would have consequences. Townsfolk would shun him, cease to do business with him. His sons and brother, Shepard, would try to change his mind.

But there came a point when a man couldn't deny truth any longer.

Will's had come after many years of questions and two final incidences.

The first had been a rainy morning the day after Elder Morton came to call in the spring of '72. Sam had headed to the barn as usual to feed their four horses, only to discover Dollop was missing.

It had taken Will a week of following tracks and talking to folks to find the horse in Morton's barn. Then Morton lied, said he'd bought the horse, didn't know it was Will's. When Will brought accusation against him before the elder board, it was Will who received the backlash, been told to retract his accusations.

He'd stewed for months afterward, unappeased by everyone's attempts to get him to give Morton the benefit of the doubt.

Then, in the summer of '78 his water allotment at the saw mill began to dwindle. He, Will Jr. and George headed upstream to find out why.

He could still feel the heat rising in his face when, after searching for two days, they discovered the dam diverting Will's water to Elder Morton's corn fields.

The pleasure of taking the man by the scruff of his collar and dunking him in the river he'd dammed up still satisfied him.

And the confirmation he needed.

He'd worked tirelessly over the years to do the church's bidding. Had the cost been for the glory of the Almighty, he'd have pressed on willingly. But in the end, he realized his backbreaking labor had profited the leaders alone.

They alone grew wealthy and powerful.

Toquerville had been his line in the sand.

He wasn't a quitting man but he'd moved the family to Beaver, where the possibilities for a fresh start were plentiful.

There his hardships eased. He prospered: he, Tilly and his children. He won her forgiveness and knew he needed to be forgiven by God.

Any religion that condoned Morton's actions, taking from men and women who had little, justifying raids on wagon trains heading west, and placed burdens on worshippers who could not possibly do all that was required, was just that – religion.

Will now had real faith.

And Tilly supported his decision to walk away.

She was a diamond, his Tilly. She'd voiced her own misgivings about the church many times. She was especially sour on plural marriage and Will couldn't blame her.

He'd added a few too many wives over the years. Planted his seed in seven women. He loved all his offspring, but he'd concluded after all, that one wife too many didn't make for a harmonious household.

Brigham Young could have his fifty and claim he needed them all to build his celestial kingdom, but for Will it was just Tilly now.

Will liked it that way.

Still, he'd worried she would leave him if he left the church. They were taught a woman needed to be married to a Mormon man in order to get to heaven. He knew she struggled with whether she believed that or not.

But when she'd found out about Morton's theft, she'd picked up her Bible and read to him about how each one will give an account for himself.

"I do not need to be married and sealed to a man in order to reach heaven myself," she'd added.

Today he was content with his wife, his land, his woodwork and his orchard.

It had been five years since he'd denounced Mormonism but he still sold a fair amount of furniture, applesauce and cider to those who were still members – some his own children. But on Sunday nights, they would still come for supper. And some were beginning to listen to what he said about the Bible.

He and Tilly would sit on the wrap-around porch he'd built for her, in the rocking chairs he'd made for them both, and marvel at the number of them. Will Jr. and his wife Sarah had four girls: Sarah, Matilda, Lydia and Mary. Emeline and her second husband Neri also had four girls: Luella, Emma, Hanna and Amy. Then there was George and Mahaley and their little girl, Metta Matilda, and Joe and Martha with their children, Thaddeus and Martha. James and his wife Sarah had given Will a namesake last year but the boy had died. And Miriam and Thomas had moved to Nevada with their kids Wallace, Ruth, Lizzy, Thom and Milo.

There'd be a whole lot more before all was said and done, Will had no doubt. And it pleased him that Will Jr. had named one of his girls after his stepmother. It tickled Tilly to no end.

No doubt about it but that she was his little spitfire Englishwoman. They'd had their trials, faced more hardship together than any two folks should have to.

And come out on this side of love.

That was a testament to his Tilly.

His union with Josephine was *her* line in the sand. Will had never crossed it again.

Now his fingertips are soiled from the dirt he'd held in his hand as he looks toward the house to see Tilly standing on her porch.

Yes, he'd made mistakes, but he was the man he was today because of them. And his hope was that his children and their children and theirs would learn from those mistakes and not repeat them. After all, he was responsible for a multitude of offspring. His descendants.

He prayed in Christ's name that they would see the signs.

CHAPTER 29

With the Rangers game blaring in the background, Granddad and Brutus are napping; Granddad in his recliner, Brutus at his feet. I quietly enter the kitchen and pull out from the refrigerator the casserole I've prepared for Granddad's supper. I place it in the oven, set the temperature and head to my room.

Ben will be here soon. I've tried to keep my mind occupied all day on thoughts other than that. My date with him. I worked on two sets of vows. One for a guy in Seattle who wants a lot of mother-nature and green earth verbiage, another for an eighty-five-year-old who is at long last marrying his childhood sweetheart. It's been creative and fun to put them together.

I've read more of William Hatcher's journal, concluding he is the kind of no-nonsense guy I would have admired. I've also researched how to restore old furniture, anything to keep me occupied and calm. Otherwise, I'd have been a nervous wreck.

When I hear Ben's truck pull up, I take a deep breath, take one last look in the mirror and leave my room. My heart is pumping something fierce when I open the front door and he enters.

"Sweet," he announces, his gaze roaming my appearance. I'm wearing a flowery blue sun-dress, mid-drift peach sweater and white pumps. Mousse and hairspray have given lift to my hair, which I've framed around my face and neck.

"You'd better say that," Granddad says from his chair.

His comment soothes my anxiety.

"I'll have her home before curfew, Carl." Ben takes my hand as I grab my handbag off the foyer table.

"Supper's in the oven. It'll beep in twenty minutes."

"Have a good time."

"Thanks, Granddad."

Ben leads the way to his truck. I appreciate the gesture when he opens the passenger side door and helps me into the seat. I can hear Steph and Linda scolding me for accepting such a chauvinistic gesture and my silent message back to them is *too bad, girls. I like it!*

Small talk gets us through dinner and the play is a funny farce at a charming 1920's style theater house.

It's after the play, after meeting Mandy and telling her how good her acting was and how much we enjoyed the show, that I begin to relax. Ben leads me to the Georgetown town square. We stroll along the shops; we enter the Georgetown Winery and purchase two glasses of chardonnay. Served in plastic glasses, we take them back out to the square and continue our walk past boutiques and pubs as live jazz music plays near the courthouse.

The ambience on the warm, fall night is superb.

"How'm I doing?" Ben asks as we stop and take a seat on a park bench. "At convincing you?"

I smile cautiously. "I have to admit this has been an impressive evening."

"But?"

"No buts."

"Let's see if I can make it more impressive." His tone is seductive, his gaze smoldering as he leans in and kisses me.

My breath catches as a current of sheer sensuous electricity flows through my veins and I feel for the first time a tingle all the way to the tips of my toes.

When the kiss ends, he sits back in the bench. "Wow. I don't know if you're impressed, but I sure am."

I laugh nervously. There is no way I am telling him just how much.

♦ ♦ ♦

Ben catches me off-guard the next morning when I'm feeding the chickens. When he walks up behind me and kisses my neck, I spin to face him, heat staining my cheeks.

"I was hoping we could pick up where we left off last night," he grins.

"Don't you have a ranch to run? Business to discuss with Granddad?" I return his smile as my heart flips over in my chest.

"I guess you still need some convincing." He tips his hat and walks back towards the barn. "Carl and I are going to look at a couple bulls. Be back later."

My satisfied sigh reverberates through the morning air. Ben – my nemesis. All this time he'd 'liked' me. Could I believe him? Trust his affection was nothing more than a passing attraction?

I needed to be cautious.

But it was getting more difficult to hold back.

♦ ♦ ♦

That next afternoon Ben asks me if I'll accompany him to the new water park with the Eagles baseball team in a few days.

"You must need another chaperone," I smile.

"You're right," he admits, pulling me close to him. "We might need one as well if things keep up like this."

"Then you'd better leave."

"I guess I'd better."

♦ ♦ ♦

Saturday night we have a date with bar-b-que and a local country-western band.

"Wear boots."

"I don't own any."

"Time to buy a pair."

"I don't two-step."

His grin leaves me breathless. "You will soon."

♦ ♦ ♦

Emory and I are knee deep in sandpaper and lacquer, pretending we are confidently restoring Gram's old sewing machine cabinet, when I look up to see Granddad staring at us from the porch.

"Hey there, getting close to supper time already? I'll finish up here."

"Naw, nowhere close," he says. "I was just watching my two beautiful granddaughters' is all. Nothing wrong with that is there?"

I smile. "Nothing at all."

Em blows hair from her face. "Watching us ruin this piece of furniture, more like it."

"Gram would be pleased as punch to see you two like this," Granddad replies. "Whether that ol' piece of wood turns out nice or not." I see a sparkle in his eyes and hear him sniff. Em and I share a glance. I'm sorry it took Gram's death to bring us closer together.

"Well, I'm getting hungry." I toss my gloves in a bucket we have filled with supplies. "And where are those two dogs of ours, anyway? Getting into something they shouldn't, is my guess." I crest the porch and take Granddad's arm. "Come on, Em. Let's go find the boys and start supper."

Later that night Granddad is in bed and the two pups doze at our feet. Emory and I sit back with a glass of wine and Google Lexington, Missouri and the *Saluda* disaster monument.

"Look at this bell tower they erected as a memorial." Em points to the photo of the tower. "I can't believe the ship's captain was so negligent that he let the boilers dry up."

"Here's the list of victims, their names and ages." I enlarge the screen so we can read the names easier.

"John Sarnge, 38, and Joseph Sarnge. He was only eight years old."

"And Matilda was engaged to John. How tragic."

Emory places her hand on my shoulder. "Shelley, we need to go there. Don't you think? I want to go to Lexington and see the Missouri River and envision Matilda on it."

"And see the memorial," I add. "Yes, Em. Let's do it. And soon. Can you take off work for a few days?"

"I think I've decided to give my two-week notice anyways. I'm so tired of waitressing. I need to move on."

"Really? Anything special you want to do? I have an idea I've been bouncing around. I was going to talk to you about it."

"You've intrigued me. Let's talk about it as we drive up 35 to Missouri."

♦ ♦ ♦

Ben joins us in the yard two weeks later to see us off. Brutus and Samson are romping at our feet, Emory giving Gail Hernandez last minute instructions on Samson's feed and care.

"Gail agreed to care for the dogs while we're gone so Granddad won't feel overwhelmed."

"And you'll be back on Wednesday?"

"We think so."

He has his Stetson on, his riding jeans; he and Granddad are picking up the bull they purchased later this morning.

"I'm going to miss you. You sure you have to do this?"

I chuckle. "I'm just going to Missouri."

"Too far."

"It'll be good for me and Em to spend time together."

"That bonding thing."

"That bonding thing."

"But I'm going to miss you," he says again. I was going to miss him too – way too much – but I wasn't telling him so, showing him so. I still wasn't comfortable enough, sure enough about where our relationship was heading. I was keeping my armor in place – my protection against rejection – just in case.

Ben was still determined to break down my defenses.

As the morning sun pours over the countryside, illuminating green grass and trees and blue sky, he puts his hands on my waist and draws me close.

"Don't you care."

"I care." I put my hands on his arms. I love the feel of his arms; firm, solid, strong. "But you're a big boy. Deal with it. And take care of Granddad?"

"Yep. Are you going to call me? Check in?"

"Do you want me to?" I can hear my own pathetic lack of self-esteem.

"You really have to ask?" He kisses my forehead. "Let me put it this way; if you don't call at least once a day I'll be calling you. Twice would be better."

"Okay." I lift my head. Ben's lips press to my own and I inhale pleasurably. "Okay then," I say when the kiss ends, needing space to cool down. "I'll call. Now let us get out of here."

"I guess if I can't persuade you to stay." He lifts my suitcase and heads for my car. "You're staying in Mulvane, Kansas tonight?"

"Yes. I have a reservation at the Hampton Inn there."

"Call when you get there?"

"I will." I love that he wants me to, but again, I don't tell him so.

Granddad and the dogs join us at my car and we say good-bye. And as Em and I drive away I glance back at the two men in my life and feel such intense joy.

And then I'm suddenly terrified – of losing them.

"What's wrong," Emory asks. "You're pale and shaking.

"I must have eaten something," I bluff. "I'm fine. Just excited."

189

She takes my word and turns on Pandora, and the rest of the day is spent driving up Interstate 35 toward our first stop in Mulvane, Kansas.

The weather is fair, traffic light after we get through the Ft. Worth road construction, and my dour mood lifts. Soon we are in girly mode – giggles and story-telling – sharing about the frogs we've dated and the good ones who got away and the craziness of social media and working jobs we dislike.

Starbucks boosts us the next brisk morning. With our favorite artists blasting over the car speakers, mine Adele, her's Taylor Swift, Em and I arrive in Lexington the following afternoon.

"Do you want to check into the hotel or go straight to the riverfront?" I ask my cousin as Adele's *Set Fire to the Rain* plays in the background. Just then we begin to cross the Blanchette Bridge on Interstate 70 and we try to see the mass of water below it over the cement barriers blocking the view.

"Let's head to the water first," Emory replies. "Look how wide the river is. Take this exit."

I steer our way off the highway, down the embankment and a few side streets until we are near the water's edge. Then we are parking and walking in a brisk cool breeze through knee high grass until we stand near the bank.

We are silent for a while as we take in the breath of the Missouri. It is not as pretty as imposing, and I try to envision floating upon it in a rickety old steamboat on a cold, late winter day. The ice floes were heavy that long-ago fateful day when our fourth great-grandmother and the Sarnge family traveled upstream.

Was she afraid even as she prepared for her wedding?

Church, God and faith had taken on new meaning before I began reading her and Grandfather William's journals. But even more after learning all they went through. Emory and I had great discussion about

Mormonism and Christianity, about devotion and sacrifice and corruption and betrayal on our drive this morning.

I'd been attending church with Granddad regularly since returning to Texas, at first for him, then out of curiosity. Now – maybe at last – I attend because I want to. I've begun to take seriously this whole relationship with God.

As I stand by the riverside, breeze against my skin, the water current swiftly passing, I can feel my grandparents talking to me through the pages of their journals. They are both telling me they are glad I've discovered them, glad I'm interested enough to get to know them.

They have much to say; that's evident in the journals they left for us. There is significant and important information to be gained by knowing them.

And they are both telling me it is time for the rest of the family to remember them again, too.

♦ ♦

A week after returning from Lexington I am hastily showering after rounding up Brutus from chasing the chickens when I stop for a moment and realize I am happy with the direction of my life.

It is a warm Autumn afternoon. I've already completed my 'regular' chores, written two sets of vows and kissed Ben goodbye. This after he'd brought Granddad and I crawfish poor-boys for lunch. In half-an-hour, I am hosting three mothers who have children with Down's Syndrome. Carmen said these women are interested in starting a therapy program for their children and they come with the skills to put it all together. I am excited to offer them the resources and let them take the program from there.

Meanwhile, Emory and I had discussed her work situation on our trip to Missouri. I'd told her I was considering opening an English tea house in honor of Gram and Matilda and all the other women in our family.

"That is a brilliant idea!" she'd exclaimed. "Want a partner?"

We now have an appointment with a local broker to view available properties. We plan to decorate with Gram's old antiques, like the sewing machine, and display her tea sets for all to see – with Granddad's blessing. I'm hoping I'll be able to stop writing wedding vows once we open and start seeing a profit.

At six, Granddad and I are headed to the high school football team's fall fundraiser. Ben is meeting us at the carwash and barbeque. I can already hear the banter that will take place between Ben and the kids and Granddad will give some young man advice about keeping his composure while on the playing field. The food will be delicious, the camaraderie fulfilling – a far cry from the Denver night scene.

I hurry out of the shower, dress and mousse my hair – and since I haven't heard Granddad come in from the barn yet, instead of heading to the kitchen to pull out the cracker and cheese platter I'd put together for my visiting mothers, I head out front.

Brutus is making another ruckus, his bark loud and constant.

"Brutus, shush," I shout. "Come here, boy."

My command fails to calm him. His bark is coming from the side of the house but I still can't see him so my sandals sinking into the soft thick grass, I round the corner – and stop cold. "Granddad!" I begin to run. "Granddad!" He is face down on the ground, unmoving, Brutus barking near his side. "Oh Granddad," I sob as I bend over his body.

CHAPTER 30

The medical examiner tells us there was nothing anyone could have done. Granddad had passed before I found him. I'd burrowed myself into Ben's chest, his arms around me more needed than ever before, as we cried together.

I keep wondering how long Brutus stood over his prone frame, calling for help for his master. That's where I stumble. Had I heard the dog earlier, would it have made a difference. I'd called 9-1-1 as soon as I'd found him.

I counter that by telling myself he was old, that we all die – once. Granddad's death was inevitable.

But this only partially comforts me.

I try to cling to my new faith. It tells me God is in control; God knew the day and time Granddad would breathe his last. This faith is center and forward right now. I either believe in God – really believe – or I don't. Unfortunately, we all have to make this choice.

Fortunately, God allows us to. That's where free will comes in.

And so, I choose, to believe.

Tilly believed in God. William did. Granddad and Gram as well. They are the wisest people I have ever known.

For his efforts and his loyalty Brutus stands beside me at Granddad's memorial service – a tearful affair of tribute and love and song and I am glad I can say Granddad is with Gram in heaven for all eternity, that now his body rests beside hers under the shady oak behind their house.

But I already miss him. I miss cooking for him and watching baseball with him. I miss hearing him in the hallway at five heading for coffee and his horses.

Ben misses him as well; misses the chess games, riding fence with him, whining about government interference with him.

Granddad had been a pretty perfect companion.

But it's apparent he missed Gram more than he'd ever let on.

After his service, friends and family return back to homes and jobs and schools and life, and those of us who were closest to him begin to adjust.

I sit with Ben one evening on the porch as an autumn breeze whips leaves from the trees and chills my hands, and as Ben wraps me in his arms, I realize how easy it would be for me to drop my barriers and just let him love me.

I resist for fear of smothering him with my need, reminding myself that just because he's helped me through the toughest trial of my life doesn't mean he's signed up to do so for the rest of his life.

I also realize he's needed me as much as I've needed him. I hope I've helped him just as much, but need isn't want.

I can't confuse the two.

"How did you think today went?" Ben asks, rocking us in the swing.

We had both been invited to the reading of Granddad's will. Nell and Emory had met us at the attorney's office, my father via a conference call.

"I'm glad his estate is in good financial shape. I know you had a lot to do with that. And I'm glad he deeded the house and land to my dad. I assumed he would, but since my dad doesn't want to live here, it could have been sold off. I didn't know my dad would ask me to stay on and run it."

"Nell didn't seem to mind either. And she'll receive a large sum of cash instead."

"She likes Austin. And since she's newly divorced the money will help her a lot. Although I know Granddad would have given her whatever she needed while he was alive."

"I'm glad you agreed to stay, you know."

I brush his words aside, not ready to deal with their possible meaning. "I'm in no hurry to leave. I'm too numb. I feel like his death has punched me hard in the gut. And made me realize how short this life can be."

"I found that out when my dad and grandparents died."

I turned to face him. "That's right. I'm sorry. It must have been so hard for you. Don't you think most of us are unprepared for death? Our generation believes we can do whatever we want, act however we want, be whatever we want - without consequence. War, to us, is a sound bite on a website, mourning a half day out of our schedule. Kids are blowing up video game people all day, every day – no feelings attached."

"I know."

"But that is so wrong. Granddad's death has taught me how real death is. My grandmother Matilda also. And God."

Ben thumbs the back of my hand. "We're supposed to feel death to the core of our beings. It's the only way we can understand how God feels when we are separated from Him."

"I'm learning that. Learning that who we are and where we go after this life is what *this* life is all about. That's what Matilda knew too – and wanted her family to understand."

When Ben is silent, I add, "I'm sorry. I shouldn't be having such a deep conversation."

"Why are you sorry? We can't run away from hard discussion, bury our heads in the sand."

"Yes, but—"

"But nothing. I should be the one you're having this conversation with. Or haven't you figured that out yet?"

◆ ◆ ◆

Late in October, I watch as the first group of *UPS AND DOWNS* takes place. There are five kids in all. Ben has loaned us two of his own horses so all five kids can ride while their parents hold the reins. Lemonade and cookies follow and afterward thanks and plans for another event.

That afternoon I greet Emory, Samson in tow, and as the dogs play, she and I climb into the attic.

We are quiet as we peruse the cluttered space. Then Em picks up a candleholder and one item after another we try to decide who had owned it, when it had been discarded, what era it had belonged in and whether we can add it to the teahouse furnishings.

"Look at this," Em has opened a small wood box. Inside, wrapped in tissue, is a pair of medals.

"They're Granddad's," I say. "He showed them to me the day Ben brought the sewing machine down. One is the Soldier's Medal, given to him when he saved another soldier from committing suicide. The other is a service ribbon."

Em sniffs. "We need to put these in a shadow box and hang them up."

"That's a great idea. I'm sure there are other items of his we could us at the teahouse as well – now that he's gone."

"Like maybe an old uniform or spiffy sports coat?"

"Yeah. But you know," I add, "He really didn't enjoy tea. He was a coffee man. Maybe we should add a coffee bar, make a masculine area?"

"Have a separate door?" Emory's eyes widen. "I love this idea. We can have an inner connection but the men can have their own retreat."

"See," I smile, tears pooling in my eyes. "Granddad is still guiding us."

Em blinks as her eyes fill and she covers her mouth.

"So, listen to this story," I say to change our mood. "I researched the Adans last night. Remember David Adans is our fourth great-grandfather?"

"Kind of."

"He was the Scottish guy who brought his family to Pennsylvania."

"That's right."

"He converted to Mormonism after they immigrated. Well in 1849 he and his wife Mary – our grandmother, left Pennsylvania for Salt Lake and guess what? She died on a steamship on the Missouri."

"What? Really?"

"From Cholera. Two of her young daughters died with her. The crew buried their bodies on the riverbank somewhere near St. Louis."

"That's insane. Those steamships were dangerous. So not only was Matilda on one, but Mary too?"

"One of her two living daughters, Margaret, is our third great-grandmother. Margaret was eight when she lost her mother and two sisters. Then David Adans married again – a month later - and they all continued on to Utah. He founded a town they named Adansville, near Beaver, and they lived in Beaver too, near Matilda."

"One big happy family."

"And if you can believe this, Margaret married a polygamist man when she was sixteen. His name was Philo Farworth. He already had two other wives and he married another woman after Margaret. She had seven children in the next ten years and then died at the age of thirty-six from pneumonia. He had thirty children all together with four women. Margaret's children were sent to live with friends and family throughout the Beaver area after her death. They didn't even live with their father."

"Good grief, what were these people thinking when they began the practice of polygamy?"

"I don't admire David Adans much for letting his daughter Margaret marry into that. And I can tell you what I think those men were thinking with, and it was anything but God-inspiring."

Em laughs. "They had a good 'ol time at the woman's expense, didn't they?"

"Didn't they? Margaret must not have had much help. All those babies and an absent husband and father. She was exhausted. I hope there is a harsh punishment for her husband and all men like. And I wonder if she knew Matilda. Matilda didn't get to Beaver until the late 1860's but Margaret would have been there."

"Wow. They could have been friends. We need to go to Beaver."

"I was thinking the same thing."

"When?"

"Soon."

Em then pulls several faded lace hankies from the wood box Granddad's medals had been in. "Look how fragile these are."

"Maybe we can display them as well. They're so pretty."

"Yes," she smiles. "Everyone should see them."

♦ ♦ ♦

"So, you're leaving me again, huh?" Ben is leading Leadfoot around the corral while I bathe Chester (and myself) with soapy water. "I can't seem to keep you in one spot."

"You'll probably be glad to see me go." I scrub the horse with a wet sponge. "Give you a break."

"A break?" He stops in his tracks. "You think I need a break from you?"

"Probably. Well... no, not like that. Just..." He smiles that smile and I nearly throw the sponge at him. "Stop teasing me."

"Fine. While you and Em are in Utah I think I'll go hunting." He resumes walking Leadfoot.

"Great idea."

"Nolan's been bugging me to join him. Just don't forget about me."

As if that were possible, I say to myself. "I'll try not to," I say out loud with my own teasing smile.

♦ ♦ ♦

Emory and I arrive in Beaver, Utah, a small, in-the-middle-of-nowhere town in the central part of the state, just as fall is turning the hillsides into the most stunning colors of magenta and red. The town is set at the base of a mountain range, a wide-open green valley stretching below it. Interstate 15 whizzes people by as they travel from Salt Lake to Las Vegas. The occasional driver pulls into the truck stop or coasts down the one main street to a forties-style diner call Arshels Cafe.

The town square is a contrast to the fast-paced freeway traffic – a quaint, well-tended few acres of history and preservation that tells the real story of how Beaver was settled in the mid-1800's. Matilda and William Hatcher and their children and children's children are still everywhere in the telling. There is a museum here. We find photos of the Hatcher Hotel and the proprietors William Hatcher Jr. and his wife Sarah. William Jr. was our grandfather's son by his second wife. Matilda raised William Jr. along with most of our grandfather's other children, sixteen in all, seven of them our grandmother's natural children. William Jr. had been the local sheriff at the turn-of-the century. Later he was credited with discovering an area now called Hole-In-The-Wall. He'd led several men on an expedition there.

Our trip is about discovery. Em and I both long to know all we can about the two people who began our family. Had Matilda not left England, had her fiancé John Sarnge not perished, our family would look much different. Had William not left Illinois, had his first two wives not left him, he and Matilda would have never married.

At the museum, we discover that Grandfather William's furniture pieces still grace homes in the area; others are in the Mormon Temple in Salt Lake. We also learn the home he had built for Matilda with the first wrap-around porch in the area is still standing.

Excited to see it, we make a quick drive through the town of modestly framed houses and stare at the remnants of our grandparents' old home. We are told the incline where it is set was called Hatcher's Hill and was surrounded by the apple orchard they cultivated.

"It's so small," Emory says. "By today's standards. But they raised all those kids here."

The house itself can't be more than a thousand square feet. It is lopsided, aged and in need of repair. But it's the porch – simple, not large – that I can see Matilda sitting on. In my mind, I see her looking out at the valley or apple orchard; maybe waiting for William, maybe serving Sunday supper to their large brood.

I take a deep breath of clean air and enjoy the gentle breeze that caresses my face, the sun's warmth on my skin. It's inspiring to see what Tilly saw.

"I wonder who owns the property now," I say as we head to Arshels. We order a piece of delicious homemade coconut crème pie as Em and I peruse an aged phone book and see a long list of Hatchers. On a whim, we head out and dare to knock on the door of a nice estate. An elderly woman answers and after we introduce ourselves, we discover she is a distant cousin. She offers lemonade and we share time going through some of her photos, listening to her stories. Then she points us to the Mountain View Cemetery just a block from her home.

We enter through the gates with expectation, slowly edging along the dirt road outlined by aged gravesites covered in green grass. We park at the end of one row and begin walking through them, looking at names. Among the crumbling headstones, we find several Hatchers from the late 1800's. We find Margaret Adans Farworth. She is our other grandmother who so tragically lost her life at the young age of thirty-six.

"Look, Em," I finally say as I discover William's headstone at long last. It is a tall granite piece with an engraved tribute.

"It's beautiful and large. The family really honored him."

"But where is Matilda?" I walk around William's stone. "Surely she was buried by him."

"She is." Em points to the backside of William's marker. "See?" Matilda's headstone is on the backside of William's.

I blink away tears. "They couldn't be any closer. That is so comforting." I place the flowers we have brought at the base of the headstone.

After several minutes of reflection, we move on, cataloging all six of William and Matilda's sons, many of their wives and children.

"Emory," I finally say as we head back to the car. "Rachel is missing. Matilda and William's only daughter isn't here."

"She wouldn't have been brought here from Toquerville. They didn't do that back then."

I can still hear the sorrow of Matilda's words as she wrote about Rachel's death some eighty miles south.

"We need to go to Toquerville. We need to find Rachel." Goosebumps edge up my skin.

◆ ◆ ◆

The next morning, we take the interstate south, winding our way through miles and miles of open country, marveling at how the early settlers were able to succeed in taking themselves, wagons and horses through, up, down and over, the steep, rocky and thickly foliaged terrain.

We turn off the interstate at the Toquerville exit, traveling another six miles of winding, hilly terrain; green and rich. Large portions of highway are banked by carved granite rock with many more boulders embedded in the ground all around us. Modern irrigation systems have turned this land into ranch country now, horse country. Nice big spreads with big houses and pastures.

As we reach the outskirts of town, I slow the car, take in the sight of nicely kept homes on either side of the main drag. A quaint Latter-Day Saint church stands on the left, a pioneer museum and statue of the Indian Chief in front of it.

"That must be Chief Toquer," Em says. "A monument to him."

"Start looking for the big boulder on a street corner," I reply. "That was one of the hints we found in Matilda's journal." I maneuver our car down one side road, then up and down each street as we look for signs of the dugout.

"There are so many black boulders I don't see how one will stand out."

"The dugout must be something built into the side of a hill, don't you think? But there aren't many hills here. So, we need a hill and a big black boulder."

We snake through the town once with no luck.

"Maybe it's further down the road. Or it's been excavated."

"Let's ask this woman." I pull up against the curb by a house where a woman is watering her outdoor plants. Emory is first out of the car.

I follow and hear her ask the woman if she knows where any still-existing dugouts might be.

Without hesitation, she points towards Westfields Road. "The west fields," she tells us, "Where the cotton fields were planted. That's where the pioneers built the dugouts."

"That makes sense." Bolstered, we thank her and return to the car. We drive down Toquerville Boulevard one more time. "The next street is Westfields Road," Emory points out. "And look, there's the big black boulder partially buried in the ground."

"How did we miss that?" My heart beats faster as I turn the corner and slow the car to a crawl. I look left, right, left again – and then I see it. I gasp. "Emory is that it?"

A three-foot high red-adobe fort greets our eyes. We see a partial door and steps leading downward. Weeds cluster around it, some sticking through holes in the adobe façade. There is no hill behind it but that doesn't mean there wasn't one long ago. A hundred fifty years ago – when William built the structure to house his wives and children.

I park the car and we cross the street, staring in awestruck wonder. The dugout is long and narrow. We circle it, red clay dirt crunching beneath our feet. A foot-wide window breaks up the exterior. It is covered with chicken wire; just large enough to allow some light inside. Another window is on the other side.

Loose adobe stone litters the tall grass and dirt but at the front a stone set of stairs steeply decline downward to a tall, thick wood door curved at the top.

"Do you think it's unlocked? Should we go inside? We're technically trespassing."

"We'll just take a peek," I reply, too tempted not to. The stairs are narrow, barely the length of my foot. The air grows colder as I descend them. At the base, I tug on the door. It opens on squeaky hinges and I peer inside, into the darkness. I step onto a dirt floor, see an old claw-foot bathtub in one corner. Discarded beer bottles and odds and end furniture litter the floor.

I bat away cobwebs and move inside the dark and dank interior. Chilled, I try to visualize living in such a place – with children; even giving birth here.

I try, but can't.

Emory moves in behind me. Just the two of us makes the place feel smaller.

"It's musty. And damp."

"And they lived here for four or five years." I move in a circle, wondering where they would have put their bedding, what would have been the kitchen. "They had Conestoga wagons. Maybe they used those for sleeping and supplies."

I shiver, reluctant to leave, needing to get out. As I move to the door and up the stairs the temperature rises and I inhale fresh air.

Back in the sunshine I pause in wonder. How could the dugout have survived all these years? How could people have lived here?

I walk the length of it, noting that the roof is made of the same red adobe stone. It is pitted and eroded and daylight seeps inside through open crevices.

As I walk around, I pick up bits and pieces of adobe, looking for artifacts. When I reach the back wall, I see an array of blooming wildflowers.

"Aren't those pretty," I say to Em, who is beside me. "I wonder who planted them?"

"And how long ago." Emory reaches down and plucks one yellow flower.

"You don't suppose these could be the flowers Matilda wrote about planting over Rachel's grave, do you?"

"That would mean— "

"Em, look at this." I stare at the back wall of the dugout as I see what appears to be a small cross etched into the adobe stone wall just above the flowerbed. Just above the mound. Moving closer I examine the indentation. I can barely contain my excitement, believing the cross is just that – an etched cross – the cross William etched above Rachel's grave.

I shiver as I realize we have found the place where Matilda and William buried their baby girl.

CHAPTER 31

The Austin airport is humming when Em and I land. We dodge other travelers as we head for baggage claim, still spinning from our discoveries in Utah.

"Mom just texted me," Em says as we step onto the escalator. "She's not picking us up. She said Ben is."

"Ben?" My heart begins to sing, even as I try to tamp it down. "Ben went hunting. Is she okay?"

"She's fine. She says Ben wanted to surprise you."

"But I thought he went hunting."

I see him as I exit the escalator. He's already waiting for us at the baggage carousel.

"Hey." He smiles, walks my way and gathers me into his arms. "A week is a long time to be apart. Too long."

"But you were doing guy stuff."

"And thinking about you every minute."

A double-shot of intoxication slams through me. Not only am I attracted to Ben physically, I am attracted to him emotionally.

Ben has a moral compass.

Has integrity.

He had put on his big-boy pants years ago and never looked back.

That kind of maturity could only be intoxicating.

"I missed you," he whispers in my ear.

Did I dare tell him I'd missed him too?

How much longer could I deny it? If only to him?

I was still stuck on self-preservation, terrified he would soon back away, wasn't really thinking that 'we' were an 'us'. If I admitted to Ben that I missed him too, would he make a bee-line in the opposite direction as fast as he could?

I pull back slightly, still considering how to reply when Emory says, "Knock it off, you two. I'm getting jealous."

Grateful, I chuckle nervously, glad for the reprieve. Ben doesn't seem to have caught on to my indecision. He takes my overnight bag in one hand, my hand in the other. "Hungry?" he asks us both. "I'm starved. Let's grab some lunch."

We stop at The Saltlick once we are away from the crowded airport area and over beef brisket sandwiches, we tell Ben all about our journey. The pictures we share show most of the story – how can anyone convey what the dugout really looks like except through pictures? Or the feeling of finding a cemetery filled with crumbling headstones with your ancestors' names on them?

"And I know – I just know the little girl – Rachel – is buried behind the dugout," I tell him. "We checked every cemetery in the area and she isn't anywhere that is recorded."

"And see," Emory adds. "Look at these photos of the wildflowers and the cross etched right there in the stone. We both got goosebumps when we saw it."

"I still get them every time I think about it."

"Maybe we could hire one of those infrared imaging companies to check out the dugout area," Ben says as he munches on a fry. "I know they've discovered human remains with that technology."

"Seriously?" Emory's eyes widen.

"Ben, that's an incredible idea." I squeeze his hand. "Costly, I'm sure. But well worth it if Rachel is found. I'll look into it."

We finish lunch and head to Granddad's.

I have a melancholy feeling when we pull into the drive but it helps to see Gail coming out of the barn. Leadfoot gallops after her, Brutus and Samson chasing them both. I wave and wait for Brutus to rush me. "Hey, boy. Oh my gosh did I miss you." I ruffle his ears and he licks my hand. Em lifts Samson and with a wave heads to her car and home.

Ben is already walking around to grab my suitcase out of the bed of his truck. Brutus darts his way, jumping on his pant leg.

"Down, boy," I tell him. Then to Ben, "Come in for a while?"

"I was beginning to wonder if you were going to ask." Ben passes by me with a brief kiss. He drops my bags in the foyer.

I begin sifting through the mail Gail has stacked on the credenza as I say, "Want some iced tea? Did you manage to kill a poor defenseless creature while hunting?"

"A couple of pesky doves." Ben follows me into the kitchen. "They'd over-populate if we didn't."

"They are a nuisance."

As I pour us each a glass of tea, Ben pulls a tug-of-war rope out of Brutus' toy pile and begins to play with him.

"Let's sit on the porch."

Autumn is ablaze now, the trees shedding summer leaves, turning shades of orange and red and yellow and brown. The humidity of summer, as well as its heat, has subsided and the porch is cool and refreshing.

I sink onto the swing, glad I'm home as Ben tosses a ball into the yard for Brutus to chase. When he sits beside me, he sets the swing in motion, then takes my hand in his. "What's your week looking like? Any meetings with Aaron?"

"Yeah. Em and I are meeting with Aaron on Thursday." Aaron is our new building contractor. "And a couple of tea distributors on Wednesday. I also have three sets of vows to write by Wednesday and two Skype interviews with people who responded to my ad about writing vows. I can't wait to hire an assistant. One day soon I won't need to write vows anymore."

"For the uncommitted grooms' you despise so much."

"Well, yeah. Is my disdain that transparent? It's just that ninety-percent of the vows I write mean nothing to the men who are going to pledge them. It's hard not to feel disenchanted."

"Is the number really that high?" Brutus drops the ball at Ben's feet. He reaches for it and throws it again, Brutus scampering after it.

"Maybe I'm exaggerating. But it feels that high. There was a guy this week that seemed very sincere."

"And don't forget you agreed to help me with my vows a while back. I'm sincere. Or I will be when I express my vows. You can't retire completely until you help me with them."

I feel the hair on my arms rise as an uncomfortable, awkward sensation runs through my frame. I'm familiar with this feeling. Have felt it way too many times before.

This was the feeling I never wanted to experience again. Was behind my reason for not letting my guard down, not telling Ben how much I cared about him.

I have an instinct to pull my hand from his. By sheer will I leave it tucked around his own. "That was a long while back." I make light of his comment. "I'd actually forgotten I'd agreed to help."

"Yeah, but I haven't." His tone is matter-of-fact, nonchalant, while I feel panic. "I do plan on getting married one day. Who better than you to help me come up with something appropriate?"

He brushes the palm of my hand with his thumb, but now his touch feels abrasive. "If you have time let's work on them tomorrow."

"Tomorrow?" Now I do pull my hand from his. I stand up, needing space between us. "You really have given this some thought. Okay then. Let's get them written." I'm all business now. And since I never invite a client to my home I add, "How about we meet at the Starbuck's in Wolf Ranch. Ten tomorrow morning? You'll need to put on your groom hat."

"Ten, huh? I might be a bit early. And they might take some time to work on so don't overbook your day, okay?"

I try not to glare at him. "My rate is pretty steep."

Ben stands and takes my arms in his hands. "Worth every cent. And I'll put on my future groom hat."

"And I'll put on my work hat."

"Okay."

"Okay. I'll see you tomorrow then."

"You're kicking me out?"

"So, to speak."

CHAPTER 32

There it was... the bursting cloud. And right over my head.

It was exactly what I'd always worried would happen. Planned for. But my accurate prediction didn't make the reality less painful.

I was feeling pretty depressed by the time I was in bed, Brutus snuggled up against me, providing me with the warmth I so needed.

I starred up at the shadowy ceiling, contemplating. The topic of Ben's vows hadn't come up since the Garden Club Gala. He'd be spending most of his time with me, so had he met someone else recently? Or been having a long-distance relationship and was ready to change that?

Maybe I'd been too clingy after all. Maybe he was weary of needing to emotionally support me, wanted instead to move on – away – from me and Granddad's ranch and all the memories here.

Endless possibilities played through my head, making sleep impossible, making me wonder, yet again, what was wrong with me – why I'd never been number one with any man for long – and why I kept setting myself up to be let down.

This time I'd been so careful.

Was I just being silly? Reading too much into Ben's message? He *had* said *future* wife - as in *way future*. But if so, he wasn't considering me for that future.

Which were the very reasons why I'd kept my distance, kept my guard up.

At least I hadn't made the mistake of telling him how much I cared about him.

My chest tightens though, when I think about letting him go. Moving on without him. And so soon after losing Granddad.

As if I had a choice.

I toss the covers aside and squeeze around Brutus, leaving him to sleep while I head to my desk and computer. I write and re-write a set of vows, then, still wound up, I Google infrared imaging.

♦ ♦ ♦

I'm pulled from a deep sleep hours later when my foggy brain becomes aware of a tap-tap-tap outside my window. With blurry vision I read four a.m. on the side-table clock. Brutus lifts his head from the pillow next to mine, then lets it fall again. When he fails to growl, I decide I must be dreaming and close my eyes again.

"Shelley." I sit up, instantly alert.

The voice I hear is muffled but distinctly male. Ben?

Brutus wastes little time bounding off the bed and to the window. He barks once, then sits down, waging his tail.

"Good Brutus," I hear from outside.

Good? I'm supposed to be the one to tell Brutus if he is good. There is, after all, someone outside my window – in the middle of the night.

Brutus whimpers. I toss my blankets aside in a huff.

"Wake your mistress. Wake Shelley," the voice – Ben - adds.

"I'm awake," I call back, a note of irritation evident in my tone. "You and I need to have a talk," I add to Brutus as I climb out of bed.

Opening the window blinds, I see Ben trying to peer inside. "What are you doing? Doing here?" My voice echoes against the closed glass.

"Mornin'." I can see his shadowy lazy smile. That smile that always weakens my knees. Sheer lack of sleep and a new resolve to distance myself from him fortifies me to be stern. "You going to let me in?"

"It's the middle of the night. What's wrong?"

"I'll meet you at the front door."

He moves away from the window before I can protest. I huff to no one but myself. I defiantly refuse to brush my hair or change from my oversized t-shirt and leggings. Instead, I stomp through the darkened house, flicking on a couple of lights as I go, Brutus beside me.

I fling the front door wide with my hand on my hip. "This better be good," I growl – because Brutus did not.

"Good morning to you, too," Ben drawls. I can only ignore the current shooting through my system because I certainly can't stop it.

With another sigh, I say, "Are you going to explain yourself?"

"I am. Just as soon as you let me in so I can brew us some coffee. And you need to hurry. Sunrise will be here before we know it."

"Sunrise?"

"Throw on some jeans, a sweatshirt and your riding boots, and... uh... brush your hair. I'll have the coffee ready by then."

"But— "

His hands caress my shoulders. "Trust me, okay?" He turns me around.

I think about protesting but allow him to push me toward my bedroom because my curiosity is too powerful to overcome. But I promise myself I will still be curt with him. Still keep my distance and my resolve.

I return to the kitchen a few minutes later, appropriately dressed and brushed, but before I can once again ask Ben why he is in my kitchen, he takes me by the arm and, sealed coffee mugs in hand, steers me toward the door.

Brutus is left munching down his breakfast as Ben leads me outside.

"Ben."

"Shhh. Listen to the quiet." He steers me down the porch where I see Sherlock and Chester saddled and waiting for us. He puts the coffee into a saddle bag and helps me mount.

I wait for him to explain what he is up to.

Instead he sets the horses in motion. "Look at all those stars," he says into the dark landscape. "Aren't they incredible?"

I peer up, seeing the night sky is still filled with a shimmering glow. My intrigue keeps me from replying.

We ride a mile or so before we veer onto a dirt path edged with dense foliage. A half mile later we ascend a hill that crests at a clearing. There he stops.

"Let's go," he says.

"Go?"

"You can dismount."

I sigh inwardly. He is already at my side, helping me down. He opens the saddle bag and pulls out our coffee and I see two lawn chairs and a blanket a few feet away. "Have a seat," he says.

"You want me to sit down?" He brought the chairs sometime earlier?

"Yeah." I am beginning to think he is delusional. Perhaps I need to go along with him until I know whether he is or not. I don't want him to get upset if I challenge him.

Ben follows and holds one chair as I sit down. He then sits in the second chair and places the blanket over us. He hands me a mug of coffee. "There. All set." He takes a gulp of coffee. "Isn't this nice?"

I stare at him. "Nice? Okay, Ben what are we doing?"

Refusing to look my way he takes another drink. "Doing? Just sitting here. Relaxing. Enjoying our coffee." He tucks the blanket more securely around my waist.

Somewhere between confused and flabbergasted, I'm not sure what else to say. What else to do. So, I take a swallow from my own cup.

Silence settles around us. It is still too early for the blue birds and the cardinals to be singing. Too early for deer to be foraging for food. Too early even for the squirrels and rabbits to be scampering about. There is only an occasional rustle in the distant trees as the breeze rattles the leaves.

I gaze around as the stars begin to fade and the landscape gradually lightens, not daring to glance Ben's way. And I soon realize from our vantage we can see lights from the valley below. From the direction of the lightening sky I guess we are looking east. Behind us it is much darker. The sky in front of us is slowly turning a hazy shade of pink and orange, the few wispy clouds hanging in the sky adding to the colorful display.

"Look at that." Ben breaks the quiet with a whisper as the sun crests above the plain. He puts his mug down and takes my hand in his.

My heart hitches and I swallow, just as much mesmerized by the big ball of flame rising in front of us as I am by the feel of Ben's warm grasp.

He effortlessly moves his thumb over my skin. "Isn't that incredible? Don't look straight at the sun or it'll damage your eyes."

My eyes aren't the only thing I'm worried about being damaged. But I silently admit that watching the sun rise is an incredible experience.

The daily event is something we take for granted. It's beautiful and breathtaking. One minute the sun is nowhere to be found and the next dawn becomes day in a swirl of colorful hues.

Without turning Ben's way, I say, "You came to my house, woke me up, to see this?"

I feel Ben's smile more than I see it. "That was the idea."

I smile back – how can I not? "Thanks."

"You're welcome. Now, what do you say we go fishing?"

Fishing?

I'm speechless as we remount and ride through one copse of cedar and juniper after another, through open meadow and back to a forest of trees, until we stop at the bank of the San Gabriel River.

"First, cinnamon rolls," he grins, grabbing a picnic basket from inside the saddle bag again and a thermos of more fresh coffee.

We sit on the bank of the river, listening to the gentle current, song birds singing in the trees, and dine on plump cinnamon rolls.

"Where did you get these?" I can't help but ask. They are delicious.

"What if I told you I made them myself?"

"I wouldn't believe you."

"That seems to be a recurring theme." He stands then, walking towards a tree before I can question his response. He pulls out a tackle box and two poles from behind the tree – more things he'd obviously placed there earlier.

"Put these on." He holds up a pair of rubber waders.

"I don't think—"

"Exactly. Don't think. Just put them on."

I struggle into the waders, still wondering what all of his effort is about. Ben slides into his own waders, baits my hook, hands me a pole and I follow him into the cold murky water.

The current tugs at my legs.

"Plant your feet so you won't fall over."

I follow Ben's instructions.

"All set?"

"I think so."

"Okay, now cast like this."

Ben casts his line into the water and I nervously do the same.

"Not bad."

I chuckle, pleased with myself for casting it accurately enough. "Now what?"

"Now we wait. Patiently."

"While you tell me what this is all about?"

He ignores my questions as the current laps around us, the quiet returning.

"I used to come here with my grandfather," Ben says instead. "Fishing with him is one of my earliest memories. My grandmother would make us lunch and we'd hike down here from the house. She'd come to check on us after a couple hours. If we had a good catch, she'd plan supper around it."

As he talks, I'm lulled by his tone, his words.

"Those were good days. After a lot of bad days."

"The death of your father?"

"That and then my mom's remarriage. That was worse on a lot of counts."

"Granddad told me a bit about it."

"Coming to the ranch was the best thing that ever happened to me. I remember the first day I met you, too. I put peanut butter in your hair. We were having some kind of party- "

"Your grandparent's anniversary."

"That's right. And my friend Mark Dalbert dared me. He had a crush on your friend— "

"Debbie. She was the granddaughter of one of Gram's friends and came to stay with us for the weekend."

"Debbie. And he was too chicken to talk to her."

"So, you attacked me instead?"

"You remember?"

"I've never forgotten. It took me days to get the stuff out. I haven't forgotten when you pushed me in this river either. In January. When a bunch of us were playing hide-and-seek.

"Oh, yeah. I'd forgotten that one. I was pretty ornery."

"I'm glad you admit it at last."

"I did apologize for standing you up at the summer dance."

"Let's see. I remember your grandfather standing with you, his hand on your shoulder as you said 'Sorry, Shelley, but I didn't know Star Wars was opening yesterday.'"

"Lame, huh?"

My pole jerks. "Oh. I have a fish!"

"Tug gently. Reel slowly." Ben wades my way and stands beside me while I tug and reel, tug and reel, until a catfish flaps out of the water.

"Hey, not a bad size." He grabs the line and fish, steering it to a bucket. He digs the hook out of the fish's mouth. I look at the thing flailing around. Gills protruding, he has buggy eyes and long whiskers. "He'll fry up nicely."

I cringe. "Can't I toss him back in?"

"You don't want him for dinner?"

"Not if I don't have to." I shake my head.

"Softy," Ben nudges me. But he takes the bucket and I wade back into the water beside him. Amid the rocky, shifting soil, I grab the bucket and empty it back into the water.

Ben takes the bucket and heads back to shore as I stand in the knee-high current.

I watch as he drops the bucket and bends down to pick up a handful of small rocks. He turns back to me with a devious grin planted on his face. "I'm still ornery," he announces and tosses a rock my way. It splashes inches away. Droplets splash my clothes.

"You are so in trouble."

"Not if you can't catch me." He tosses another rock.

"That's not fair."

His smile enlarges as my gaze narrows. I bend forward and push handfuls of water toward shore, hoping the spray will breach the distance. He easily side-steps my effort, his chuckle musical, flowing over the riverbank to my ears.

It's not fair," I say again, this time to myself. How will I ever let him go?

I splash my way out of the water, a difficult thing in waders and rocky soil. "When I catch you..."

Ben drops the remaining rocks from his hand and ducks behind a tree. He laughs. "Are you going to chase me?"

Am I? "I am." I take off after him. He makes it easy when after a brief chase he surrenders, turning to face me and catching me as I nearly collide with him. "You are so in trouble," I tell him again.

He takes my face between his hands and says, "Promise?" and my heart trips. He dips his head and his lips find mine.

This is *so not fair*. I can't even muster enough angst to pull away.

His arm snakes around my waist and draws me closer, his kiss lingering. And I am melting... melting...

"Hey Shell- "

I push away from him, trying desperately to remember that he is going to make me write vows for another woman.

He is going to betray me.

"I need to go home." I say firmly. I need air, need cool air and a cool head and his closeness is depleting both.

Ben takes a deep breath himself. He kisses me lightly and steps back. "I guess Gail has had time to bring over some fresh clothes for you by now. So, yeah, let's head up to my place and change."

"Gail? What are you talking about?"

"I texted her yesterday and asked her to bring some of your clothes to my house."

"She was in on this little, this little..." I don't even know what this is, how to finish my sentence.

"Wise of me, huh?"

"Not even close."

"But you'll forgive me."

"I'm not so sure. What are you up to?"

He glances at his watch. "We'd better hurry."

He takes my hand and pulls me along. "Ben, where are we going?"

"To collect our fishing gear and coffee mugs."

"And then?"

He stops and plants another kiss on my lips. "Guess you'll find out."

I have phone calls to make and vows to write and chickens to feed, and well, even the fridge needs cleaning. Why then do I follow blindly after him? All of this is going to cause me more heartache. Lots more heartache.

Is he deliberately being cruel? Wanting me to know just how much I am going to miss out on when he dumps me?

I help him gather our paraphernalia and trudge up the bank toward the horses. We feed them each an apple, give them some fresh water and remount.

"Trust me," he says again as I stare at him for answers.

A half-mile later we reach his ranch. I self-consciously follow him inside his house. Into his domain. His life.

I am now completely out of my element.

"The guest room is right here," he says, leading me down a hallway. "And look, Gail came through." On the bed lay my blue capris, a half-sleeve peasant blouse and – God love her – my makeup bag. Sandals rest on the hardwood floor.

"The bath is right through that door. Shower and dress. I'll do the same. You have twenty minutes."

Okay, fine, I am a fool.

After today I'll be a fool no more. But on this day, I can't stop myself. I'll digest everything tomorrow.

Eighteen minutes later his truck horn has me scurrying.

We are soon cruising down Williams Drive, jazz music adding to the comfortable ambience.

"When do you plan on telling me where we're going?"

"Well since you asked, this is my day to help out at the food bank."

"Food bank?"

"At *The Caring Place*. It's Georgetown's local assistance center. And since they can always use more help, I didn't think you'd mind lending a hand as well."

How can I complain about that? "Okay."

I'm no longer surprised by Ben's wide-range of activities and service. Nor by the warm reception he receives when we enter the assistance compound. I quickly learn *The Caring Place* provides clothing, food and shelter to the needy. There is also a thrift shop on sight.

Ben leads me to an assembly line area where volunteers are preparing boxes filled with food pantry items. He introduces me to the staff and volunteers, some of whom I already know through Granddad, and we join in, for the next two hours filling boxes with supplies.

When we leave, I've already committed to returning to help again. I'd enjoyed doing a small part to help others.

Ben takes my hand as we head back to the parking lot. I try to pull away, finally having my equilibrium back. But when he squeezes, I yield.

"Hungry?" he asks. My fullness from the cinnamon roll has subsided hours ago.

"I'll grab something at home."

"We're not going home yet. We have a couple more stops to make."

"But I need to get home. This has been nice but—"

"But you'd rather spend the day with someone else?"

"No, but—. That's not fair. You can't put me on the spot like that. I have chickens to feed, and Brutus—"

"Gail has everything under control."

"You'd better be giving her a bonus then."

"Trust me."

"You keep saying that."

"Then do it."

My apprehension skyrockets. I can sense a downfall coming. "Where are we going now?"

"To the lake."

"The lake? Fishing again?"

"No. Lunch."

I can only go along with him. Confounded and uneasy, I sit by as Ben drives down Interstate 35 to the Lady Bird Lake turn off. We park again and I'm led toward a floating restaurant. We're greeted at the gangplank, sat at a nice window table overlooking the blue water and watch kayakers and fishermen as we dine on fresh fish tacos, spicy salsa and sip on rum punch.

"Fabulous," Ben says when he leans back in his chair. "You want anything else?"

"Not a thing. I'm stuffed."

Ben takes my hand. "Let's walk some of this off then."

We leave the restaurant behind and walk along the wood-platform walking trail around the lake as the sun begins to set, turning the western sky a hue-filled orange and yellow. I can't remember another time in my life where I have viewed both ascent and descent. Both with the man I love.

I can only imagine how many times my grandmother Matilda was exposed to sunrises and sunsets as she traveled wide open expanses of sea and land.

The air chills as we walk. I rub my arm just as Ben says, "So there is one more place we need to visit. Then we'll head home. Are you okay with that?"

"One more," I reply.

Soon Ben is maneuvering into traffic, staying on Austin's crowded downtown roads. Rush hour traffic is heavy, street lights long and bothersome.

The peacefulness from the lake's atmosphere slips away as homeless men with signs, step close to the cars. Some want to wash our windows, some ask for a job, others don't bother to make any excuse at all as they ask for money.

Ben ignores the men, which surprises me until he says, "I learned a long time ago to give to the shelters instead of the individuals who will usually just take what they can get and spend it on drugs or booze."

I nod, wondering why there are so many homeless men on Austin's streets. Then, a few short miles later Ben steers us into a large parking lot. "Isn't this the hospital?" I ask.

"Seton. Yeah." Ben squeezes my hand.

"Why are we here?" My apprehension increases. I hadn't "I'm not comfortable in this setting. Just leave me here and go do what you need to do."

"Shell, we're here to see Matt Henley and his family. Remember when he was injured during scrimmage last week?"

I did. Matt was one of the high school football players. He'd been knocked out during practice before the team barbeque. One of the other coaches had taken him to the emergency room.

"Well, they ran some tests and found out he has a heart defect."

"Oh. Wow. Still, you go on without me. I don't know this family—"

"Come with me."

Baffled by Ben's behavior all day and exhaustion setting in, I open my own door and move at a fast pace through the mega parking structure towards the hospital entry.

I can't talk. Don't want to talk. I want to go home. Not face what the Henley's are facing.

We walk through the electric doors and are confronted by a multitude of people moving about, going down one corridor or another, towards elevators, laboratories, Pediatrics, Oncology.

Illness is everywhere; sorrow, suffering and disillusionment at every turn.

Ben takes my hand but this time I pull away. I don't want his contact. Can't handle his contact now.

"Hey," he offers. He pulls me to a stop and faces me. "It's all right." His smile reaches his eyes and I calm inside. "I'm right here," he adds.

"But for how long?" I can't believe it when I hear the words spoken. "Forget I asked that. Shouldn't we pick up some flowers in the gift shop?"

"I sent some yesterday."

I take a deep breath of stale air and when Ben takes my hand again, I let him. Then we are moving up the elevator and stopping outside a door in the Pediatric Wing's cardiac unit.

"Here we are. And just so you know, Matt's dad is one of the Vets who come to the ranch."

I take a deep breath again. Ben pushes on the half-closed door. "Anyone here?" he calls. "Hey, Matt. How's it going?"

Matt Henley is sitting up in his bed as we enter, his mom I assume, spooning Jell-O into his mouth. He smiles at Ben."

"I'd rather be at school."

"Now that's a miracle," his mom says.

Ben introduces me to Lenore, as Matt's dad, Everett, stands from the seat he is occupying. He extends his left hand for me to shake and I see he doesn't have a right arm. The shorts he wears reveal he doesn't have a right leg either. Everett and Lenore's young daughter is coloring in a book placed on another chair.

"Surgery is set for tomorrow morning," Everett tells us. "They'll replace his heart-valve."

"And then he'll be good as new," Lenore adds. I can see her chin quiver and the tears in her eyes – the fear in her eyes.

"Piece of cake," Ben says.

"And Matt has company. Another kid next door has the same problem. It's a whole new world in here."

"Daddy, Mommy's crying again." Leah leaves her crayons and the chair and wraps her arms around her mother tightly.

"Sometimes we need to cry," Everett soothes. He rubs his daughter's back. "Sometimes tears are good."

"And you know what, Leah?" Ben adds. "God holds each tear we cry in the palm of His hand."

I blink rapidly, my throat clogging. I don't have a word to say – I don't know these people, can't offer any kind of support – except, well, maybe prayers. Not something I promise lightly these days.

I make a mental note to pray for Matt and his family tomorrow morning, first thing.

Then Ben asks if he can lead the family in prayer. This is so new to me, so foreign. But I love how strong Ben is. How real his faith is.

We all gather around Matt's bed and hold hands as Ben begins. Afterwards, Ben promises Matt a trip to watch the Aggies play a home game in College Station once he's healed enough.

"Really?" Matt's excitement shines in his brown eyes.

"You bet."

"That is so cool. I'll be ready real fast then."

"I'll be waiting."

We say our good-byes soon after. We retrace our steps and I can't get outside fast enough.

The sun has all but set when I do, my mood as solemn as the dusk, as heavy as the sorrow inside the hospital.

I am more than ready to go home, my emotions all over the place.

I sink into the truck seat with a sigh, staring straight ahead even though I can feel Ben in front of the open door. His fingers caress my rigid jaw.

"Tough scene back there, huh?" I don't want to talk, don't want his touch – but I lean into it anyways and feel my tension begin to subside. "Let's go home," he adds. "A glass of wine and a nice fire is what we both need right now."

Soon we are driving down the darkened highway, oncoming headlights rushing by, a wordless jazz tune filtering through the speakers. I consider telling Ben I've had enough for one day – enough for a lifetime – but I don't want to be alone now; his offer of a fire and wine too inviting to resist.

Hopefully, that will settle me enough to curl up with Brutus and forget about today.

Ben pulls into his driveway before I realize he is not taking me to my house. I don't have the energy to protest so in the quiet of the night, I follow him inside. I can see a fire already flaming in the living room fireplace. It draws me closer.

As Ben flips on a few lights, I hear him moving around in the kitchen. I take up space on the leather sofa in front of the crackling fire, tuck my feet beneath me and pull a knitted afghan over my lap. Ben shadows the fire, offers me a glass of red wine as he sits beside me, moving my legs across his lap.

"Are you sure Gail was feeding the chickens?" I take a sip of Merlot, try not to enjoy the feel of his hand on my leg.

"Promise," Ben replies.

"And Brutus? Was he cooped up all day?"

"She took him out several times."

I want to relax but I'm still dazed. The flames mesmerize me. "You need to explain this. This. Today."

"Okay."

"No more talking in circles?"

"No."

Ben takes my wine glass and sets both of them on the coffee table. He puts his arm around me and draws me nearer to him. I want to pull back. I want to lean in to him. I do neither as my nerves tense.

"Today was – is - about getting you to trust me. Simple as that."

"Trust you." I state the words he'd said. Mostly so I can digest them. My voice is gravelly to my own ears and I curl my toes.

"Trust me. Something you don't – haven't done yet."

"I trust you." I did – sort of. "You've shown yourself to be loyal, like with Granddad, and with this entire community."

"That's not the same thing and you know it. You know what I'm talking about."

I wasn't about to admit it. "Ben—"

"Shelley, you don't trust me with your heart."

Every nerve in my body stands on end. I grab onto the afghan for support and slide my legs from his lap. "My heart." I stare at the flames. "You snubbed me for months. Treated me as if I were a persistent hang-nail. Then suddenly you wanted to date me, woo me and dare I say 'court' me. You led me to believe we – meaning you and me - might go somewhere in this life together. And then – just when I'm hooked, just when all my defenses are beginning to crumble in a heap - you tell me you want me to help you write wedding vows for your *future wife*. Wedding vows. For your future wife?" I turn my head and stare at him. "And I'm supposed to trust you with my heart?"

"Yeah. Yes, you are." His words are matter-of-fact, pointed.

"Oh, for the love of..." I stand up, exasperated.

"Slow down." Ben stands beside me, turns me and places his hands on my shoulders. "I know I made a few mistakes early on. I knew I needed to make up for those. That's what I was doing today."

"Explain that for me then. Exactly. Because what I've been doing is spinning all day. And I'm tired of spinning."

"Then stop." He holds me firmly still. "We shared a pleasant ride on our horses today, right? And saw the starry night sky together? And the exact moment when the sun rose?"

I sigh and nod. "We did."

"Then we went fishing together?"

I nod again.

"Had to put on waders and maneuver through the muck. After that we lent a helping hand, trying to help out the less fortunate. From there we went on to have a nice lunch on smooth waters."

"Ben."

"Here me out. We then left to offer hope and encouragement to a family in need. Got stuck in traffic, got frustrated. Saw a seamier side of life in a rough part of the city. Were faced with the weak, the sick, the frail. We navigated corridors of sorrow and sadness. Saw Matt, saw Everett and their family and knew at any moment we could be walking in their shoes."

"Yes." I drop my gaze, shamed and fearful.

Ben gently lifts my chin, his thumb moving across my jaw. I sink into the sweetness of it, close my eyes briefly, wanting to stay in the moment forever.

"And now," Ben adds, "we're back on stable ground again, enjoying a calm evening, a bit of wine and a warm fire."

I stop his thumb with my hand. "And your point, after all you've said, is?"

Ben smiles and his eyes sparkle as he peers at me. "Those are my wedding vows, Shelley. Mine to you."

My intake of air is abrupt.

"Together we're going to ride together. Enjoy starry nights together and see brilliant sunrises. We're going to share calm evenings and adventurous days. We're also going to have to wade through the muck sometimes. Have days that are strung together by nothing more than determination. We're going to be immersed in situations that break our hearts and make us want to run for cover. We're going to have to offer help sometimes and accept help sometimes.

"When we have kids - I want three or four if you're willing – they will stretch us. And we will face challenges like Everett and Lenore. You might face challenges like Lenore, her husband so injured she can't stretch anymore.

"The thing is, Shelley, I'm going to be here for all of it. I'm not going anywhere without you. You can trust me until the day God takes me out of this world – and after. Until then, it's going to be me and you and then our kids and hopefully theirs. Those are the vows I'm making you. No need to write them out on a piece of paper. No need for fluffiness or pretty words."

He pauses and takes my hands in his. "I was running from you for a long time. I stopped. You've been running from me longer. Refusing to let yourself love me. To tell me you missed me. Keeping up that wall you've built around your heart. I want you to stop running now. It's time to trust in me, Shelley. I've loved you since the day I smeared peanut butter in your hair. I think you love me. And I want us to share our lives together as husband and wife."

CHAPTER 33

Our teahouse contractor, Aaron Hall, finishes latching the sign and dismounts the ladder, looking upward. "How does that look?" he asks.

"*Tilly's English Tea House*," I read out loud. Scrolled letters with a sketched image of my Victorian-era grandmother, one of her in her mid-twenties, greets my eyes. It hangs above the sidewalk on Austin Avenue in the Georgetown square, in front of our new establishment.

"It's perfect," Emory adds.

"I like the sign next door better," Ben grins and wraps his arm around my shoulders. "*The Buck Stops Here Coffee Bar*. Now that's a great name." A buck's head is etched into the swinging sign. The buck has a large rack of antlers.

"That is a great name," Aaron replies. He moves beside Emory. He's thirty-ish, handsome and has a successful construction firm. "Who came up with it?"

Ben and I smile at each other. It's apparent we're both thinking back to the day he proposed.

"Ben and I were supposed to have a meeting at the well-known coffee house, or so I thought," I explained.

"But I had other plans that altered our direction," Ben adds. "The name is a spin on that."

"But it was Shell's idea to have a teahouse and coffee bar," Emory says.

"And yours to have two entrances."

"The concept is brilliant." Aaron removes his baseball cap and wipes his brow. "I'm looking forward to walking up to a saloon-style bar and ordering a mug of coffee."

"No expresso for you?" Emory teases and I can see a spark between them.

"Nor a caramel-latte with extra foam."

"I'm with you, Aaron," Ben agrees. "Ready to head inside?"

I inhale, excited and nervous. "You first, Em," I offer. She unlocks the door leading into *Tilly's English Tea House* and steps onto the aged and creaking wood floor. I follow behind, flipping on the lights. The old storefront had needed all new electrical outlets installed as well as an entire facelift. But now, among the other quaint boutiques and specialty stores, we have a place for every one of Gram's odds and ends, Granddad's medals, family heirlooms and vintage furnishings. We have Gram's tea sets scattered throughout on secure shelving and will use new sets we bought in Fredericksburg, Lorena and Gruene for our guests. In the five tea rooms we've laid out one is in honor of Matilda – our family's heroine. Her picture is on the wall as are other old family photos, along with excerpts from her journal and documents that tell her story. A second room is dedicated to Gram and her heyday. Still another is for young girls, where they can have tea parties of their own, princess attire included.

The coffee bar is connected but separated by a half wall. More masculine in style, we have it decorated with Wild West wanted posters, wildlife scenes. Photos of our grandfathers and Civil War ancestors are also scattered about. The long salon-style mahogany bar is the center piece and heavy-duty over-sized coffee mugs line the back.

"Hey."

My heart flutters at the sound of Ben's voice next to my ear.

My fiancée's voice.

I still pinch myself and rub the engagement ring I'm wearing.

"Are you daydreaming?"

"Just enjoying the moment." I smile.

He kisses me. "I'll start unloading the truck."

"Okay." My great-great grandmother's restored sewing machine will add the final touch to *Tilly's*.

As I watch him leave, Alice walks in. Alice, a plump older woman with a ruddy complexion and jovial demeanor, is the baker we hired to supply all our food offerings. "Good morning," she greets. "This is so exciting. Opening day is just a week away. Show me where I'll be delivering my scones, tea cakes, finger sandwiches and fruit tarts?"

"Follow me, Alice," Emory answers.

As they head toward the back, silence surrounds me. I look around, satisfied. I can't wait to share *Tilly's* place with the world. To give Matilda a voice. One she never had while she was alive. I want them to love and admire the Grand Dame of our family as much as I do.

On our opening day, midway through seating a long line of guests and listening to chatter and tickling tea cups, two other things happen to rock my world. The first is a phone call from the resort in Maui confirming my reservation for a small, beachfront wedding.

I hang up, try to gather myself as my heart flutters and I marvel at being on this side of love.

This side of love – the side of commitment and trust. The side where fear has no foothold and the 'come what may's' come with a sense of peace.

I do trust Ben now. With my heart. And I'll marry him with all of it wide open.

More importantly, I'll trust God with my heart as well. After all – He did create it.

My phone rings again a moment later. With the noise escalating in the main room, I head for the back storage-area and employee break room.

"Yes, this is Shelley Gatewood."

"Hello, Shelley. Jim Bonner, Bonner Infrared Imaging."

"Mr. Bonner. How is the search going?"

"Well, Shelley, you know we had some issues with the owner of the Toquerville property at first. Then they signed a release for us to scan the dugout area."

"Yes. The owner isn't protesting again, is he?"

"No. He's been watching us. I think he's curious."

"Then?"

"And you know this soil is very rocky. It's taken us more time because of all the red adobe rock in the area. It's made it difficult to define the images we've found and our equipment has been utilized to the maximum."

"Okay. Did something break?"

"No, nothing like that. We just wanted to make certain, that we were very thorough before we gave our defining opinion."

"And do you have one yet? An opinion I mean? About Rachel be buried there?" I'm on pins and needles now. I don't want him to tell me the scanners haven't been successful.

"Not an opinion, actually. If fact, I have definitive proof."

"Proof? What kind of proof? That she isn't there?"

"No, no. You're misunderstanding me."

"What do you mean?"

"What I mean is we have definitive proof that a child was buried behind the dugout. We found bone fragments. We had them analyzed. They are human."

"Rachel," I whisper, tears pooling in my eyes. "We found you." Louder I say, "You found her?"

"Yes. I believe so."

CHAPTER 34

Beaver, Utah
September, 1896

I received two letters today. Both were bittersweet.

They always are these days.

The first was from Louisa, she no longer the frightened young girl who did not want to board the *Kennebec*. Indeed, she is a grandmother now. She is still living in Salt Lake, near her sister Sarah. The two have stayed close all these years, after living with William and I until their own marriages. They helped me birth my babes and I helped them with theirs, and they remain the daughters of my heart unto this day. Now a letter or two on occasion keeps us close.

Today Louisa shared that Jonathan's inquiries concerning Ellen were finally answered. None of us had heard from her after her marriage and move to the California territory in sixty-eight. She, her young daughter and husband were supposed to have met up with Jonathan but they never arrived. Now, it appears she perished along the way.

"Jonathan found her grave and spoke to her daughter, Louise," Louisa wrote. "She took sick not far from his stead."

"Ah Ellen," I whisper. "Always the independent one."

Jonathan was still well, he and his wife farming on his land in California, her letter went on. He had never had any children.

The news was enough. It had to be.

My second letter was from England. And yet, before I began to read it, I was reminded of the first letter I ever received after departing my homeland.

It had found me in the wilderness at Ft. Laramie. Feeling uncertain and afraid, I had needed that letter so.

From my mama, it was.

The words were rich and comforting, scented with fragrance that was distinctly hers. A fragrance that lingers with me today.

It was in response to the post written by Nurse Filmore relaying the news of the *Saluda* tragedy. Just one of many posts I'd sent over the months. Posts entrusted to others, mostly strangers. Never knowing if they would find their way home.

The first I'd written had been on the ship *Kennebec* on the first evening John Sarnge, the children and I had sailed away from Liverpool. I'd been uncertain and afraid that night, too.

Today's letter came to me from my namesake Matilda Jane. She and I had been conversing for several years now, she eager to share the news about the generations of nieces and nephews I'd never met.

When I finally read the contents, it conveyed the sad news that my beloved sister Rachel – Matilda Jane's mother – had passed from this life.

I set my tea cup on the table as my eyes welled up and my throat thickened.

Rachel. How much we were to one another as children and adults.

I was glad my heart of hearts was at ease. I've learned that much after all these years.

After all, I now know that those who have gone before us are merely a breath away.

It is a simple thing we do, breathing. Repeatedly and without thought, we breathe in and breathe out until at last, we breathe no more. We do so by the grace of our Creator. Nothing more. And knowing that He never designed us to even die once is great solace. But for the fall of mankind we would never have had to experience the separation death brings. But knowing that once we cease to breathe, we are in the presence of God is the only comfort I need.

My own day is soon coming, I do believe. I am old, have lived long. I have seen much and despaired of all, and felt great bursts of exhilaration in this life. William and I have many grandchildren, and they children of their own now, and when I look back on it all, I am in wonder of how it all began.

Had we seen into the future all those years ago, the costs, the perils, the twists and turns, would we have changed our course?

I am glad I did not know what each tomorrow would bring.

Instead I can only pray for the generations of this large family of his and mine. And hope they understand that we tried our best. We sought to be wise, we deemed to be good, and we learned from our mistakes.

The Bible tells us sin is visited to the fifth generation. I hope it will not take that long for our family to be purged of the errors William and I made.

I hope they will read about our travails and not repeat them.

The accounts we leave them are meant to help them along their way.

CHAPTER 35

Present Day
Beaver, Utah

Emory and I stand beside Matilda's grave, the new smaller mound of freshly turned dirt beside it. Ben keeps his arm around me, knowing my emotions are getting the best of me. My tissue is no match for my tears.

After Jim Bonner sent the fragments his team discovered to a California lab with DNA from my dad, we knew for certain Baby Rachel had been found.

We have just concluded a small ceremony interring her next to her parents at long last.

With us are the cousins Emory and I met on our visit to Beaver last fall. Mom and Dad and Aunt Nell are here as well, Emory sniffling against her mother's shoulder.

I take a deep cleansing breath, overwhelmed with satisfaction and joy.

Matilda is content.

Matilda is at peace.

The last mystery of her life is resolved; her baby girl restored to her.

I understand they were truly reunited long ago; I have no doubt they have been together since the moment Matilda left this earth. God in his graciousness, in His redemptive plan made a way for that. Matilda was confident in that, William as well – rejecting the teachings of a religion that told them otherwise.

But for me, it is good to honor Tilly this way. To bring Rachel to rest with her six brothers, many half brothers and sisters, and parents.

As a gentle breeze swirls leaves and thick green grass, with my husband's presence to comfort me, I am content. Tilly surrounds me at home and here.

And new life grows in my womb.

Perhaps the firstborn girl of a new generation. Perhaps a new Matilda.

AFTERWORD

Dear Reader,

How is it possible to know the mindset of another human being? One who lived one-hundred and fifty years before you? It isn't, obviously. Therefore, this work is a work of fiction but it is solidly based on fact. I can honestly say that Matilda, my great-great-great-grandmother, spoke to me as I was researching her life. Her husband, my great-great-great grandfather William, did as well, through the events of his life and the conclusions that lie therein. Matilda's was subtler. It is easy to conclude that she made her earlier decisions based on both emotion and practicality. As example; was it better for her to return to England after the *Saluda* exploded or continue on, knowing supplies were waiting in Council Bluffs? It is easy to conclude she could not and would not abandon the orphaned children after John's death. We know this because she stayed with them and took them with her. She cared for them deeply, naming one son after Joseph, her eight-year-old charge who died on the *Saluda*. She was gracious enough to name her firstborn (George) after the brother of her husband's second wife. We know that she had a mind of her own and made decisions wisely. She concluded that the Mormon doctrine was erroneous, remaining with William after he was excommunicated instead of unsealing herself to him and sealing herself to another man as was the practice at that time. More so, she was never able to go to the Mormon temple to be sealed to her only daughter; something she most certainly would have done had she feared never being with Rachel in heaven.

Matilda did not leave a journal. What she left were snippets that I pieced together during my three-year journey to discover her life. William did leave a journal – the date of his ex-communication written for all to see and understand. It is because of this that I felt so compelled to tell their story. I did so with no small amount of angst. I do not condemn people who profess the Mormon faith. Many of them are my relatives. However, I do abhor their leaders – as I hope I've conveyed within. They have led millions astray.

I must thank my daughter, Jennifer, for helping me 'find' Matilda. It was Jennifer who gave me the gift of an ancestry website, which allowed me to discover our family. In the beginning, I admit, I wasn't much enthused with the gift. But after being diagnosed with genetic-based breast cancer, I wanted to find out if any family members had the same. My search led to such a discovery, but the bigger discovery were the men and women I could soon put faces and stories to; those who had come and gone and been forgotten. Matilda was one of them and I believe she needed to be re-discovered. It is no small co-incidence that I have always had an interest in England and especially the Victorian era. It certainly cannot be a co-incidence that I am a published novelist and that my first two books took place in Victorian, England. The next five books were set in the Old West. All my published books are historical romances. What better a romance than Matilda's story? I now feel this grandmother of mine has been calling to me my entire life – not in a mystical, nonsensical way, for I do not believe in such things. Rather, in a deeply-rooted resemblance of love and faith. Her story – and William's - needed to be told – and I was the one chosen to tell it.

Their story for the future generations of our family is all important, but on a more down-to-earth-level, it is fascinating. *She* is fascinating, as is her family. I give much credit to my great aunt for her research and public postings of it. I used much of this to learn about our family.

The letters from Matilda's sister Rachel and brother Benjamin are real. My aunt discovered them on one of her pilgrimages to England. They give us such rich insight into the family and I'm thankful they were publicly available.

It was heart wrenching to learn about Matilda's sister Caroline – hard enough to lose one child let-alone two and a husband. Margaret Adans was no less tragic; a girl when she married a seasoned polygamist who was never a real husband to her or father to her seven children. Both women endured much.

The rest of the family is no less fascinating; William was quite the rugged frontiersman. He was indeed a carpenter and his furnishings still exist today.

Shelley and Ben and the entire 'present' day story is pure fiction but I hope you enjoyed the contrast of Shelley's generation and Matilda's.

One other note: Baby Rachel has never been found as was portrayed. I do believe she is buried behind the dugout but I have never attempted to find out. Writing that she had been found and interred next to her parents is my own feeble way of attempting to conclude this story with a happily ever after.

In closing, we have to wonder if Matilda and William, by the end of their lives, understood the legacy they were leaving. And in the end, that is the question we all face.

Made in the USA
Coppell, TX
30 October 2019

10715046R00134